# Destiny of a Warrior

## by

## Mary Morgan

*Legends of the Fenian Warriors,*
*Book 4*

**Destiny of a Warrior**

Cover Art by *Debbie Taylor*

The Wild Rose Press, Inc.
PO Box 708
Adams Basin, NY 14410-0708
Visit us at www.thewildrosepress.com

Publishing History
First Fantasy Rose Edition, 2019
Print ISBN 978-1-5092-2647-4
Digital ISBN 978-1-5092-2648-1

*Legends of the Fenian Warriors, Book 4*
Published in the United States of America

Tossing the pinecone aside, Aidan stood. His instincts screamed at him to do something to prevent her from further inspecting the stone. Only he knew the significance. And he now understood why he was sent here. In all his travels, not one human had documented his time among them. Or so he believed. Upon his arrival, he longed to pulverize the stones to shards of dust after viewing the back. The altar stone had remained buried under moss, dirt, and ivy. The same was true with the tallest stone at its base.

He fought against extending his hand outward and sinking the area a thousand feet underground. Making quick strides to Rose, he came to an abrupt halt. Her face was ashen as she knelt behind the stone, sketching an entire scene on her notepad. One side mirrored the stones, but on the opposite page, her hand drew an epic vista.

The blood pounded inside his head, and he dared to draw in a breath. With each stroke of her hand, an image came to life, and his greatest fear unfolded. Slowly, Aidan lifted his hand. The power built and traveled down his arm. He had to destroy the picture. Banish the past vision from her mind. Eradicate all knowledge of him. Seal the door to the past from the present.

*The truth must never be revealed.*

But when Rose lifted her gaze to meet his, Aidan's heart stopped. For the first time in his life, he was torn between duty and his own personal needs.

"I am sorry," he stated in a strangled voice.

## Praise for The Fenian Warriors Series

"This story is a great mix of settings and scenes from medieval Scotland, fantasy, and romance all wrapped in one. Forbidden love, the fae, solid world-building, a steamy romance, what more can fantasy fans want?"

*~Majanka Verstraete for InD'tale Magazine*
~*~

"Mary Morgan has penned such an emotional fantasy romance, I cried. A moving tale, *TRIAL OF A WARRIOR* is a forbidden romance with warring races, treachery and deceit."

*~N.N. Light Book Heaven*
~*~

"I didn't think I could like these warriors and this world more, but I was wrong. This one is even better than the first."

*~Cyrene for Uncaged Book Reviews*
~*~

"Morgan's world building floats the reader in a magical world, fantasy, yet not. Her characters are so fleshed-out, I could touch them. Her scenes are descriptive—some being very emotional, which put me to tears."

*~Booktalk with Eileen*
~*~

"Conn MacRoich and Ivy O'Callaghan are two of the most strong, vibrant characters that I have ever read as they try to unravel secrets, right wrongs and deny a sizzling attraction that heats up the pages."

*~Stormy Vixen*

# Dedication

With deep appreciation on my five-year anniversary of being a published author, I dedicate this book to all my readers across the globe. Many of you have traveled this road with me from the very first book. You've encouraged, cheered, and shared your thoughts and love for my stories. May I continue to bring you many more romantic tales—ones filled with hope, redemption, and always a happily ever after. Thank you with love!

As a special acknowledgement, I'd like to express my admiration to my publisher, The Wild Rose Press, Inc. They granted this writer her greatest wish by giving me my first contract. Thank you, Rhonda Penders and RJ Morris, two amazing women who are the captains of our Rose Garden.

Thanks also to Lisa Dawn, marketing extraordinaire! You're always there 24/7! To Debbie Taylor, a phenomenal graphic designer who has given me the most amazing covers! I cry each time I receive a new one from you.

But most of all, my gratitude goes out to my dear editor, Amanda Barnett. I will never forget our first conversation. I took a leap of *faith* on that day and have never regretted being under your tutelage. You have taught me so much, not only as a writer but as a friend, too. Cheers to many more anniversaries!

## Glossary of the Fae Realm~The Tuatha Dé Danann

CATHEDRAL OF TREES: A place of worship and where royal ceremonies are held.

COURTS OF THE FAE: Special chambers where the Fae Order discuss and advise on the laws.

FAE APOTHECARY: A special healer and where one can purchase or create medicinal herbal remedies.

FAE COUNCIL: A group of nine Fae members who proceed and advise over the laws, especially those governed by the Fenian Warriors.

HALL OF REMEMBRANCE: A place the Fae visit to reflect on their life's journey.

KEEPER OF KNOWLEDGE: Archibald McKibben, Bard of the Fae. He is responsible for keeping a historical record of all events pertaining to the Fae within both worlds—human and Fae.

LIBRARY OF THE ANCIENTS: All the knowledge the Fae brought with them to Ireland.

PLEASURE GARDENS: A vast, luscious garden where the Fae may find others for sexual pleasures.

REALM OF SORROWS: When a Fae becomes trapped in his own misery and sorrow. Ultimately, they become a shadow of their former self and go mad.

ROOM OF REFLECTION: The Fae prison.

ROYAL HOUSES: On the planet of Taralyn—the Fae homeland—each of the nine continents maintained a royal house and family. These houses governed their own continents, but all were ruled by the King and Queen of the Fae.

Prologue

In the beginning…when the world was new, Fae and humans lived peacefully together, but as the centuries passed, fear and distrust evolved. The Fae continued to love the humans, but they believed it was time to safeguard the realms. Therefore, they appointed the Fenian Warriors to protect the domain between human and faery. But most importantly, these warriors were to assist the humans and steer a new course in the mortal world.

When evil threatened to destroy a clan, country, or civilization, the Fae council called upon these warriors. This group of elite Fae had the power to travel through the Veil of Ages, supporting those in need. They were not to alter the timeline or what the Fae believed to be the life strings of a human. To do so, would be catastrophic.

Ancient and powerful, the Brotherhood of the Fenian Warriors was second only to the Fae King and Queen's powers. They have lived amongst us for thousands of years—watching, aiding, guiding. They could live in the guise of a professor, lawyer, knight, tavern owner, or a simple farmer.

Whatever was required, the warriors did so without complaint. If so much as a whisper of negativity reached their leader, they were banished from the Brotherhood.

In the early formation of the Fenian Warriors, many were chosen to enter the Brotherhood. Yet, some argued as to who should lead this vast number of Fae. A council of nine Fae elders was appointed to oversee the debate regarding a leader. The elders agreed that whoever was chosen had to have qualities which were impeccable. No blemish could stain his life history.

They were given nine days to make their decision. In the end, one Fae stood out in stark contrast to all those who were considered. It was a unanimous decision.

Aidan Kerrigan, older brother to Queen Nuala, was deemed the perfect Fae to govern the Fenian Warriors. His code of ethics rivaled none. Steadfast and loyal to his people and the Brotherhood—not one could find fault in him. In addition, his royal bloodline was vast, and he was one of the few to be born on their homeland of Taralyn within the great cosmos.

So on the summer festival marking the five thousandth year of the Fae living on earth, King Ansgar made Aidan the supreme leader over the Brotherhood. He was bestowed with more powers, making him almost an equal to the King of the Fae.

Over the centuries, admiration grew for the leader of the Fenian Warriors. Honorable, loyal, brave, courageous—words uttered by all when his name was mentioned.

Until one day, when the sun and moon became one on both worlds, and a shift in the Fae realm transpired.

The Fae forgot about the prophecy. No one cared about the whispers on a darkened midday. Nor did any seek out the seer for her wisdom or hear the weeping of the priestesses within the temple of Mother Danu.

The warm air turned frigid in seconds, and not one Fae paused to understand the meaning of what was about to occur.

Yet, one human female did notice in her world.

When she stumbled along a path one spring afternoon in awe of the glorious solar eclipse, the Fates shredded the loom of two individuals—one human and the other a Fae.

The rift in their lives would be glorious *and* catastrophic. Neither would be prepared for the future they faced, or the impact they would have for future generations.

In the end, their fated meeting would bring about the greatest downfall of one of the most revered warriors ever.

And the Fae realm would never be the same again.

Chapter One

*Beneath the Hill of Tara, Ireland, Early spring— the season of growth and renewal in the Fae realm.*

His fingers moved deftly over the hilt of his sword, aching to unsheathe the blade and sever the hand from the warrior's body. Watching the scene unfold in the training camp below, Aidan Kerrigan drew in a sharp hiss. The wind slapped at his face, mocking him to make his move against the defiant Fae. Branches smacked his back in an effort to sway him from his concealment within the trees. He barely registered the wolf's low growl behind him.

Nevertheless, Aidan was a seasoned warrior, not some young lad showing off his prowess in front of his peers and those others whom Aidan had fashioned into hardened Fenian Warriors. No, he would not rush in, though his instinct begged him to do so. He would choose the right moment to reveal himself.

"Why is there always one who defies my orders?" he uttered with contempt.

And the question Aidan posed was immediately answered.

"Because this is how you pluck those who are unworthy to continue with their training in the Brotherhood."

Aidan gripped the hilt more firmly, refusing to

acknowledge his friend and kept his sight riveted on the scene below. "Then explain why those not *worthy* are the ones who possess the most power?"

"Power is intoxicating. Even the strongest cannot deflect the energy all the time."

Arching a brow, Aidan glanced sharply at the Fae. "Do you speak from experience, Flynn? Or was this part of your elusive training when you left the Brotherhood to study under the king's guards?"

A shadow of annoyance passed briefly over his friend's features. "Intoxication in any form is a hindrance to the Fae. Power can fill our bodies, flood our veins, and heighten our senses."

"As with any drug, woman, *or* libation," countered Aidan, releasing his grip on the sword. "This is why I order all initiates to undergo a year without all three. If I deem they cannot control their *basic* urges, then they are not creditable to continue with their training."

"So with the first brush of Fenian power, you believe they should harness the intensity of the feeling?"

Shifting his stance, Aidan clasped his hands behind his back. "Instantly. With one thought, a warrior could obliterate a man into ashes within seconds in the human world. The power should not control the warrior. Are you wavering from your own training, Flynn?"

His friend rubbed a hand over his jaw. "Until my last breath, I shall always recall the rush of power when it first entered my body after the seclusion."

"You did not answer my question."

"No. But for a fraction of a second, I almost let loose the power," Flynn acknowledged.

Aidan eyed his friend warily. What possessed him

to make such a confession? And why now? "Is there a reason you're admitting to this declaration?"

Flynn sighed heavily. "It is a pity. Loman is a strong warrior. In addition, he is blood kin to my own royal house. I only sought to share my story in hopes you would find mercy and allow him to remain."

"Yours was a split-second indecisiveness." Aidan cast his hand outward. "The warrior making a mock display of authority over the others is vastly different. There is no comparison. Furthermore, Loman continues to build the energy without thought to the repercussions. As you know me so well, Flynn, I give *no* mercy to any warrior in training."

His friend shifted his stance, but remained silent.

The wolf padded around in front of Aidan.

"Your companion's interest has grown," commented Flynn.

Aidan shrugged. "Even the animal can sense the misuse of power."

"Or his next feast."

The wolf as well as Aidan snapped their gazes toward Flynn.

"This wolf is a higher species than those in the human world," declared Aidan.

"You should not have brought him into the Fae realm," argued Flynn.

The wolf snickered and returned its attention to the group of Fae below.

Aidan fought the smile forming on his mouth. "The man or beast? Which one should not have been permitted into the kingdom?"

Flynn arched a brow. "Are they not one and the same?"

"His clan is interested in observing the training we do with the young warriors. It was the same with the Dragon Knights. We brought them here for a short time to witness and learn." Aidan waved a hand dismissively. "Dragons, wolves, does it matter?"

"I'd rather deal with dragons," admitted Flynn, folding his arms across his chest.

Aidan chuckled softly. When he requested to bring a member from Clan Sutherland to the Fae realm to survey the training within the Brotherhood, all argued against the preposterous idea. The council judged it unsafe to have a Highlander from the Wolves of Sutherland wander among the Fae and animals, striking at any for his meal. Regardless of Aidan's assurance they would not act upon their predatory instinct to kill for their meal, the council denied his appeal.

Therefore, Aidan took his petition to the king and won. The council was not pleased.

Apparently, Flynn regarded the wolf as a hunter and not an elite warrior—trained in the art of all forms of combat. He had yet to share with his friend that Magnar was also the war chieftain for his clan.

"He has made a vow not to *devour* any Fae while in our homeland," Aidan remarked.

"I do not find your statement amusing," stated Flynn dryly. "Can he not observe in human form?"

In a soft blur of gray shadows, the wolf shimmered into a man. All seven feet of him, and totally naked, he fisted his hands on his hips and glared at Flynn. "Will ye be more comfortable now that I am in my human skin?"

"I was *comfortable* before," argued Flynn.

Magnar sniffed the air. "Liar."

7

Flynn's eyes flashed silver, and he took a step toward the man.

Aidan put a fist to his mouth to stifle the laughter, eager to watch the display of power between his friends. "Be warned, Magnar moves as fast as you or I."

"Ahh…it has been eons since I've challenged anyone in the training lists," proclaimed Flynn.

Magnar relaxed his stance. "And I only confront those I consider *worthy*."

"Arrogant bastard."

"Aye, but do ye not have any *Fae* curse words?"

Flynn shrugged. "You would not comprehend their meaning."

"It will be a pleasure beating ye in the lists." Magnar's smile turned predatory as he shifted back into his wolf form.

Aidan smacked his friend on the shoulder. "Save the event for when I can gather the other warriors."

Flynn pinched the bridge of his nose. "A spectator sport was not what I intended to—"

A blast of power had both men stumbling back. Aidan was the first to recover, and he scanned the area below. Loman had increased the sphere of energy into a massive swirling globe, effectively showing off his power. However, he was unable to control the building orb—the sparks of energy bolted outward in all directions.

Withdrawing his sword, Aidan emerged forth from the trees. "Release the power!"

Slowly turning, Loman's features went from triumphant to wariness, but he refused to relent.

Aidan held his sword upward. "Do as I command!"

Lightning seared the azure sky, and the other

warriors took a step back from Loman.

"Is this not what we trained for?" asked Loman, attempting to harness the energy and failing miserably. Several trees were obliterated into ashes, and one of the warriors put a protective magical shield around the others.

Aidan's fury grew. The warrior refused to do as he ordered. Storming down the hill, he raised his sword outward, aiming not at Loman, but the orb. As he steadily approached, he kept his focus on the warrior. "You defy me?"

Loman refused to acknowledge him. Sweat beaded his brow, and his jaw clenched.

Directing his blade at the energy, Aidan bellowed, "*Finalen absolute*!"

The sphere exploded in an array of golden shards of light. Many of the warriors shielded their eyes from the intensity, but Aidan remained fixed in his position. His sword arm radiated with the residual effect. Lowering his blade to the ground, he forced what was left of the energy into the land.

Loman balled his fists. "I was not ready—"

Swiftly leveling his blade against the warrior's throat, Aidan hissed out, "You did not heed my words. A grave error of misjudgment."

"Call it a learning one," retorted Loman.

It took all of Aidan's control not to shove the blade into the defiant Fae's skin. "A lesson which will haunt you in your later years."

He lifted his left hand, and the ceremonially dagger used in initiations appeared magically. A sliver of blue light emanated from the tip of the blade.

Loman's eyes widened in fear. "No," he

whispered, understanding the consequences.

Aidan tapped the dagger on each of the warrior's shoulders. "You are hereby discharged from all power and rights within the Brotherhood. The markings which were bestowed on you at your commencement are now stripped." The air blistered with the energy, and he took a step back. "Flynn, please escort Loman out of the training lists and beyond the gates of the Brotherhood. We shall send your personal belongings to your home."

"You cannot do this to me!"

The ground rumbled as Aidan tried to control his temper. "Furthermore, I judge it wise you spend some reflective time in the Hall of Remembrance. There, you can witness the events that led to your downfall in the Brotherhood *and* reflect."

As Flynn placed a hand on Loman's shoulder, the warrior shrugged out of his grasp. "I shall present my complaints to the council. They will give their final order."

"Remove him now," ordered Aidan with deadly calm.

Loman had no chance to utter another retort as Flynn removed them both in a flash of light.

Slowly, Aidan swept his gaze to the group of gathered warriors. "Did not one of you attempt to thwart this Fae's abuse of power?"

"To do so would have encouraged his strength and skill," responded Conn, stepping forward. "In truth, we warned him of the consequences last evening when he bragged of the magic he had harnessed."

Aidan ignored his nephew. He expected Conn to be the one to give the account, but he had hoped two others would venture forward. All the warriors looked to Conn, considering he was once Prince of the Fae. In spite of his lineage, his nephew renounced his heritage the instant he became a Fenian Warrior. Ironically, Conn became the spokesperson for each situation or query Aidan posed to the group.

"*We?*" echoed Aidan.

Taren nodded. "I was in agreement with Conn."

The others acknowledged their agreement with a nod or voice.

Scanning the area of warriors, Aidan searched for the two he deemed should have halted Loman's misuse of power, along with Conn. Those three had been successful in harnessing the Fenian power quickly and assured Aidan they would assist the others in maintaining the strength to not bend to the energy's will.

"Where are Liam and Rory?" demanded Aidan. As he waited for a response, he magically rid himself of the ceremonial dagger and sheathed his sword.

"Uncertain," replied Conn.

Aidan leveled a hard stare at his nephew. The lie was evident in the shift within his eyes, and yet, he could not find fault for Conn protecting the two warriors. As they must be allies in the human realm, the warriors' trust in each other was tantamount for their survival.

Conn clasped his hands behind his back. "Give the order and I shall search for them."

"No," he stated with aggravation. "Return to your quarters. Each of you will spend one day in solitary to reflect on this situation." Aidan's gaze settled slowly on each warrior. "Next time another warrior dares to defy an order, I will not be so lenient. Furthermore, I blame each of you for not preventing this destructive display of power. You all stood and observed, instead of preventing your brother. Enthralled by his exhibition is a ploy used by the Dark One at the last battle. Therefore, by your demonstration of not interfering, you showed how unskilled you are to face any battle."

"If I may interject," offered Conn.

Aidan shook his head. "This is not a discussion open to debate. It is a lesson to ponder and learn. The Brotherhood has lost a warrior. You all stood and witnessed the event transpire. It does not matter if you tried to oppose Loman yesterday, last week, or last month." He pointed to the scorched marks where trees once stood. "What concerns me is that you all stood as silent witnesses. Not *one* of you tried to stop the warrior. Or persuade him to relent."

Conn fisted his hands by his side, but nodded.

"You are dismissed," ordered Aidan.

In a silent whisper, each warrior vanished from the training lists. Aidan gave a curt nod to Magnar, and the wolf vanished through the pine trees.

Only then did Aidan let out a frustrated sigh before wandering to the blackened area. Bending on one knee, he placed his palm upon the ground. "Forgive me, Mother Danu." A breeze of roses kissed his cheek. When Aidan lifted his hand, tiny green shoots burst forth from the ashes of destruction.

Slowly standing, he waved his hand outward and magically transported to the Angora Waterfalls.

Mists sprayed him while he stood on the rocky ledge. Stripping free from his vest and leather pants, the echo of the falls roared around him. He rubbed a hand vigorously over his face, attempting to rid himself of the disquiet that had lodged recently within him. Frustration seethed inside him over the path and training of the Fenian Warriors, but there was something else. It was elusive—one moment he believed he had grasped this unrest, and the other times, he blamed it on his direction with the Brotherhood.

Never before had the tides of his life been at war. Usually, there was an ebb and flow. He understood his direction and purpose. Yet lately, he was prone to discontentment. Perchance, he should visit the seer and ask her advice. Would she tell him what he was seeking?

He shook his head slowly. "How can I seek answers when I do not know the question?"

Glancing upward, Aidan watched the graceful flight of a white songbird. Delicate in its beauty and melody, it continued on its path through the air. He thought it odd the unique bird would attempt to fly near the cascading waterfalls.

He stared at the bird. "Are you a portent of a new direction? A new path I must follow?"

The songbird gave a shrill cry and flew off in a different direction.

As he lowered his sight to the water below, Aidan rid himself of all his frustration and dove into the waterfall.

Chapter Two

*"Even without the sight from a Fenian Warrior's eyes, he must be able to follow the path within his heart."*

~Edicts of the Fenian Warriors

The luring tune and heady floral aroma had an intoxicating effect on Aidan as he slipped under the archway leading into the Pleasure Gardens. His body trembled with need, aching to strip his clothing free from his body and seek out the tempting carnal pleasures. He forced his gaze away from the beauty gliding her fingers over the strings of the harp as his cock swelled even more. The lyrical welcome lured him to come near, but he willed his body to refrain from reaching out to her. Her sheer gauzy robe did nothing to conceal her rosy pert nipples enticing him to feast upon them. She winked at him as she continued singing the song.

As he directed his sight elsewhere, Aidan noticed the lovers under a tree heavy with peaches. The woman straddled the man in a provocative pose, feeding him portions of the fruit. She trailed a piece over her lush breast, enticing the man to taste both—fruit and flesh. Aidan fought the urge to join them and suckle the sticky juices from her skin.

Averting his gaze, he followed the dewy grass

across the bridge to a more intimate part of the gardens. He stepped around the fountain of ambrosia, bubbling with the cool, sweet scent of honey and spices. More lovers were crowded around, enjoying the delights of the enthralling liquor. Wildflowers dotted the scenery, encouraging some to gather the flowers and arrange them into garlands for their lover's head.

When the magical whisper of a soft kiss touched the back of his neck, his skin tingled. A groan escaped his lips, and he turned around.

Her smile was seductive as she approached. "It has been eons since you've visited, Aidan Kerrigan. What brings the *mighty* leader of the Fenian Warriors into the Pleasure Gardens?"

"Mina," he acknowledged, trying not to take in her luscious form—minus any clothing. "Perhaps you can assist me?"

She laughed, and Aidan realized his mistake in the question he posed.

Trailing her fingers over his silver torc and down his chest, she whispered, "I have long waited for this day. You shall be my greatest conquest. To give you pleasure like no other."

The sensual atmosphere clouded his mind. Aidan was not making himself clear. He clasped his hands behind his back, not trusting himself. "I'm in search of the elusive MacGregor brothers."

Mina pouted, brushing her hand over his agonizing erection. "Can they give you better pleasure than I?"

He choked on the laughter and held his palms up in surrender. "I am not a Fae prone to the likes of other males. I'm merely here to escort them back to the Brotherhood."

Taking advantage of his weakness, Mina took his hands and placed them on her full breasts. "A pity you do not have the time to indulge in what the gardens have to offer."

Aidan smiled. "Time to partake in these pleasures is something I no longer can afford." Squeezing her breasts slightly, he released his hands and cupped her chin. "Where are they?"

Sadness briefly flashed in her eyes. "Is this not their time to quench their sexual desires before you send them into the world with humans?"

Aidan fought the barb he wanted to lash out at the woman. She was deliberately avoiding his question. Furthermore, Liam and Rory had no right discussing their status outside the walls of the Brotherhood. "If they are unable to quench their lustful thirst within a twenty-four hour time period, I deem they are not suitable to remain warriors."

"Do not pass blame on them," she protested and quickly added, "They were given a special cup of the ambrosia elixir."

He arched a brow in disdain. "Why were they given the invigorating drink? Surely they did not need any assistance in seeking their pleasures."

Mina looked affronted. "Of course not! They offered to sample the ancient mixture, so it was made available to them."

"But you neglected on explaining the effects of the ambrosia," mused Aidan, watching her reaction to the truth.

A blush stained her cheeks, and she shrugged. "We wanted them to remember their experience in the gardens while they were above."

"We?" Aidan almost choked on the word. Once again, he found the word distasteful.

"Yes." Annoyance passed over her features. "The maidens who are skilled in techniques in maintaining an erection for—"

"Enough!" Aidan bit out. "I am well aware of their…*unique* talents."

Her sensual smile returned. "Then you can comprehend how the days have blurred in the arms of these Fae women. You cannot find fault with your warriors."

"Your logic is sound, but you did nothing to explain the potent effects of the ambrosia. Without it, I am confident the MacGregor brothers would have achieved their satisfaction and returned in the appropriate amount of time."

Mina studied him for several moments. "You are correct, Aidan. Regardless, the blame is mine, not theirs. I gave them the drink without supplying the knowledge. If your order must be to punish someone, I will happily surrender my body into your care. I will become your personal submissive slave."

"What a grand proposal." Leaning near, he whispered, "My punishment for you is one year banished from the Pleasure Gardens?"

She gasped and staggered back. "You…you would not dare?"

"A challenge?"

Lifting her chin in defiance, Mina glared at him. "I retract my earlier *suggestion*. Follow me."

Aidan's mouth twitched in humor. Though her offer was tempting, he would never submit another Fae to quench his own pleasures. They came willingly with their own carnal desires, and not as a bargaining chip. Unfortunately, after he took leadership over the Fenian Warriors, women stopped appearing at the door of his chambers. The truth reached him one day when he bumped into an acquaintance who had frequented his bed many an evening. When he asked why she never returned, her response was she and others feared he would find human females to sample. They had no wish to share the great Aidan Kerrigan with a human. They considered it beneath him to take a female from the realm above. He called the rumor preposterous and sealed his chamber doors to any further liaisons within the Fae realm.

Watching Mina stroll seductively down a moss-covered path, Aidan almost called her back to him. He'd take her rough and quickly, sating both their needs. He shook his head to rid himself of the lustful image of her body bent over and his cock thrusting deep into her slick folds.

His hand shook as he wiped it over his brow. Taking a deep breath, Aidan released it slowly. "Perchance another time," he uttered softly and did his best to harness the sexual tension within his body.

"I am waiting," she announced with impatience.

Aidan kept silent as he proceeded to make his way to her. Mina stood at a door carved within a massive oak tree. She bent and retrieved a golden key at the base of the giant. After opening the door, she stepped aside. "Do not tarry too long, or you may find that your body will betray you and stay with the others," she warned.

"Leave the door open," he commanded as he swept past her.

"It is not done," she countered.

He glanced over his shoulder. "Must I remind you of your past failure?"

Narrowing her eyes, she responded, "As you wish, Aidan Kerrigan. I shall stand guard."

Giving her a curt nod, he followed the narrow, wooded path filled with song and enticing scents.

His cock strained even more against his pants. Fighting the urges that plagued him the moment he entered the gardens, Aidan swept his gaze around the sensual interior. Water lapped gently over the stones within the stream. Scents of lovemaking and soft groans filled his being, and he swallowed.

Annoyance became his shield. "Present yourselves, Liam and Rory MacGregor!"

The ground rumbled beneath him, and a muttered curse came from beyond a cluster of amber trees.

Liam was the first to stumble forth, clutching only his tunic. "Aidan?" His tone a mangled version of itself.

Ignoring the warrior, he pointed to a position where he wanted the Fae to stand, and bellowed, "I will not order you again Rory MacGregor!"

Feminine laughter floated toward Aidan, and Rory staggered forth from the trees. "By the hounds, can we not have privacy?"

"I deem five long days is enough seclusion to slake your need, MacGregor," protested Aidan.

Rory had donned his tunic and ran a hand through his hair. "*One* day," he corrected.

Without warning, Aidan leveled a burst of power at Rory. The warrior slammed into a tree, gasping for breath.

Aidan shot Liam a warning look when he attempted to retrieve his brother from his prone position on the ground.

"Is your head now clear, Fenian Warrior?" snapped Aidan, fisting his hands on his hips.

"Yes," he grumbled, rubbing a hand vigorously over his face.

Aidan regarded Liam. "And yours, warrior?"

"Absolutely."

"Good. Let us depart."

As they made a hasty departure through the Pleasure Gardens, Mina followed. When they reached the exit, she touched Aidan's arm. "Do not be a stranger. Your body is meant for exquisite passion and enjoyment."

Grasping her fingers, he placed a light kiss over her knuckles. "Farewell."

She dipped her head and closed the door behind him.

Inhaling deeply, Aidan cleared the last remnants of the gardens from his body and mind. He turned and observed the strained expressions on the MacGregor brothers. Each had the appearance of too much intoxication—from drink and women. He was sorely tempted to order them directly to the training lists.

Aidan folded his arms over his chest. "Who suggested drinking from the ancient well of ambrosia?"

Both warriors straightened, but remained silent. Wariness showed within their eyes.

Shaking his head, Aidan fought his impatience over their lack of response. "Since your minds remain clouded, I will indulge you with this information. After drinking the potent elixir, you lost all sense of time and place. In reality, your one day of leave consisted of *five*."

Rory shifted his stance. "Are we to be banished from the Brotherhood for this grave error?"

"An interesting question, MacGregor." Aidan moved aside and steadily made his way down the path.

The warriors followed alongside him. After an hour wandering through the Fae hills, Liam slowed his steps. "Is there a reason we're walking and not magically transporting to the Brotherhood?"

Aidan smirked, but resumed his pace. "Another fascinating question."

When the second hour approached, Rory halted and bent over. Sweat poured off his brow.

"Is there a problem, *Fenian Warrior*?" inquired Aidan.

A muscle twitched in Rory's jaw as he slowly straightened. "No."

"Excellent," professed Aidan. "It's only ten more miles to the Angora Waterfalls."

Both brothers exchanged looks of horror, but swiftly masked their expressions and descended the path to the meadow leading to the falls.

Onward they traversed, and Aidan had to contain his mirth when one or the other would stumble, groan, or utter a foul curse after tripping over an exposed tree root or stone in their path. His mood had lightened considerably the farther they went, enjoying the pitiful reactions from the two brothers. If his plan succeeded, they would sweat out the elixir's potent effects by the time they reached the water.

When the roar of the waterfalls reached them, Rory muttered, "Finally."

Aidan pressed forward, brushing aside the thick foliage. Entering the serene place, he followed the stone path leading upward.

"Are we to climb the steep area?" asked Rory.

Ignoring the MacGregor, Aidan continued his ascent. After reaching the top, he rid himself of his tunic. Folding his arms over his chest, he shouted, "You both have twenty seconds to reach the top, or we shall begin this journey all over again! And no magic!"

Both brothers glanced at each other, and the race for the top began in earnest. Liam shoved his brother back and jumped on the second stone step, making quick strides. Yet, Rory swiftly regained his stance and dashed to the other side of the waterfalls. Each determined to be the first to the top, and Aidan fought the smile forming on his mouth.

The MacGregor brothers were back in competition to best the other.

Once, Liam stumbled, but righted himself and resumed the trek upward. Despite how much Rory complained during their journey, he still managed to make it to the top before Liam.

"Should you not be over here?" barked out Liam, wiping a hand down the back of his neck.

Rory roared with laughter. "Of course, little brother." With a flick of his wrist, he transported himself to Liam's side.

Liam jabbed a finger into his chest. "As always, you cheated. Might I remind you, I am the same size as you."

His brother shrugged in good humor. "I did not use magic to climb the stones, only to be by your side. Furthermore, Aidan did not mention which side of the waterfall to ascend. And as you are the youngest in our family, I considered using the term, *little brother* to annoy you."

Pleased to see the brothers back to their semi-normal selves, Aidan clamped a hand on each warrior's shoulder. "Let this be a lesson to you both. I shall not tolerate another incident like this one again. Nor will I fetch you myself. In the future, I will send the council guards."

All traces of humor vanished from Rory and Liam, and they nodded solemnly.

"This week was one where many learned valuable lessons on the path to being a Fenian Warrior. Not only must you learn to control your carnal urges, but also the power you will possess and wield. I dismissed Loman from the Brotherhood for ignoring a direct order and misuse of his powers. I deem the situation might have been avoided if you both were there to thwart the warrior's lack of discretion when building the energy."

Liam narrowed his eyes. "He did not listen to me when I explained the danger. His arrogance was his downfall."

"As yours could have been," countered Aidan.

"You have my word this will not happen again," stated Liam.

"And mine as well," affirmed Rory.

"Good. Now swim five hundred laps through the healing waters to rid the last traces of the elixir from your veins, and we shall speak no more of this incident. After you have completed your task, you may transport yourselves magically to your chamber within the Brotherhood." Without giving them a chance to utter a complaint, Aidan pushed them both over the waterfall.

Their combined cries of displeasure echoed within the mists and roar of the water.

Aidan settled himself on a nearby boulder. He had no need to supervise the MacGregor brothers any further. Leaning forward, he cast his sight across the expanse of the river below. Once again, a flicker of discontentment wove a thread within his soul. Quickly banishing it on a sigh, he glanced over his shoulder.

The leaves fluttered in the warm spring air, and a white stag with golden horns appeared. His regal stature and horns suggested his leadership among the others within the forest. Aidan stood slowly. He waited patiently for the animal to approach. However, it remained rooted in its position.

"What quest must I seek? Do you bring a message from Mother Danu, or are you merely passing through?" Though Aidan judged it was the latter. The great Goddess normally chose to communicate with him in floral scents and song.

As the soft afternoon light spilled over its form, the animal transformed into a stag—resembling the ones living in the human world.

Frustration overrode curiosity. "My purpose is here—to train the Fenian Warriors. There are others who can assist the humans in their world. Seek them out."

Blinding pain seared into his thoughts, and Aidan closed his eyes.

*"It is your destiny, Fenian Warrior."*

Chapter Three

*"Snip the petals from the foxglove, bluebells, and primrose. Toss with sprigs of rosemary and scatter along a path around your home."*

*~Society of the Thistle*

*Glasgow, Scotland ~ Spring 1986*

"If you had let me trim your hair, none of this would have happened," declared Lily between fits of laughter.

"Get the bloody animals away from me! The length of my hair has nothing to do with this awful situation."

"Rose MacLaren! Those are *our* beloved goats. For shame."

"They're eating my hair *and* clothes. I'm trapped," complained Rose, doing her best to free herself from the assault of the animals surrounding her in their enclosure.

Her sister continued to laugh at the scene, instead of trying to help her out of her current predicament. "You should have let me tend to them, instead of wading out in your good clothes." She sputtered on hysterical fits of laughter. "At least you had the common sense to put on your wellies."

"They had to be fed, and I didn't see any of the others helping."

Lily wagged a finger at her. "Sorry we can't be like you and rise from our beds at the first call of the songbird. Or the streak of sunlight which graces the morn."

"Ouch! I swear by the Goddess, Lily, if you don't help me this instant, I'm going to tell Deacon that you fancy him." She tugged, attempting to turn around, but to no avail.

Her sister sobered instantly. "You would not dare?"

Rose winced from the pain, trying to pull her hair free from the mouths of two stubborn animals. "Did I say fancy? I meant to say lust. Or is it love? Yes, I believe you l.o.v.e him."

"You're a wicked sister! You know I *despise* the man!" Lily stormed off into the barn continuing with her litany of objections.

Now it was Rose's turn to laugh. However, the effort cost her, and she yelped in pain. "Blast it all!"

Her sister soon returned carrying a sack containing sweet carrots from the garden. After tossing most of the vegetables into a corner, she coaxed the remaining few animals away from Rose's skirt and hair with remnants of what was left in the bag.

"Finally." Rose twisted the mass of hair around the front of her body, inspecting the ends. "Sweet Brigid! What a sodden mess."

Lily snorted. "Looks like you'll need that trim after all."

Rose darted an incredulous look at her sister. "I won't let you near me with any form of shears."

"You wound me, Sister," Lily teased as she climbed over the fence and ran off toward the barn. "I can't help it my eyesight is worse than yours."

Grumbling another curse, Rose rapidly exited the pen, securing the gate behind her. Not only was her hair in shambles, but also her clothes. As she glanced upward at the sun's direction, she realized she was late again for her class on Herbology at the university. "It's not like I need the knowledge," she muttered, wiping the grime from her hands onto her skirt and heading toward the cluster of elm trees. "I believe I can recite the Latin name of every herb, foliage, and tree in Scotland."

"But not those in the rest of the world," argued the female voice behind her.

Rose stumbled, but quickly righted herself, and then turned on her friend. "Honestly, Maeve? Did you swoop down from the air to scare me?"

Her friend glared at her. "Did you wake up this morning intending on being spiteful to everyone you encountered?"

Blowing out a frustrated breath, Rose went to a large boulder beneath one of the trees. "I'm sorry. Can I blame my foul mood on the impending full moon?"

"No, it won't work for an explanation. You of all people know how to harness the energy of the Goddess during this time." Maeve motioned her to move down, so she could sit next to her.

Rose wiped her nose with the back of her hand. "I'm distracted and unable to focus. My nerves are jumbled, and I can't make any sense of the dreams I'm having."

"Dreams? Not visions?"

Rose plucked a leaf from her hair, feeling the heat rise along her neck. "I seriously doubt a vision would contain three moons."

"It could be the triple Goddess," mused Maeve. She tapped a finger to her mouth. "Or she's informing you to attend the Beltaine festival outside the city."

"And an extremely tall man?" Rose dared not look at her friend.

"Have you seen him before?" Her question held a note of curiosity.

Inspecting her hands, Rose replied. "Never. Though, his features were hidden and his back turned toward me."

"And this bothers you?"

Rose swallowed and stood. "His voice was commanding, powerful, *intoxicating*." She darted a glance over her shoulder. "Yet, I didn't understand any of the words. He spoke in a foreign tongue."

Maeve arched a brow. "A sensual dream?"

Rose threw her hands up in frustration. "With whom? I haven't dated anyone in over a year, and I have no desire to meet anyone. I'm far too busy."

"How long have you had this particular dream?"

"A week."

Maeve patted the boulder. "Come sit and give me the details."

"I can't. Each time I reflect on the dream, my nerves become frazzled." Rose twisted her hands together.

"Have you written them down?"

"Goodness no! I never write down my visions."

Maeve pointed a finger at her. "But you said they were *dreams*, which is important in any journal."

Wiping a hand over her brow, Rose debated if she should draw the image. "Perhaps I should sketch the details?"

Smiling, Maeve nodded. "My next suggestion. Can you share anything else?"

She glanced upward at the sunlight streaming down through the canopy of trees. "It begins with a flash of brilliant light, expanding to reveal a mound. I am drawn by the beauty of the area. When I step through, darkness descends around me, and the stars glitter like diamonds in the black sky. I remain standing and watch as three moons rise over the crest, illuminating the man standing in the middle of the hill. His hands are lifted as if in reverence."

Clasping her hands to her rapidly beating heart, Rose added, "His stance spoke volumes. His hair was dark as ebony, and a body that looks chiseled from the Gods. He is without a shirt, and his voice—deep and sensual—echoes to my soul. The markings on his back are reminiscent of Celtic spirals, so I understand he follows the same path as we do."

Silently, Rose returned to her friend's side. "He speaks to me every night, and though I do not understand the words, his meaning is clear."

"He is coming for you, Rose," confirmed Maeve.

"For what purpose? Does he herald a new beginning? A path?" Rose shook her head slowly. "Surely, he must be a God honoring the Goddess and wants me to do the same. Or I am seeing a dream from the past."

Maeve poked her in the arm. "This vision has stirred emotions in you."

"Dream," corrected Rose once again and stood. She slammed the door on the images and feelings within her body. "Whenever I have a vision, it's only once. They never repeat, so I have to conclude it's only a recurring dream."

"And I disagree," argued Maeve, rising to stand by her side. "You are drawn to him, his words, and the three moons. By the way this has you rattled, I can only presume it's a portent of something coming your way."

How could Rose dispute her friend's wisdom and counsel? Maeve's gift of intuition and inner sight was often more powerful than hers. There were times when she longed to possess another gift like the other women in The Society of the Thistle. Trying to discern meanings from the visions left her baffled and frustrated.

Rose chewed on her bottom lip as she made her way back to the main house. "I don't need a man in my life. It's only the God and Goddess sending me a dream."

"The more you fight the tide of prophecy, the more it will bring you under. Accept the message or drown and miss the meaning, Rose."

"How can I understand when I don't know the language?" she shouted over her shoulder.

"Don't let fear rule your heart! The next time you dream, walk forward."

"Damn it all," whispered Rose, and then regretted the outburst. A vision or dream came from the Goddess, and it should not be treated with disrespect. "Forgive me, Goddess. I shall do my best to decipher this message. Yet, why do you send it to me over and over each night?"

Distracted by her earlier conversation with her friend, Rose almost collided into the oncoming bicyclist. "Oh! Sorry, Colleen," she blurted out, darting out of the way.

The woman gave her a smile and waved in passing, heading around the back of the main house. "Enough of men and moons. I'll dwell on the meaning later."

Rose entered the mudroom of the massive two-story house. Depositing her boots alongside all the other pairs, she ran up the stairs to her room. After stripping free from her clothes, she inspected her skirt. Muttering a curse, she tossed it in the rubbish bin. At least her blouse had survived the munching attack from the goats. She hastily cleaned up and surveyed the damage done to her hair. Retrieving a pair of shears, she left in search of one of the other women living with them.

Lily greeted her at the bottom of the staircase, presenting her with a fresh-baked scone. "A peace offering for not attempting to free you earlier."

The aroma of cinnamon and spices wafted by her, and her stomach protested. "And I'm sorry for threatening you with romantic lies about Deacon." Her mouth twitched in humor. "Though, you should have seen the look on your face."

Lily smacked her playfully. "Good thing I love you."

After placing a kiss on her sister's cheek, Rose accepted the warm scone. "I love you, too." Taking a bite, she savored the sweetness and closed her eyes. "Mmm…you make the best, sis."

"Why, thank you. But I must confess that Katie made these."

Rose snapped open her eyes and brushed a few crumbs away from her mouth. "Seriously?"

"Yes, and with minimal supervision. Not only is

she a splendid empath, but a fine baker." Lily linked her arm through hers. "What's on the agenda for the Society since you're not going to class today?"

Rose devoured the rest of the scone. "We could look over the plans on the newest project near Aberdeen?"

"The one in the wooded area? The village of Corridon?" inquired Lily, moving them along the corridor.

"Correct. I'm anxious to find out what the ruins mean and see if there's a connection with the dig nearby outside of Glasgow. I heard a student mention peculiar writing on the stones here that are similar to the ones recently uncovered in Corridon."

Frowning, Lily tugged on her arm. "Our instructions were to inspect the plants and other rare specimens and flowers on both sites."

"And we will, but if there are ancient writings on any of the standing stones surrounding the ruins, we might be able to glimpse what type of foliage was growing there thousands of years ago." Rose steered them into the library and toward the desk.

"Since when does the Society concern itself with the writing on ancient stones? You do realize there is already an archaeological team there, right? Furthermore, I thought your classes kept you from these projects."

"So I've been told by Professor Linton. And I've made the decision to drop my *one* class at the university in favor of doing this research." She placed the shears on the desk. Reaching for her glasses, Rose inspected a map of the area. She pointed to a space about a half-kilometer from the area they were given permission to survey. "It's in the direct path of the site we're working on, so I don't see why we can't record notes from the stones."

Lily braced her hands on the desk, studying the map. "Have you forgotten about the warning from the last mishap?"

"Tsk, tsk, such formal language."

"I'm serious, Rose," warned her sister. "The university could have banned us from any future excavations. You had no right inserting your beliefs that it was first Vikings, not Saxons who settled along the banks of the Kaylean River."

"There were runes and other objects fashioned by the Vikings which could not be ignored," protested Rose.

"Regardless, they could have forbidden us to ever come to a site again after your heated debate with the professor. We are fortunate to be able to view the area where the standing stones are, as well as in Corridon. I fear Maeve and I are going to have our hands full with keeping you restrained."

Sinking into the cushioned chair, Rose regarded her sister. "The Society is an ancient order—eight hundred years old—established by a powerful laird for his clan, specifically his wife. We should be granted more respect, instead of being pushed aside. We're the descendants from the original order created centuries ago. In addition, the man hated I proved him wrong months later."

Lily arched a brow. "They don't like our pagan ways."

"This isn't the middle ages where they burned witches," Rose argued, rubbing her temples.

"Thankfully, the administration at the university would not order a burning, but they can certainly leave us out of anymore findings. To be excluded from these would send a message to other places in the country and they could ban us as well."

"The universities are more tolerant of our Order in Boston," grumbled Rose.

"There's no one there challenging them," countered Lily, pulling up a chair and sitting down.

An idea blossomed within Rose. "What we need is an insider related to the project."

Lily shook her head vehemently. "Absolutely not! I will not be friendly with Deacon."

Reaching across the desk, Rose grabbed her sister's hand. "Though I may have teased—"

"*Threatened*," corrected Lily.

"Yes, yes, but I would not ask you to be pleasant to the man for the sake of gaining access. Is there anyone else you can think of? They are more forthcoming with you in the archaeological group than with me."

"I did hear Professor Linton state they were bringing several more assistants onto the team, so let me do some covert research."

"Perfect." Rose released her sister's hand and stood. "And I give you my solemn vow to behave myself on this new assignment."

"Are you sure I can't trim those jagged ends for you?" asked Lily, standing and coming alongside her. "I will endeavor to do my best and wear my glasses."

Rose patted her sister's cheek affectionately. "As much as I love you, I believe it's wiser to have one of the other women assist me."

"Rose *Aine* MacLaren, you wound me once again,"

pouted Lily, though her eyes danced with mirth.

"Bah! I know your devious side, Lily *Diana* MacLaren. You've been aching to cut my locks to my shoulders since we were young lasses playing in fields of wildflowers."

"And you landed in a patch of nettles," added Lily, cupping a hand over her mouth.

"A dreadful incident," remarked Rose, doing her best not to laugh. "At least mother had the good sense not to chop off all my hair."

"I tried to convince her otherwise!" shouted Lily.

"Thank the stars she refused to listen to you."

As Rose departed the library, her sister's laughter followed her down the hall.

Chapter Four

*"Happiness is often times fleeting. A code of honor is immortal."*

~Edicts of the Fenian Warriors

Aidan paced within the chambers, darting a glance at the prism of light streaming through the stained-glass window. A rainbow of colors danced along the floor, creating a magical effect inside the room. After listening patiently to the proposal, he sought answers to the many questions tumbling through his mind, especially the ones pertaining to the Standing Stones of Corridon. He paused and lifted his hand to the light. "Why the twentieth century in Scotland, Loran?"

When his friend and member of the Fae council remained quiet, Aidan turned around. For a moment, sorrow brushed across the Fae's features. Loran quickly masked his emotions and rubbed a hand over his chin. "This missive comes from the High Seer. She states there is a situation that must be contained."

Aidan frowned. "But why did she request me?"

"Uncertain," replied Loran. "As you are aware, the seer rarely divulges all of the vision."

"How true," muttered Aidan. "Has King Ansgar been informed?"

"Yes, and he did have his reservations."

Walking to the window, Aidan leaned against the

ledge. "If the king does not wish to see me take on this mission, I will happily turn it over to Ronan, Conn, and Flynn to assess the situation in the mortal realm."

"The king was reminded that though you are the leader of the warriors, you are not above your duty to oversee important timelines in the human world. In addition, you have land near the site, do you not?"

Growing frustrated with the lack of information Loran was supplying, Aidan fisted his hands on his hips. "Yes. I have a castle in the hills of Aberdeenshire, though I have not visited in centuries. What exactly do these particular stones reveal in Scotland?"

"The Fae realm and our origins."

Aidan abruptly pushed away from the window. "Who would dare violate our rules?"

His friend shrugged. "Any one of the ancient civilizations on Earth, but I deem it was the Picts."

Aidan waved his hand in dismissal. "There has never been a recorded account found from these people. It must be another ancient tribe."

"Then only the best warrior should be sent to disprove my theory."

Chuckling softly, Aidan shook his head. "Do not flatter me, old friend."

"Why the objections? You have not visited above for many years."

"Others need to be trained, and I have no need to venture to the mortal realm."

Loran fidgeted with the quill on his desk. "Is it beneath you?"

"Of course not, but my duties are required here."

"Regardless, the order has been given *and* granted. If you oppose this assignment, then I suggest you take your argument to the king."

Aidan returned his attention to Loran's garden outside the window. Seeking counsel from King Ansgar was often not favorable, especially after his son Conn entered the Brotherhood. Their conversations remained clipped and terse. The king had no wish for his only son to renounce his heritage to the kingdom. Aidan considered if Ansgar put part of the blame on allowing Conn to join the elite group as his fault. No matter the argument he made to Ansgar, his mind had already been set.

And the division between the king and Aidan began.

Aidan retreated from the ledge. "I shall make arrangements for someone to be in charge of the Fenian Warriors. Am I permitted to bring any other warriors?"

Loran nodded slowly. "Yes. Whom did you have in mind?"

"Since this pertains to historical events, I judge it wise to bring Liam."

"I concur," agreed Loran. "Your journey begins at the light of the next day. Though I believe Rory will not look favorably on being left out of a historical dig."

Aidan glanced sharply over his shoulder. "The *MacGregor* brothers need to spend some time apart."

His friend remained silent and continued to fidget with items on his desk.

Crossing the room to Loran, he studied the elder's features. "Is there more you care to impart to me?"

Chuckling softly, Loran placed a hand on Aidan's shoulder. "Do not attempt to analyze my features. My concerns are with this mission."

"Do you sense danger? A threat to the kingdom?"

His friend shrugged and retrieved a scroll from the shelves in back of his desk. "As you recall, centuries ago it was a woman who claimed to have the knowledge of the stars—of people who descended to Eire and inhabited the island. She even documented the event on parchment." Loran tapped the scroll against his fingers. "Thankfully, it was retrieved for safekeeping."

"If required, we shall bury the stone artifact into the ground," suggested Aidan.

"And to have it surface later?" Loran shook his head. "No. Assess the situation and determine if the translation needs to be altered in any form, but only by the human archaeologists—not Fae magic. Convince them of another meaning."

Aidan gestured to the parchment. "We can always collect the stone and preserve it for safekeeping in our realm."

Loran arched a brow in disdain. "Obtaining a large stone tablet, which has most likely been catalogued, photographed, and discussed by the Earth's news media, is far more difficult than snatching a piece of parchment from the tent of an eighth century bard."

"Merely a thought. Or we could cause the elements to destroy the stone…" Aidan paused and folded his arms across his chest. "No. That theory won't work either. Photographs and such."

"Precisely."

Waving a hand in the air, Aidan added, "I'm positive the issue will present a solution when we have examined the situation."

"Keep within the Fae laws," advised Loran, dropping the scroll onto his desk.

"The leader of the Fenian Warriors shall always abide by the codes." After giving the elder a mock salute, Aidan vanished in a sliver of light.

\*\*\*\*

The air swarmed with bees, and the scent of honeysuckle floated by Aidan as he proceeded down the curved path within the royal gardens. Spring had always been his favorite, and he smiled as his steps took him past new growth in the flower garden. As was always the custom with his sister, Nuala, she favored her garden during the early morning.

He brushed his fingers over the lavender wands flowing lazily with the warm breeze. Whenever he visited, a sense of peace and calm descended within his soul. Flowers of every kind sprouted forth in abundance, presenting a fusion of colors.

Bending to inhale the heady floral scent of a rose, Aidan was tempted to pluck the petals.

"Do not encourage or tamper with the growth of the flowers in my garden," warned Nuala.

He peered over the rose bushes, finding his sister on her hands and knees, kneading the soil near a cluster of bluebells. She was barefoot and wearing a simple gown. "I would not dare," he teased, coming around in front of her. "Does the Queen of the Fae enjoy playing in the dirt?"

His sister tossed a lump of soil in his direction, and he swiftly maneuvered out of the way. "Your aim is off, *wee* sister."

Nuala trailed a path in the dirt with her finger. The ground rumbled beneath Aidan, sending him sprawling backward onto the ground. She stood and flicked her wrists to magically rid the dirt from her hands. "Never underestimate the power of the queen, regardless if she happens to be your sibling."

Aidan placed his hands over his bent knees and roared with laughter. "Duly noted." Standing, he gave a slight bow. "My queen."

Nuala chuckled softly and went to embrace him. "It is good to see you, Aidan."

Cradling her head against his chest, he exhaled slowly. Guilt plagued him. "I have been away far too long."

"Agreed," she uttered softly. "But I presume your duties will always keep you away, since the Brotherhood is your home and position."

After breaking free, Aidan cast his gaze outward to the garden. "Conn is doing extremely well in the Brotherhood. Your son has chosen his path."

"As I expected," she mused and walked along the path between the bluebells.

Aidan followed her. His sister passed under a trellis thick with ivy and primroses and gestured for him to sit beside her on a rose quartz bench. Water flowed in a gentle current from the river behind them.

Leaning forward, Aidan braced his forearms on his thighs. "I have forgotten how serene the royal gardens can be on one's spirit."

"All Fae gardens in the realm are tranquil. You find this particular landscape appealing because you have not visited the blossoming of the land in some time."

He glanced sideways at her. "You have a special touch, Nuala."

"The season of rebirth brings us all home again," she declared, trailing her fingers over the primroses.

"I suppose."

She frowned and clasped her hands together in her lap. "What troubles you, Aidan?"

"Unsure."

"Specify," she ordered.

"What have your visions told you about me?"

She regarded him coolly. "Answer *my* question."

Standing abruptly, Aidan paced within the bucolic setting. "Discontentment, uncertainty, threads which are elusive and do not present themselves."

"You need to run barefoot across the land," suggested Nuala.

Halting before her, he folded his arms over his chest. "I am not a lad who needs some playtime."

Nuala waved a hand dismissively. "No. You are a Fae and connected to the land. You have forgotten in your quest to hone and sharpen the Fenian Warriors."

"I am fully aware of my *connection*. Nevertheless, I have no time to dwell on reflective contemplation. A situation requires my attention in the human world."

Nuala lowered her head. "I have heard the news."

Tipping her chin up with his finger, Aidan asked, "From Ansgar *or* a vision?"

"Both." She took his hand and stood. "I cannot see the vision clearly, Aidan."

Confused by her statement, he shrugged. "Why does this concern you? The mission requires a delicate, but firm assessment. As soon as it is concluded, I will return home."

Pushing away from him, Nuala walked down a moss-covered path toward the river. Sunlight radiated off his Fae sister as if she drew it to her. He darted across the path and reached for her hand. "You have not answered any of my questions."

A smile tugged at the corner of her mouth. "Which ones? As one of the seers, I am bound by their laws and can choose not to reveal my visions."

He placed her hand over his heart. "And as my sister you have sworn to always divulge anything that comes from the Goddess in a vision regarding me."

Nuala attempted to free her hand, but Aidan kept a firm hold. "A pledge sworn *before* I became the queen and a seer," she protested.

He released her hand and walked to the river. An amethyst winked from the water's edge, and Aidan bent to retrieve the gem. "Is there anything you can share?" he asked, inspecting the stone between his fingers.

"Your destiny awaits, and sadly, I don't foresee you returning to our home anytime soon."

*Destiny?* There was that word again. It had woven its way into him daily ever since the stag had made its appearance. He glanced over his shoulder. "Can you see the path ahead? I require guidance, Nuala."

She tilted her head to the side, studying him for several heartbeats. "Only a glimpse. Do not move. Do not speak."

Moving gracefully farther along the river's edge, she went to the largest expanse of the water. Nuala bent and scooped up a portion of the fine white sand, which extended out on either side of the river. As she stepped into the water, she let the glistening particles slip free from her fingers. The radiance around his sister shimmered, and the flow of the river ceased, sealing them in a cocoon of time.

Aidan feared to breathe as he watched in awe. A mirror of images blurred in a kaleidoscope of jeweled colors, and the air cooled considerably around him. Voices echoed within the water, along with vehicles from the human world. A brilliant flash of light was followed by darkness, along with musical laughter and singing he had never heard before. The female's gaiety whispered against his soul, and Aidan's heart pounded erratically. He kept his gaze locked in the middle of the river, searching for her face within the multi-faceted images.

When the first glimmer of light danced across the sky, Aidan was held spellbound by the beauty that materialized in front of him. Flowing silver-blonde hair floated with each movement of her body. She kept her back to him as she continued to lure him forward with her siren's song. He yearned to lend his voice to the melody.

Instinctively, he lifted his hand toward her, determined to see her face.

A wave of energy sent Aidan spiraling through the air. Once more, he landed with a thud against the ground. Lights, sounds, and dizziness swamped him. Several moments passed before he was able to recover. He blinked, trying to access his surroundings. Shielding his eyes, he stared into the mournful face of his sister.

"You should not have attempted to reach out," she chastised.

Aidan stood slowly. Confused over the vision, he asked, "Why was I drawn to her? Is she Fae?"

"I cannot decipher a vision."

He grasped her hands. Coldness seeped into him. "Then why the solemn veneer?"

"I can offer you no more, Aidan. I've shown you a *possible* future. Only you can make the determination if it is the right journey to follow."

"Give me *something*," he pleaded.

Tears misted her eyes. "No matter the path you choose, it will lead to destruction."

He released her hands as if he had been burned. His sister's words were like a knife to his heart, and he took a hesitant step back.

"Then I will send another on this mission."

Her smile held sadness. "You of all Fae understand that once a path is taken, you cannot alter its ending."

His laugh was bitter. Clasping his hands behind his back, he stared at the flowing river. "I have *yet* to make the journey."

"Wrong," she argued. "The Fates set in motion your timeline the moment you accepted this assignment."

"Regardless, I shall find another to take my place," he snapped.

"Will the *great* Fenian Warrior allow fear to guide him? You mistook the meaning of the word destruction. There are other interpretations."

Aidan met her gaze, seeing the censure within. "If there was any positive explanation to glean from this vision, I am confident your demeanor would not have been filled with remorse."

Eyes that blazed with anger glared at him. "Your time spent in the Brotherhood has hardened you, *Brother*. You see black and white. Good versus evil. Right and wrong. Obviously, your mind is clouded with the rigorous training required by the warriors." Turning her back on him, she stormed away from the water and through the trees.

Blowing out a frustrated breath, he pleaded,

"Nuala, wait."

She halted and glanced over her shoulder. "I have no wish to banter harsh words before you depart."

He chuckled softly. "You're so sure I'm going to leave?"

Mirth replaced the anger in her features. "Yes. Of that, I am positive. You have never retreated from a challenge, especially one that involves you. Stop using your title of leadership over the Fenian Warriors as an excuse to step back from a quest."

Aidan rubbed a hand down the back of his neck. Though his sister was younger than he was, she often proved herself the wisest one in their family. "Any parting words of wisdom, my queen?"

Nuala smiled fully. "Look between the dark and light. Find the colors of your life, Aidan. And remember, out of the ashes of destruction, a new life is always born." Blowing him a kiss, she vanished in a colorful arc of lights.

"Farewell, *dear sister*."

Chapter Five

*"Do not disregard a weed as ominous to the garden. The very plant could be your salvation in cultivating a new flower."*

*~Society of the Thistle*

Rose drew her coat more firmly around her body, surveying the excavation in the early morning light. The damp, cool air swirled around her, and a tremor of unease settled like a lodestone within her body. She crouched down and scanned the area where many of the standing stones were positioned in a horseshoe pattern facing toward the east. "They greet the rising of the sun and moon," she explained softly.

"I agree," Lily acknowledged, bending down next to her. She pointed to a stone slab partially exposed in the dirt and positioned flat on the ground. "A witness stone to the ancients?"

"Possibly, though we need to further inspect the writings and the stones in Corridon." She mentally noted the land around the stones—from grasses, wildflowers, and the subtle sloping of the ground.

Lily glanced at her watch. "We have one hour before the team arrives."

"Are you certain Kevin can be trusted? He won't demand anything in return for this favor of allowing us to survey the dig?"

Her sister stood. "One drink at the Raven Pub."

Standing, Rose thrust her hands in her pockets. "By the smile on your face, I say you got off easy."

Lily rocked back and forth on her feet. "I would not mind buying him several."

Snorting, Rose dug into her satchel and pulled out her notebook and pen. "A new conquest for you?"

"He has dreamy eyes." Lily sighed.

"Too handsome for my tastes. And his hair is always so neat."

Her sister shrugged. "He's the professor's assistant and has to look respectable."

Rose wandered carefully between the standing stones, avoiding another patch of ground that had been sectioned and roped off. "Take as many pictures as you can."

"I brought several canisters of film, so we're good," responded Lily. "What about the foliage around the area?"

"Definitely." She frowned in concentration. "I wish we could take samples of the dirt beneath the stones."

"Your *wish* is my command."

Rose stared at her sister in disbelief. "You brought specimen bags?"

Lily gave her sister a wink. "I think of everything."

Excitement flared within Rose, and she went immediately to the tallest standing stone. She glanced over her shoulder and then back again. "This one faces directly centered to the slab on the ground."

"There are nine stones, including the one still in the ground," remarked Lily. "I heard they mirror the ones in Corridon, though smaller."

Smiling, Rose examined the faint markings on the

standing stone. "The number nine is sacred to the druids. Part of this resembles the ancient writing of Ogham." Taking her finger, she traced the pattern in an attempt to discern a vision, message, or even an image.

Leaves swirled in a dance around her and the stone. Rose continued to inspect the strange markings. Graffiti marred the surface from those who wanted to carve their lasting imprint into the stone with their names, and she bit out a soft curse. These were sacred, and she found the idea of anyone taking a blade, pick, or any other tool to the stone offensive.

"Hallowed," she muttered, brushing her fingers over the cool stone. When no visual image came into her thoughts, Rose jotted down her first impressions in her notebook. Drawings of animals, along with an odd Ogham letter flew across the page.

Moving along to the outermost standing stone, Rose scanned the area from the bottom up. Trying to discern ancient writing mixed with graffiti was frustrating and time consuming. Then an idea struck her.

"Thirty minutes," announced her sister.

Rose made a mental note of the time and hastened to the back of the tallest stone. She gasped, almost dropping her notebook. Three circles appeared in an arc toward the top. The markings were more distinct than the others, though faded from time. Her skin prickled with awareness as she scribbled down a few notes. "Photograph the back of all these stones, Lily."

"The back?"

Rose pointed. "Yes, especially this stone." Bending down on one knee, she pulled back the shrubs and grasses hiding more of the markings. This time, her hands shook. Three circles were carved in a reverse fashion. However, her fascination was not so much the circles, but the figure of a man standing below them.

The blood pounded in Rose's ears, and lights glittered all around her. The landscape faded away, and in its place stood the man from her dreams. His voice rang loud as he lifted his hands to the night sky. The air was warm and sweet, beckoning Rose to join him. She found herself one within the vision and stood. Her gaze was directed to the rising of not one, but three moons. Each shimmered with a radiance so blinding, Rose had to shield her eyes. Mesmerized by the scene unfolding before her, she longed to join the man and started forward. Though she could not comprehend his words, she understood the meaning. Love, peace, reverence, and *power*. He drew the energy of the moons into his body, illuminating the markings on his back and arms.

As she approached, Rose lifted her head in awe of his height. Her hand reached outward, aching to brush her fingers against his skin and over the strange tattoo markings. Shouting filled her mind, and she shook her head to clear the disturbance. Yet, the intensity of the words increased.

Rose cupped her ears with her hands. "Stop calling my name!"

Pain seared into Rose's body, and she let out a guttural cry. Gasping for breath, she blinked in confusion. Rolling on her side, she fought the bile burning her throat. Sweat beaded her brow as her hands dug into the soft grasses.

"For the love of the Goddess, what happened?" she demanded, her voice sounding hoarse to her ears. Attempting to sit up, the pain slammed back into her.

She leaned her head forward, clenching her jaw.

"You had a seizure," sobbed Lily, wiping strands of hair out of Rose's face. "Does it have anything to do with these images on the back of this standing stone?"

Rose squeezed her eyes shut, trying to force the pain away. It had been a decade since she'd had any, so why would they return now?

"We'll continue this conversation later. We need to leave," whispered Lily, tugging gently on her arm. "I've got your notebook."

Unable to acknowledge her sister further, Rose simply nodded and partially opened her eyes. With Lily's help, she stood on shaky limbs.

"Keep your arm tucked within mine and walk slowly," encouraged her sister.

When they made their way safely out of the archaeological dig, Rose's shoulders slumped. She didn't utter one word until Lily packed their items into the car. Massaging her temples, she fumbled for her thoughts and words. "No…*nothing*…disturbed?"

"No," clipped out Lily. "The site is preserved the way we found it."

Silence descended like heavy mists as they drove away from the site.

Trying to control the shaking in her body was futile. Eventually, the tremors would cease, so Rose tried to steady her breathing.

Lily flipped the heater switch on, and Rose held her hands over the vents. The blessed heat seeped into her skin as her body began to relax.

"Here, take a nip." Lily shoved a flask into her hands. "Afterward, you can clean the dirt from your hands with wipes in my bag."

Rose gave her sister an incredulous look, but took the offering.

"I always carry the flask for medicinal purposes," stated her sister, and quickly added, "It helps to ward off the early morning chill."

Opening the flask, Rose took a small sip of the whisky. The liquid seared a path down her throat. The heat flared quickly throughout her body and calmed her racing heart. Settling back in her seat, she focused on the passing scenery. Sheep grazed along the rolling hills, many with newborn lambs at their side. Wildflowers sprouted in abundance, reminding Rose of the renewal of spring. A time of new beginnings, hope, and adventures.

When the first drop of rain splattered against the window, Rose watched the drop of water trail down the windshield. A trickle of water in time, followed by more.

"Can you talk about the vision?"

Lost in her thoughts, Rose barely registered her sister's question. After taking another sip of the delicious amber liquid, she tucked the flask inside her coat pocket. She drew in a huge breath and exhaled slowly. "It's the same one I've been having for over a week. Except this time at the dig, I felt the sensation of being there."

"Well that explains why you've been cross lately." Lily slammed on the brakes. "Sweet Brigid, keep on moving!"

Rose braced her hands on the dash as she gave her sister a dubious look. "They're only sheep with their babes. And we are on a country road." Reaching for her sister's satchel, she retrieved the package of wipes and cleaned her hands.

"And who is tending to them?" demanded Lily, waving her hand outward. "Since they're taking their time trekking across the road, explain this vision." She turned off the engine and leaned back.

Between the heater, whisky, and the thought of the man in her vision, Rose immediately rolled down the window. "I'm standing—"

Her sister grabbed her arm. "*You're* in the vision? This is a first."

Rose nodded. "As I was saying, I'm standing at the bottom of a hill. There is a man—"

"Man," echoed Lily.

Rose glared at her sister.

"Sorry," mumbled Lily. "Please continue, and I'll remain silent."

Returning her gaze to outside the window, Rose resumed her thoughts, and then repeated everything she had explained to Maeve days ago. Rose glanced sideways at her sister. "When I saw three moons and an image of a man carved on the standing stone, I *went* into the image—literally. I could feel the grass under my feet and the warmth of the night air brush against my face. His words lured me toward him."

"A message from the Goddess?" asked Lily softly.

"That's what Maeve said, too." Rose leaned out the window and brushed her hand over a passing sheep.

"You spoke with Maeve, but not me? Your sister?"

Hearing the hurt in Lily's voice, she turned around and grabbed her sister's hands. "At first, I thought these visions were dreams, so I didn't think to mention them to you. When I was rude to Maeve the other day, I told her I had not been sleeping well and explained why."

Lily squeezed Rose's hands. "You've never had a recurring vision, so I can understand why you would believe it's a dream. It's definitely connected to the standing stones, and you've been led to the place within your visions. But a man? What is his purpose?"

Rose drew back and leaned her head on the back of the seat. "Maybe I'm supposed to observe the Beltaine festival? This was Maeve's suggestion."

Tapping her fingers on the steering wheel, Lily pursed her lips. "That might be true. Then again, the similarities between the standing stones and your vision, is a connection you cannot ignore. This goes much deeper. Could the man be a leader of the tribe who erected the stones? A chieftain or druid? The dig has a significant purpose, and we need to study this further."

"So I've gathered," Rose responded dryly.

"Any descriptive qualities about this man? Young? Old?"

The heat blossomed in Rose's neck and traveled up to her cheeks. Once again, she turned away from her sister, allowing the cool rain to sprinkle her face. "Huge, massive in stance and physique with shoulder-length ebony hair. His back and arms are covered in tattoos." She swallowed. "And in this recent vision, they glowed with the power of the full moons."

"Can't be a Pict then. Too big. Maybe a God honoring the Goddess?"

"With tattoos?" Rose drummed her fingers on the car door.

"You keep referencing these tattoos. What do they look like?"

"Tribal, ancient—"

Lily poked her in the arm. "Not the meaning, but the visual."

"Celtic spirals and jagged designs. There is part of a dragon's body across his back. At least this is my first impression. The tattoos travel down the length of his back." Rose's face prickled more with heat, recalling the image of his fine ass in the pants he wore. The material molded his body to perfection.

"If I hadn't seen the images on the standing stone, I would have believed this to be a lustful dream," proclaimed Lily.

Rose glanced sharply at her sister. "*Lustful*? Whatever do you mean?"

"Ahh…look. The sheep have cleared to the opposite side of the road." Starting the car engine, Lily replied, "Your face says it all, dear sister. But what do I know? I wasn't there."

Silence became their companion on the journey back to their hostel outside of Glasgow. Both considered it wiser to be closer to the dig, instead of traveling the long roads and traffic from the Society.

The sun broke free from the dreary clouds as Lily maneuvered the car into a space near their room. When Rose stepped out of the vehicle, she lifted her head to the warmth. Sunlight graced the area, and she smiled.

"Are you feeling better?" inquired Lily, taking her arm.

Concern reflected in her sister's eyes. "I know you're worried about the seizure, but I'm all right."

"You haven't had one in a decade."

Rose patted her sister's hand. "You don't have to remind me. Though I'm grateful you were there to pull me back. I have to pay more attention to the sensations before I attempt to force a vision."

"Good." Releasing her hold, Lily added, "Care for a pint and a meal after I go over some notes? Maeve is joining us, along with Alex from the university."

"Unsure. I'm going to take advantage of the sunlight and take a walk. There's a bookstore down the street, and I'd like to pop in and see if they have historical books on the area or surrounding town.

"You do realize Alex is smitten with you?"

Rose gave her sister a speculative glance. "It's Maeve he's interested in, not me. And he's not my type."

"I wonder if you'll ever find *your type* of man, Rose MacLaren. Would you like my opinion?"

Rose snorted in disgust. "As if I could hold you back from spouting your views."

"You spend far too much time drifting in and out of old books and the past. Ancient knights no longer exist in this century. Quit being so particular."

Her sister's words stung. Rose held back the barb she longed to fling out, gripping her purse more firmly. "I'm quite content without a man in my life."

Lily sighed and checked her watch. "If you don't show in a couple hours, I'll claim your pint."

"Perfect."

"And see if they have any information regarding the castle near the Aberdeen dig in Corridon," recommended Lily as she walked away. "We'll drive out there tomorrow."

"Castle?"

Lily gestured a hand in the air. "Any castle located next to an ancient dig is worth investigating."

"Intriguing, and here I thought I was the only one

interested in ancient ruins," commented Rose as she made her way across the street to the row of shops that dotted the lane.

Scents of fresh-baked bread and cinnamon teased her as she strolled along. Temptation beckoned her for one warm bun, and she quickly went inside the shop to make a purchase. As she left the bakery, she savored the sugary treat. Humming a tune while she ate, Rose's steps slowed. The gentle breeze stilled, and the sky darkened.

"Not more rain," she complained, licking the last of the cinnamon and sugar from her fingers.

Continuing on her path to the bookstore, Rose sang a light tune. Women smiled in passing, and one elderly man gave her a wink as he stepped out of a shop. She refused to think of the oncoming rain, her vision, *or* the dig. The fresh air lifted her spirits, banishing the earlier weakness and tremors.

Regardless of her good mood, the day receded into a cloak of darkness, and Rose lifted her gaze. "Sweet stars," she gasped. "How did I forget about the solar eclipse?"

Doing her best not to look directly at the sun and moon as one, she shielded her eyes, captivated by the event.

So engrossed in a blur of thoughts and not paying attention to the road, Rose stumbled on the curb and pitched forward. Her only thought was to protect her face as she squeezed her eyes shut, preparing for the impact. Yet, it wasn't the hard pavement that greeted her.

Strong, warm arms lifted her high into the air, crushing her to his chest. She inhaled sharply. The scent of woods filled her, and her head spun. She blinked in an attempt to recover her senses.

"Sorry," she mumbled. When Rose lifted her head, her mouth slacked open. Lavender eyes flecked with silver stared back at her.

"Are you unwell?"

The soft burr of his question brushed over her skin in a warm caress. She snapped her mouth closed and shook her head. She pointed behind him. "Solar eclipse."

His smile came slowly, and Rose thought she was going to swoon.

"The sun and moon are one," he acknowledged.

She could only nod like some meek and daft lass. "Beaut...*beautiful*."

"Agreed."

Rose shivered, but not from the chill in the air. Never before had she had an immediate attraction to a man. The heat flared around her neck and rose to her face. She quickly averted his intense gaze. She realized the man was tall by their surroundings, and then swiftly returned her attention to him. Well over six feet tall, with a good set of shoulders and ebony hair that rivaled the night sky. It fell in soft waves around his ears, and her fingers ached to wrap around the strands. She noted the silver torc of a dragon around his neck and pondered the possibility that her rescuer was a God fashioned from the air.

"Goodness. You're extremely tall," she blurted out and then swiftly cupped a hand over her mouth in embarrassment.

Feeling the rumble of his laughter against her hand on his chest, Rose felt the burning sting of humiliation throughout her body and turned her face away. "Forgive my outburst."

"Contrary. I find it refreshing. And I stand near seven feet tall."

There it was again. The deep burr of his words. Not quite Scottish or Irish, but something familiar.

Gaining her wits, she returned her attention to his face. "Thank you, *Sir Knight*, for rescuing me and saving me from disaster." *Seven feet! Sweet Brigid!*

This time, the man smiled fully. "I am happy to have been of some assistance."

Even with the shadow of a light beard, she could detect the dimple on his right cheek, and Rose smiled in return. "The Fates interceded."

His smile faded just as the first ray of light emerged from the sun—ending the total solar eclipse. He gently brought her down to the ground. "Regardless, you were fortunate I was here to break your fall."

Feeling foolish for keeping her hands still attached to the man, Rose took a step back and straightened her coat. "Thank you, again." When she hastily turned around and started forward, his words made her pause.

"Would you care for a pint?"

Startled by his question, Rose responded, "I believe I should be the one to offer *you* a pint. Furthermore, I don't know your name." She took in every nuance of his form, doing her best not to touch her heated face with her cool hands.

His mouth twitched in humor as he approached. He gave a slight bow. "*Sir* Aidan Kerrigan."

Rose bit her lip in an attempt to contain her laughter. "I'm Rose MacLaren."

"*Rose*. A lovely name for a maiden."

She glanced over her shoulder at the bookstore. Indecision clashed with priorities.

"Is there something that requires your attention first?"

Quickly snapping her attention to the man, Rose answered, "I need to research a book. Can I meet you afterward?"

"Sorry, no."

Crestfallen by his response, Rose nodded. "Perhaps another time."

In one swift move, Aidan reached for her hand and tucked it in the crook of his arm. "Why don't I accompany you to Seamus Books? I know the owner, so perchance he can be of assistance in your search."

Rose studied the man's face, noting the shift of colors in his gorgeous eyes. They had a mesmerizing effect. The heat of his body seeped into hers, along with a prickle of awareness.

"I accept your company, but only if you'll allow me to buy you a pint."

He arched a brow in challenge. "A knight *never* takes coin from a lady."

Chapter Six

*"When a decision does not present itself, let logic cast the deciding vote."*
*~Edicts of the Fenian Warriors*

Every thought in his mind rebelled against escorting Rose MacLaren into the bookstore. But the words tumbled free before he could snatch them back. From the moment he turned the corner on Buchannan Street and witnessed the lovely lass wandering without purpose and gazing upward singing a tune, Aidan became enchanted. She lured him forward with song and beauty—a siren's song to tempt a warrior, and he succumbed to the temptress.

*What possessed him to consider taking her for a pint?*

When he held Rose in his arms, her scent filled him. One of spices and flowers. Heady and seductive. It required every ounce of willpower not to ravage her mouth in a succulent exploration.

*I was a fool for not accepting the sexual favors from Mina.*

Aidan held the door open for Rose to enter as he recalled the vision his sister had presented to him earlier. Was he to be her guardian? Would she bring about destruction to another human? Was he fated to intercede and set her on a course not of her choosing?

Usually matters concerning humans were discussed within the Brotherhood and the council. This predicament presented a host of consequences.

*Only part of the journey to the mission I'm conducting.*

"I dinnae appreciate the cold air entering my shop," protested a familiar voice.

Snapping out of his thoughts, Aidan closed the door behind him. "Forgive my insensitivities to your condition, Seamus."

"Like ye care about me old bones." The old man approached. "What can I help ye locate today, Aidan?"

Arching a brow at Seamus, he replied, "You wound me, old friend." He turned, gesturing to Rose. "This lovely lass requires assistance in researching a book."

Seamus straightened and ran a hand through what little hair he had left on his head. "Does the *lady* have a name? Though what she is doing with ye is perplexing."

Rose laughed, the sound reminding Aidan of bells.

She stepped forward and presented her hand to Seamus. "I'm Rose MacLaren from the Society of the Thistle. We're doing research on a nearby archaeological dig, and I was curious if you had any books on the history of this area and any books on the area around Aberdeen. Are you the owner?"

Seamus grasped her hand with both of his. "Aye. We have heard the news about the research being conducted, but I did not realize the Society had taken an interest."

Aidan stepped nearer. "You are a member of the Society?"

A frown marred her features. "Did I not state it clearly with my introduction?"

"Forgive me. I'm astonished they have members who are so young."

"There is an entire bookshelf dedicated to the history of the village and surrounding land," Seamus offered. "I do have a small section with books on Aberdeen, Arbroath, and Stonehaven."

Returning her attention to Seamus, she smiled. "Wonderful." She glanced over the man's shoulders. "In what direction?"

"Let me take ye there."

Aidan followed slowly. He knew the bookstore well. However, the old man had become besotted with the lovely lass—not that he could find fault, since he had also fallen under her charm. Therefore, he allowed Seamus to take over. Aidan had to harness in his emotions. They were leading him astray.

Rose halted among the section on ancient castles of Scotland. She brushed her hands over the spines. "Would you have any books on a castle located near Corridon near Aberdeen? It's located near the other archaeological site."

Aidan leaned against the bookcase. "No."

"Excuse me?" She gave him a baffled look.

For a brief moment, Aidan noted the hue of her green eyes go from pale to dark shards of emeralds in seconds.

Seamus reached for her arm. "I am sorry, but there are no books referencing *Balleycove* Castle." They started forward.

"I can provide you with any details of the castle," stated Aidan. "Is there a reason for your curiosity?"

She halted, removing her arm from Seamus' hold.

"It would depend on your knowledge of the castle, grounds, *and* foliage." Her tone was skeptical as she studied him.

"I can assure you, I am fully capable of answering *all* of your questions."

"Why don't ye tell her why ye are so bloody knowledgeable?" snapped Seamus and wandered to the back of the store.

She folded her arms across her chest. "Do tell."

Aidan tilted his head to the side. "I *own* Balleycove."

Her eyes grew wide. "Are you the Laird?"

Seamus snorted loudly, and Aidan narrowed his eyes at the man's rude outburst. "No. I'm merely the owner of the estate."

"How long has it been in your family?" Rose took a step toward him.

Amused by her question, he leaned near her ear. "Centuries."

She trembled and turned to meet his gaze. "Isn't Kerrigan an Irish name?"

"Smart lass," he admitted, sorely tempted to brush his fingers over her rosy cheeks.

"And?"

"*And*," he echoed.

Swallowing, Rose continued. "And the Scots actually allowed an Irish family to remain all these centuries on their land?"

Aidan clasped his hands behind his back and straightened. "They were loyal to the kings and clans. They could not refuse."

She arched a brow. "But not to Ireland?"

How could he explain he was devoted to both countries? Revered and honored the land on each? Simple. He could not. "I am loyal to all countries, which includes England."

"You answered the question as if it pertains to you, personally. Your current ownership of the land is not rife with civil wars going on between the three countries as it was centuries ago. I'm assuming your ancestors were also steadfast in their loyalty to Ireland?"

The lass was perceptive, and Aidan grew restless. When did he lose control of the conversation? "My ancestors were great negotiators and managed to maintain certain privileges here in Scotland *and* Ireland." Again, how could he possibly explain that magic was a deciding factor in negotiations for the land and castle?

"Fascinating. You must share more."

"Here are a few books that would be of interest," interrupted Seamus, handing her the stack.

"Wonderful." She glanced around the bookstore. "Would you have a chair or table? I'd like to peruse these first, before I make a purchase."

"There is a quiet alcove beyond the mythology section." Once again, Seamus took her arm and led her away. "Take your time."

Aidan strolled along perfectly content to study the lass from behind, admiring the view while Seamus escorted Rose to a nearby chair. The man continued to prattle on about the books he had chosen for her. Finally, his old friend left.

Approaching her side, Aidan glanced down at the book she had chosen first. "Standing stones of Bran?

Why the interest?"

Rose continued to flip through the pages. "The Society is working on the area with the university, along with the site in Corridon."

Aidan removed a chair from around the corner and placed it next to Rose. Taking a seat, he examined the pictures. "What are you looking for? These photos were taken within the past ten years, so they won't be able to help you ascertain what plants grew around the landscape hundreds of years ago."

"Obviously, you are familiar with the work of the Society," she observed. Holding the book closer to her face, she inspected the picture of the standing stones.

"Yes, but I don't believe their research extends to the stone ruins."

She dismissed him with a wave of her hand. "One cannot be so sure. There could be a drawing of a particular flower or something to assist us. If we were permitted to take soil samples, there might be evidence of vegetation changes due to human activity and pollen changes in the soil. We cannot say for certain what they ate, because plant material rarely survives and is easily missed in excavations. But we can find clues in the occasional nut shell, seed husk, or other remains in a clay pot."

A tremor of unease prickled across Aidan's skin as her attention remained fixed on the tallest standing stone. No matter what she spouted, Rose's curiosity extended beyond the botanical. "If I may ask, what are you looking for?"

She pursed her lips. "There are no pictures of the back of the stones."

Aidan fisted his hands on his thighs. *Why the*

*fascination, Rose MacLaren?* "The back of the stones have no conclusive meaning."

After placing the book on a side table, she reached for another tome. "Many scholars have overlooked a miniscule marking believing it to be a flaw in the stone. Have you actually witnessed them up close? Do you understand their meaning?"

"Yes," he responded abruptly. "They are merely scratches and graffiti."

Shaking her head slowly, she leaned back in her chair and flipped through the pages. "Are you an expert, Aidan?"

"Yes."

Rose snapped her attention to him. "Oh."

"I have been brought on as part of the team from the university to assess their findings," he confirmed. "Along with my vast knowledge of Balleycove, I am also an archaeologist, specifically pertaining to ancient *standing stones.*"

Her face turned the shade of crimson roses and she made to stand. "Sorry, I must be going. I…I forgot there was an errand my sister requested of me."

Aidan reached for her hand, forcing her to sit back down. Every instinct in him urged him to let her go, but his own curiosity and concern took over. "What are you afraid of?"

She gave him a haughty look. "Nothing!"

"Then why the sudden change in demeanor when I told you I was part of the team?"

"What change? There was none."

*You lie, Rose MacLaren.* "Let us start again," urged Aidan. "Tell me your fascination with the standing stones, and I promise to keep your secret."

"*Secret*? I don't understand your meaning."

Leaning forward, Aidan clasped his hands together. "The Society of the Thistle has been given permission to inspect the area *away* from the standing stones. Professor Linton was clear in his instructions to me. It appears as if you've ventured *near* the stones."

Worry reflected in the depths of her green eyes, but she did not avert her gaze. "I think this conversation is over." After retrieving one of the books, Rose stood slowly.

Aidan rose from his chair, blocking her exit. He had no desire to frighten her. Trying to converse with the lass was beginning to give him a headache. "Regardless of what I've just admitted to you, I will assist you in your research."

Clutching the book to her chest, she asked, "For what purpose? Is there a favor you seek in return?"

*A kiss given freely?* He swiftly banished the thought. "You have already agreed to a pint. If you have no objections, I can share my knowledge of Balleycove with you then."

Indecision battled briefly within her eyes. Then her smile came slowly. "Only if you let me pay."

"Ahh…the battle lines have been drawn. Then I accept your offer this once, Rose MacLaren." Stepping aside, he gestured for her to proceed.

"Let me make my purchase first," she stated.

As she made her way to the front of the store, Aidan rubbed a hand over his chin. Her scent lingered in the small enclosure. Closing his eyes, he sealed all emotions, including the heady lustful ones. They were an unnecessary distraction. *Focus, harness, bind the emotions until there are none.*

When he opened them, Aidan followed the woman.

After Rose made her purchase, she promised to come back and peruse the other sections of the bookstore. Seamus was besotted with her and grasped her hand in apparent appreciation.

He spared Aidan a glance. "You should consider writing a book about Balleycove."

"And as I have stated on numerous occasions, I have no desire to have my lineage recorded for others," responded Aidan dryly.

The man merely shrugged and thanked Rose once again.

Aidan opened the door, allowing her to step out into the sunshine. A chill breeze swept over them, and he inhaled the scent of rain on the horizon.

"I find it peculiar that an archaeologist—one with a castle—has no yearning to write the history of his own estate and surrounding land," declared Rose, as she attempted to pull the collar of her coat more closely around her neck.

Without hesitation, Aidan brushed away her locks and assisted her. "I know everything there is about my land," he declared.

She glanced at him sideways. "You explore the past, but have no wish for others to research or learn from your land and ancestors?"

"Precisely."

"Is Balleycove a secret fortress with immense treasures?"

Aidan tried to fight the smile forming on his mouth. "Actually, most of my research includes ancient artifacts. There is not much to glean from the castle or land. It's merely a medieval structure."

Rose abruptly grabbed his arm. "*Medieval?*"

He cast his gaze to where her small hand held him firmly. "Is this another one of your fascinations besides exploring standing stones?"

"Sorry," she mumbled and removed her hand. "Yes, a deep interest with anything medieval. Though my sister would object and tell you it's more an obsession."

"Does this medieval fixation rule you?" he asked, taking her arm and guiding her across the street toward the pub.

She snorted. "I've often told her I'm a woman displaced out of time. The Society studies the past. Therefore, my love for a specific time-period is merely acceptable. Even Maeve has an interest in the medieval years."

"Is Maeve your sister?"

"No. Just one of the women living with us at the Society. Lily is my sister's name."

"Any other sisters who are named after flowers?" inquired Aidan as he opened the door to the pub.

Rose laughed. Rich, warm, sensual, and Aidan's fortress of steel cracked open again.

"No," she replied and glanced around the interior. "What is the name of this pub?"

"Cuchulainn's Hounds," uttered Aidan softly.

"Celtic mythology." Rose clasped her hand over her heart. "Another *fascination* of mine. It's perfect! Did you know that Cuchulainn trained under the great woman warrior, Scáthach on an island on the west coast of Scotland? Possibly the Isle of Skye?"

"So I've been told."

*What would you say, Rose MacLaren, if I told you I*

70

*was one of those warriors who assisted the great female warrior in her training of the Red Branch warriors?*

And within the darkened interior of the pub, Aidan realized the journey he now faced was a path he could never have foreseen.

One of destiny or destruction. But for whom?

Chapter Seven

*"Be wary of plucking a flower from the ground.
You might inadvertently spread the seeds of blight to
another blossoming bud."*

*~Society of the Thistle*

Surveying the sinfully tall, dark man over the rim
of her beer, Rose tried desperately to listen to the
cadence of his voice. There was an odd fluency to the
pitch. Not quite Scottish, nor Irish, but a familiarity—
one she had heard previously. Unfortunately, her intent
to focus on his words became lost whenever she stared
into his eyes.

Exotic, spellbinding, rare, *and* mesmerizing. One
moment she detected their lavender hue and then the
next, shards of silver. She was locked in this hypnotic
trance.

"Are you lost after the one sip of beer you've
tasted? Or have my words about Balleycove left you
without words, leaving you bored?"

Rose blinked in embarrassment. After taking a
huge swallow of her drink, she placed the glass down
on the table. "I must admit your home—*castle* sounds
intriguing. It's a pity there have been no written
records."

"My family thought otherwise."

"And you're just following along?"

Aidan leaned forward, smiling. "Why the interest in Balleycove?"

She shrugged dismissively. "A link to the ancient stones?"

His good humor vanished. "The fortress was built in the twelfth century, and the standing stones have stood guard thousands of years before my home was thought of."

Rose fingered the utensils on the table. "One never knows. Perchance your ancestors knew about those who carved the symbols on the stones."

"Regardless, the knowledge died with them," he offered quietly.

"What are your plans in regard to the stones?" Obviously, the man had knowledge, and Rose was intent on prying forth the information. Flirting was not in her arsenal, but she wouldn't discount it with Aidan Kerrigan.

"To observe and study the position, relating to the stars."

"Are you an astronomer, too?" she inquired, intrigued further by his background of knowledge.

"Yes. And you?"

"No. My expertise is with history and botany. We at the Society like to combine both. Each is an integral part to learning more about the land and people who dwelled in their surroundings." Rose leaned forward. "Though I must profess, I have a keen interest in learning about the stars and planets."

"It is a vast universe," he remarked, taking another draw from his beer.

Rose smacked the wood with her hand. "Exactly what I've been saying for years." Waving her hand upward, she added, "Surely we can't be the only ones in the universe, right?"

Aidan placed his glass down. "Are you speaking of aliens?"

Rolling her eyes at his choice of terminology, she leaned back. "The word smacks of creatures with large eyes, no ears, and green skin. I tend to think of them as other civilizations that colonized other worlds."

He arched a dark brow in amusement. "And what would you do if you came upon one of these people from another world? Show them around your *bonny* Scotland?"

Rose frowned. Was the man mocking her? "It's more your land than mine. Most of my relatives came over from Ireland only a thousand years ago."

"You have not answered my question. Would you flee? Or attempt a greeting?"

Aidan leaned his massive forearms on the maple table, studying her. Dwarfed by his close presence, Rose pressed herself farther back against the cushioned booth. His eyes shifted colors, and she refused to turn away from the intensity of his gaze. She swallowed. "You have the most mesmerizing eyes, Aidan."

He blinked several times as if coming out of a trance.

"Care for a menu?" asked the server approaching their table and tapping a pencil to her notebook.

Aidan recovered quickly. "What's the special today, Pam?"

Giving Aidan a wink, she replied, "Your favorite. Irish stout stew and dill bread."

"Minus the meat, correct?"

Pam leveled the pencil at him. "I'm shocked you

would even ask, Aidan." She leaned against the table. "We always have a special menu prepared for you when you're in the village."

He chuckled softly. "One can never assume, lass. Furthermore, I don't believe I'm the only one who doesn't eat meat."

"A pity. By your strong form, I would have thought you to be a carnivore."

Aidan pushed his glass toward Pam. "To ingest other animals is not on my menu for strength."

*Is this another conquest of yours, Aidan Kerrigan?* Rose wondered. If the woman scooted any closer to him, she'd be sitting in his lap. Apparently, Pam had forgotten there was another body occupying the booth. "What's the soup of the day?"

Pam glanced over her shoulder at Rose. "Beef vegetable."

Scrunching her nose up at the thought of anything with meat, she stated, "I'll take a cup of the vegetarian stew, salad with a side of blue cheese dressing, and an order of dill bread."

Pam pointed to their almost empty glasses. "Another round?"

"Only if I pay for the additional pints," declared Aidan.

"Deal," announced Rose.

The woman swiftly departed, and Rose fidgeted once again with the eating utensils. "The village people know you well."

"Generations have known me…*my family*."

Rose gave him a skeptical look. "Generations? You must be ancient."

Mirth reflected in his eyes. "Positively."

Pam returned with two more pints, giving Aidan a beaming smile before leaving once again.

"You have an admirer," mentioned Rose, reaching for her pint and taking a huge gulp.

Aidan sputtered on his beer. Wiping his mouth with the back of his hand, he put his glass down. "Not that I care, but do *you* care, Rose MacLaren?"

She swiftly directed her attention elsewhere. "Sorry. It's one of my flaws. Speaking without reflecting first. My sister calls it *word vomit* and corrects me profusely."

Aidan's laughter echoed all around her. Finishing her pint, she placed the glass on the table and folded her arms over her chest. She angled her head to the side and glared at him. "I do not see the humor in professing a flaw."

All traces of mirth vanished from his face. In one swift movement, Aidan grasped her hand. "Humor is good for the soul, Rose, regardless where it is found. I was not laughing at you. I find your honesty...*refreshing*. But you have yet to answer my two questions."

Rose's chest constricted. The warmth from his hand invaded her skin, sending shards of pleasurable pinpricks throughout her body.

"Rose?" He rolled her name off his tongue in a low voice.

"I have forgotten the questions," she confessed softly.

His thumb rubbed across the vein on her wrist, causing her to tremble. "If you came across an *alien*, what would you do? And do you care if others *flirt* with me?"

*Stop this instant, Rose MacLaren! You've just met the man. This is far too intimate.* He oozed a sexual power, holding her captive with his seductive looks, touch, and charisma.

Recovering her wits, she replied, "I would welcome the conversation." She swallowed, forcing the lie from her lips. "As for others charmed by your looks and flirting outright with you, I could care less. I hardly know you."

Aidan released her hand as if he had been burned. His demeanor shifted, and he leaned back.

Silence descended between them like a heavy cloak. Rose eyed her empty glass, longing for something to quench the lump in her throat. What was wrong with her? *Foolish girl. You've had too much to drink and nothing to eat.*

Rose reached for her napkin and placed it in her lap. "Food is taking too long," she complained, searching the crowded pub for their server.

When Aidan remained quiet, Rose stole a glance at him. The intensity of his gaze on her startled her. She sensed he was battling some great decision.

Placing his hands on the table, he made to leave. "Forgive me, Rose, but I deem it would be best—"

"By the hounds, there you are, Aidan!" shouted a man strolling toward their booth. "Did you forget our meeting with the professor?" He fisted his hands on his hips, studying first Aidan and then Rose.

Her internal alarm went off with the mention of the professor. Tossing her napkin onto the table, Rose started to scoot out of the booth. "If you'll excuse me, I think I'll pass on the meal and head home."

The man blocked her exit. "My apologies. I did not

consider Aidan might have made other plans." He stuck his hand outward. "My name is Liam MacGregor and you are…"

Rose lifted her head, in awe of the man whose height rivaled the giant sitting across from her. His smile lit up his entire face, and she returned the gesture. "Happy to meet you, Liam. I am—"

"Rose MacLaren," interjected Aidan. "You can offer my apologies to the professor. I will contact him in the morning."

Liam ignored Aidan, taking a firm hold of her hand. "What a lovely name, *Rose*." Mischief glittered in his eyes. "How did you meet this *old* man?"

Laughter bubbled up within Rose as he released her hand. "He rescued me from falling flat on my face."

"Do tell," encouraged Liam, sitting down beside her in the booth.

"Don't you have somewhere *or* something else to do?" Aidan asked brusquely.

Liam winked at Rose before turning his attention to Aidan. "Actually, no. Since you've missed the meeting, I have nothing on my agenda this evening. Is this a date?"

"No," blurted out Rose and Aidan in unison.

"Excellent." He beamed. Raising his hand, he shouted, "Pam, bring me a round of pints and two drams of your finest whisky!"

The woman waved in acknowledgement from the bar area.

"You're not staying." Aidan's statement sounded more like a growl.

Liam shrugged. "Why not?" Turning toward Rose, he leaned his head against his hand. "You must share how this old man saved you from harm. Sounds like a story told in faery tales."

Rose spared a glance at Aidan, noting the fury in his gaze when he stared at Liam and pondered his behavior. Liam was pleasant, charming, and sexy. *You need food, MacLaren. Not men to gape over.*

She returned her attention to Liam. "It's simple. I was looking at the solar eclipse and not paying attention. Aidan broke my fall."

"Intriguing," mused Liam. "A spectacular eclipse, so I was told."

Pam arrived, carrying a tray with more drinks. "Whose tab is this on?" she asked, placing the pints and drams in the middle.

Liam pointed to Aidan. "His turn this evening."

Pam frowned in obvious confusion. "But last evening Aidan paid."

Lifting the dram, Liam gave Pam a wink. "We do everything in threes."

*Great Goddess. What's with all the winking?* Rose placed her hands around the cool glass to temper the rising heat in her face.

Pam rolled her eyes and tucked the tray under her arm. "Unless you have any objections, Aidan, I'll add everything on your tab."

Rose lifted her hand. "I will pay for the first round."

"No." Aidan speared her with a look of steel. "You can pay the next time. Yes, Pam, put the entire bill on my tab."

Rose narrowed her eyes at the man. "That was *not* our agreement. And what makes you think I'll meet with you again?"

Aidan's smile came slow and seductive. "Because you will."

Liam tossed back his dram. After placing the glass down, he glanced at both of them. "How long have you known each other?"

"A few hours," admitted Rose, keeping her gaze on Aidan.

"Sounds to me like you've known each other far longer," he teased, reaching for his pint. "*Sláinte Mhath*!"

Rose lifted her pint to the toast and took a hesitant sip. What she craved was food, not more drink. Furthermore, she was beginning to regret her decision to have a pint with Aidan Kerrigan. The man was a dominating brute—behaving like a medieval barbarian.

"Do you live nearby?" asked Liam.

"She works at the Society of the Thistle," stated Aidan.

Liam sharply assessed Rose. "I hear the Society is interested in the surrounding dig, currently being excavated."

"Rose has a keen interest in the standing stones," added Aidan. "She plans to further her studies with the stones in Corridon, as well."

Liam's gaze widened. "Oh…interesting."

Slamming her glass onto the table, Rose glared at Aidan. "Do me the honor of allowing *me* to answer the questions."

Aidan held his hands up in surrender. "My apologies."

Since her secret was out, she no longer cared and prayed her explanation would suffice and not get back to the professor. "Yes, the Society is examining the foliage around the dig, but sometimes there might be an additional clue or marking to indicate what type of plant or flower grew in the area. My sister and I are staying for a couple days to take samples. She will photograph the surrounding area."

Liam guzzled deeply from his glass. After placing his glass on the table, he shook his head. "There's nothing on the stones that can be of value to your research."

"Unless you know the work we do, your statement is incorrect," argued Rose.

"Have you already studied the stones?" asked Liam, yet his gaze was fixed on Aidan.

"Yes," she acknowledged, already regretting the affirmation. *You should have lied!*

"And were your findings any help in your research?"

*Not in my research, but my visions.* "Yes," she lied. "Of course, I will examine them further when we return to the Society."

She picked up her glass, studying Aidan over the rim. His penetrating gaze made her nervous. Could he read her thoughts? She took a sip of her drink.

Aidan folded his arms over his chest. "You must share your knowledge with the professor."

A tremor of fear crept down the back of her neck, and she set her glass down. Now that her secret was out, their chances of being able to examine anything were finished. Her hands twisted the napkin in her lap, and her sister's words earlier came back to haunt her. What if they denied the Society access to any more research? Rose refused to be a coward or to ruin an opportunity for the Society.

She lifted her head high. "Until I have studied everything further, I don't believe my findings will be acceptable to the university. Therefore, there is no need to concern yourselves or the professor with what we are researching."

Aidan arched a dark brow at her. "Perhaps in time, you will share your knowledge with me."

"Only if you consider offering yours as well."

He leaned his forearms on the table. "When we meet again, Rose, I shall."

"So sure of yourself."

His laughter caressed her skin. "Always," he responded.

Rose stole a glance at Liam. The man had an odd expression on his face as he stared with intent at Aidan.

Pam approached, bringing a tray heavy with plates of food. "Did you care for anything, Liam, or is the drink going to be your meal?"

Rubbing a hand over his face, he smiled. "Bring me the same as they're having and an additional round of drinks."

"Good," the woman replied and skirted to another table to take an order.

Rose inhaled the delicious aroma from the cup of stew, eager to dive into her meal. After taking her first bite, she let out a soft moan. The combination of stout mixed with the potatoes and vegetables was delicious. As she continued to savor her meal, she closed her eyes on a sigh with each bite. When she lifted her sight to the other men, they were gaping at her like a specimen.

Quickly wiping her mouth with her napkin, she asked, "Did I splash some on my face?"

"No, lass," uttered Aidan softly. "I have never

witnessed anyone enjoy a meal with…such *relish*."

"Nor I," affirmed Liam and reached for Aidan's half-finished pint and downed the remainder. "I think I'll go help Pam with our additional drinks," he offered, slipping out of the booth.

"I was hungry," she blurted out, dropping her spoon into the cup. Reaching for a slice of dill bread, she tried to mask her embarrassment as she focused on buttering her piece of bread.

Aidan grasped her hand, stilling her movements. "It was only a comment. There is no need to be defensive. I enjoyed watching you."

Rose swallowed, unable to form any words. Even with Liam's absence, once again, the space in the booth was too confining. Aidan's massive presence dominated the small enclosure. She merely nodded.

When he released her hand, Rose took a bite of the warm bread, aching to sample the man across from her.

Chapter Eight

*"When emotions cloud your viewpoint, encase them in a sphere of protection, and toss them outward to the winds."*

*~Edicts of the Fenian Warriors*

"What were you thinking?" demanded Liam, blocking another blow from Aidan.

"Now why would you profess such a question? And I do not favor you calling me an *old man* in front of Rose." Aidan thrust forward with his sword, attempting to unbalance the warrior.

Liam swiftly deflected the blade. "Because she is not the reason we've been sent here. Your fixation on the lass does not pertain to our situation. And you are *old*," he mocked.

"We have yet to determine what action to take with the stones. Rose might hold the key." He leaned to the side, narrowly missing an attack from Liam. Swiftly rounding on the warrior, Aidan slammed his hilt onto his back. "I might be old, but I will ask you to refrain from mentioning my age in front of the lass."

Stumbling forward, Liam then turned around. "You should have visited the Pleasure Gardens. Your lust is impeding your thoughts, *great leader*."

Aidan lifted his hand, letting the ball of energy swirl in a tempest within his palm. How he longed to rip the tongue from the warrior.

Liam aimed his sword at the energy. "Has the mighty Aidan Kerrigan lost control?"

Crushing the power within his fist, Aidan swiftly leveled a blow to Liam's jaw. "Never."

Staggering backward, Liam rubbed a hand over his chin. "Liar."

He rushed forward, but Aidan continued to dominate the training. The clash of blades echoed all around the enclosure within the castle's list. As Aidan tried to contain his growing ire over Liam's words, the warrior intensified his attack.

"Too much drink last evening, warrior?" taunted Aidan.

His foe remained quiet, lunging outward with his blade.

Aidan wielded his sword high. "I believe it was the additional dram that has you seeing double right now."

Liam's eyes blazed. "Might I remind you that *you* drank my last dram of whisky?"

"To keep you from falling over and making a fool of yourself in front of the lass," countered Aidan, as he deflected yet another blow.

"You're correct," agreed Liam and swiftly pointed his sword at Aidan. "I plan to make amends by asking her out to see the band, Wicked Pipers. I must present myself in good form."

Aidan let out a hiss. "You will not ask her to go *anywhere* with you!"

Liam's smile turned wicked. "Why? Surely you don't have a Fae claim on the *lass*? My year of sexual absence in the human world ended decades ago, so I see her free for the taking."

Dropping his sword, Aidan let out a great roar and charged at Liam. When the warrior lifted his sword, Aidan smacked it out of his hand with a wave of power. His hand went to the man's throat. "There will be no talk of bedding *Rose MacLaren*," he ordered, though he barely recognized his own words.

"Yo-yo-*you* win," stuttered Liam in a strangled voice. "She is yours."

Releasing his hold on the warrior, Aidan stumbled back and glanced down at his hands. They shook not from rage, but from the loss of his iron-clad control. He raked a shaky hand through his hair and retrieved Liam's sword. "There are no winners today, and Rose MacLaren is *not* mine." Aidan held the sword outward.

Taking his blade, Liam saluted him. "I concur." He started to sheath his sword and then stilled his movements. "If I may inquire, why does this human female appear to have you mystified?"

His observation unnerved Aidan. He pointed to Liam's sword. "Do you fear retaliation for your question? I can assure you I shall not lash out further."

Liam blew out a curse and completely sheathed his blade. "I was being cautious."

"My puzzlement is over her concern with *studying* the stones. No more. She has seen and photographed them." Aidan brushed past Liam and retrieved a cloth from the bench. Wiping his face off, he tossed it aside.

"Why? Their markings were left by the ancient Picts eons ago. What reference could she deduce? She studies plants."

Aidan cast his gaze to the sky. "Wrong. I fear she will be the one to connect the tallest standing stone to the altar stone. Until I saw the markings with my own eyes, I concluded they weren't the Picts. They chose not to record or transcribe anything. Yet, the stones are evident of Fae lore. The altar stone records the constellations of *our* world. One of them listened to our stories told over a campfire and carved them into the stones." He glanced over his shoulder. "Call it intuition, but none of the others within the professor's group are making any similarities. They'll conclude they're gibberish. Perchance symbols for a ritual. But the lass is unique. Therefore, my deductions have led me to believe Rose is on a path of uncovering an ancient secret."

Liam wiped a hand across his brow. "Then we must thwart her plan to inspect the area. The professor must be alerted, so he can oust her from the dig."

Aidan winced, unsure if this was the best plan of defense. "Rose is inquisitive. Keeping her and the Society from the area might encourage her to continue to inspect the stones on her own."

"Then a guard must be posted," demanded Liam.

Chuckling softly, Aidan exited the lists and made strides across the bailey. "I don't believe a guard could halt the progress *or* curiosity of Rose MacLaren!" he shouted.

"So what is the plan of attack? Earthquake to bury and destroy the stones?" asked Liam, running alongside him.

Aidan shook his head. "Steer the lovely lass in another direction. Give her a possible scenario. Watch, observe, and guide her on another thought process."

"What about the professor?"

Halting his stride, Aidan clamped a hand on the warrior's shoulder. "Use your charm and persuasive words to have the professor *permit* the Society in on the full dig."

"Wonderful," he replied, sarcastically.

"Are you not up for the challenge?"

Liam narrowed his eyes in thought. "Why don't we create another dig for the lady to direct her fascination?"

Aidan released his hold and entered the castle. "I deem any other dig would not hold her interest. She possesses a gift for insight. I fear she'd sense the ruse."

"Sweet Mother Danu! Great. Next, she'll proclaim to the human world she has discovered Fae Warriors living among the humans."

"It's happened before," admitted Aidan, ascending the stairs to his chambers.

"If I'm to prepare the professor, what are your plans for today?" asked Liam, following alongside him.

Smiling, Aidan responded, "A visit to see the two members from the Society of the Thistle and give them the good news about working on the site."

"Why am I not shocked? Though aren't you making an assumption the professor will agree?" Liam remarked, making his way toward his own chambers.

"Use your power of persuasion, MacGregor. I'll give you one hour to comply, before I bring the lovely lasses to the dig site."

****

"Maeve says a cure for too much drink is a chocolate shake and cheeseburger," suggested Lily, cupping her hand over the phone.

"I'd gag at the smell," moaned Rose, splashing cold water on her face and neck.

"Colleen recommends tomato juice mixed with a

raw egg and pickle juice. Then hold your nose and drink the tonic in one gulp."

"Goodness, that's horrid." Rose sat down on the edge of tub.

Lily peered around the entryway of the bathroom. "Or I could run out to the market and find some herbs?"

"Have you consulted *everyone* at the Society?" complained Rose, massaging her temples to alleviate the pain.

"Almost. Let me hang-up the phone."

"You're a wicked sister. I bet you all think this is hilarious that I've finally succumbed to having what you all famously have experienced—a hangover."

"Now Rose…" Her sister entered and sat down beside her. "Did I berate you in any way? Get angry when you didn't arrive back to the hotel until after midnight? And yet, did you think to call your sister, so she would not worry?"

"Ha." Rose cast a skeptical glance at her sister. "You only arrived five minutes before my entrance."

Lily snickered and smacked Rose's leg. "You're always the reasonable one when working on a site. One drink. Early to bed and up before dawn. No dating, yada, yada. In all honesty, I'm curious about the man you had dinner and *drinks* with."

"No one special. And it wasn't a date."

"Really? Then why did you keep repeating his name in your sleep?"

"I did?" blurted out Rose.

"Oh, yes. Aidan, Aidan, *Aidan*."

"I met him at the bookstore and found out he's part of the dig."

Her sister's smile vanished. "Did you say anything

about the standing stones? Was this an investigation to pry information from him?"

Rose bit her lower lip. "It sorta leaked out we were interested."

"Crap!" Lily stood and began to pace in the small enclosure. "I think it's time to head back home."

"No!" Abruptly standing, Rose reached for a cloth and went back to the basin. After running it under cool water, she wrung it out and placed it on the back of her neck. "I'll take a cup of coffee, toast, and an aspirin."

"Why?"

Rose met her sister's gaze within the mirror. "I have seen the image of my visions on that standing stone. I'm not about to retreat without an explanation or another vision."

"Be careful," warned Lily, placing a gentle hand on her shoulder. "Forcing the information can leave you battered and trigger migraines."

Rose dropped the cloth in the basin. "Don't worry. I know what I'm doing."

Indecision wavered across her sister's features for a moment, and then she smiled. "Then tell me more about this Aidan."

Shrugging, Rose moved out of the bathroom. She had no wish to be put under Lily's microscope. She waved her hand dismissively. "You know. Tall, dark hair, knowledgeable. Aidan Kerrigan is also the owner of Balleycove Castle near the dig in Corridon." After hastily removing her T-shirt, she rummaged through her suitcase and pulled out jeans and a pale green sweater. Tossing the jeans onto the bed, she pulled the sweater over her head. "He's nothing spectacular."

"How many drinks did you have with him?"

"Three beers and a dram of whisky," confessed Rose.

Her sister clucked her tongue in obvious disapproval. "I'll go fetch you that tea and toast from the café next door. Imagine you having drinks with the owner of a *castle*. You must share more when I return."

"Coffee," she corrected, keeping her focus on tidying up her suitcase.

As the door of their room closed softly, Rose collapsed onto the bed. Never would she divulge her immediate attraction to Aidan Kerrigan to her sister. Ever. The man was merely a means to obtain valuable information. "Nothing more," she muttered, though she doubted her words.

A knock on the door caused Rose to lift her head. On a groan, she called out, "Did you forget your key or misplace it again, Lily?"

She made the effort to get off the bed, and when she opened the door, her anger turned to one of shock. Aidan Kerrigan's great shadow darkened the door's entrance. His gaze went from her eyes and traveled the length of her body.

"Is this how you greet all your guests, Rose?"

Her eyes widened in alarm. "Oh!" Slamming the door on the man, she dashed over to the bed and yanked on her jeans. And to add further to her embarrassment, Lily's voice echoed in the corridor. Running into the bathroom, she quickly swept a passing glance over her hair and face. "Awful," she muttered, twisting the long mass of hair into a knot. Searching the bathroom counter in a panic, she plucked a hairclip and pins from her sister's case and secured everything.

"You have a visitor," announced Lily upon

entering.

Taking a deep breath, Rose released it slowly and strolled into the room.

"Forgot my money," confessed Lily, digging in her purse.

The corners of Aidan's mouth twitched in mirth, and Rose gave up trying to fight the heat rising to her face. She lifted her chin and stared at him—daring him to burst out in laughter.

"Good morning, Aidan," she greeted.

He coughed into his hand. "Actually, it's early afternoon."

Her humiliation now complete, Rose folded her arms over her chest. "Is there a reason why you're here?"

"Did I not say we would see each other again?"

"I took it to mean something else," she argued, keeping her eyes fixed on his. *Do not retreat. Do not let him intimidate you with his size. Do not swoon!*

His smile was slow in coming. "I accept. Dinner tonight after I let you inspect the standing stones in Corridon."

Rose snorted in disgust. The man was not following the conversation. Making up his own set of rules. "Absolutely not. I think—" She blinked, finally recalling all the words he had spoken. She grasped his forearm. "You are going to let me study the stones—in Corridon?"

Aidan glanced over her shoulder at her sister. "Did I not express myself clearly?"

"You sure did," admitted her sister.

Rose beamed. "I don't know what powers of persuasion you used over the professor, but thank you."

He dipped his head. "You're welcome."

Lily nearly pushed her out of the way as she thrust her hand out toward the man. "I'm Rose's sister, Lily. It's nice to meet you."

"And you, as well."

Rose chuckled softly. "Give me a few moments to gather my supplies, and I'll meet you outside."

Her sister continued to banter with Aidan as they strolled out of the room, giving Rose time to brush her teeth and apply some lip gloss. After retrieving her boots by the side of the tub, she went to the small desk by the bed to check the supplies in her satchel. Picking up her journal by the lamp, she stuffed it inside.

Lily stepped back in the room and leaned against the door. "Oh, sister…"

"What?"

"You don't lie very well."

Rose shrugged. "I don't know what you're referring to." Sitting down in a chair, she put on her boots.

"Sadly, I won't be able to see how this adventure will play out here," declared Lily.

"You're speaking in riddles." Rose stood and slung the satchel over her arm.

"I received news last evening that the new client is here from America. Arrived a week in advance. They're requesting a meeting with Maeve and me, so I'm leaving now. I'll call the hotel in Corridon and have them change the reservation to one. Sorry I won't be able to assist you."

"No worries. I only need a day or two at the most, especially since the professor has given me access to the stones."

Lily pushed away from the door. After pinching her sister's arm, she glared at her. "You must be blind or you're lying."

"Ouch! Your brain must be addled," declared Rose. "Whatever are you referring to?"

"Be careful of *Mr. Nobody*, Rose MacLaren. Your face betrays your feelings. If you have not noticed, Aidan is one gorgeous man."

Rose swallowed. *Noticed, filed, and tucked away.* "I will ring the Society when I'm ready to return and someone can pick me up."

When she stepped outside the door, Rose paused and looked at her sister. "He's not the adventure I'm seeking."

"I think you've already taken the first step."

Her sister's words continued to echo within Rose's mind as she made her way out of the hostel and into Aidan Kerrigan's vehicle.

Chapter Nine

*"To study the footpath of an ancient civilization, you must travel the road with a keen insight to the landscape of the past, not present."*

*~Society of the Thistle*

The busy highway blurred behind them as the vista opened to reveal the lush hills of Corridon. From the moment Rose entered the car, Aidan could sense the uneasiness from his traveling companion. She continued to fidget with the strap on her satchel, keeping her gaze fixated on the passing scenery, and remaining silent. Was she contemplating her greeting earlier in only a sweater that barely reached the tops of her thighs? The vision she presented him roused his lust in an instant. Aidan yearned to lift her into his arms and whisk her away to some remote part of his castle—preferably his chambers, and feast on her body.

Slamming the door on the image, Aidan cleared his throat. "Your enthusiasm to view the site has left you without speech, Rose."

"What?" she asked softly, turning her attention to him.

Her eyes mirrored the deep forests of his homeland, and Aidan swiftly glanced away. "You're quiet."

Rose laughed nervously. "Sorry. I guess I don't

have much to say at the moment."

"What are your plans when you get there?" he asked, attempting to draw her into a conversation.

She huffed out a breath. "Observe, notate, photograph, and contemplate the surrounding area."

"Efficient, precise, to the point." *What has you wound so tight, lass?*

Wisps of silver-blonde tendrils had escaped from the braided hair on her head, and Aidan's fingers itched to hold them against his skin. Instead, he returned his attention to the road in front of them. Horses grazed in the surrounding hills, the afternoon sunlight shimmering on their dark manes. The soothing view of land and animals quieted his inner turmoil. The beast of lust had emerged constantly in Rose's presence, and he found it difficult to harness his desire for her, and to keep his other emotions in check.

*Enough! Bind and control. She's merely a human.*

When Rose's stomach protested loudly, Aidan pulled the vehicle to the side of the road.

"Why are you stopping?" complained Rose. "Have you rescinded your offer in taking me to the dig site? Surely it's not much farther."

Aidan stepped out of the car, choosing not to respond to her cutting remark. "Would you care for coffee or tea with your cucumber and watercress sandwich?"

Her eyes lit up. "You have coffee? Food?" She removed her satchel, dumping it onto the floor of the vehicle.

He tried to contain his humor. "Yes."

"I'll take coffee, please. Do you need some help?" she asked, exiting the vehicle and coming to stand beside him.

Aidan opened the back door and pulled forth a thermos. Handing it to her, he then proceeded to bring out two sandwiches. Motioning toward the fence, he suggested, "Let's eat out in the sunshine."

"Excellent." She beamed.

"Do you require cream or sugar with your coffee?"

She shook her head, and more of her locks came tumbling free. "Nope, unless you have cinnamon?"

"Cinnamon?" He closed the car door and started forward.

Rose lifted her head to the sunshine. "Helps to curb the bitterness."

Aidan nodded slowly. "Interesting…"

When they reached the fence, Rose immediately dove into the coffee. After pouring a full cup, she inhaled and sipped it slowly. He stood in fascination, watching her ritual. When he held out the sandwich, she shook her head. "I must have a full cup inside my system first." She gave him the most glorious smile. "Thank you. I fear I would have been difficult to be around without any food or coffee. I can be moody before my first cup."

"I did not notice," he lied, placing her sandwich on a wide portion of the fence post.

He took in their surroundings and spotted several colts in the distance near a barn. A young colt darted past its mother with a playfulness that was full of innocence. "New life," he pointed out between bites of his food.

"Aren't they adorable," she exclaimed. "I have not ridden in some time."

"How long has it been?"

"Several weeks," she declared, pouring some more coffee into the cup. She offered the steaming liquid to him. "Your turn."

Taking the cup, he nodded his thanks. "Do you ride daily?"

"Weather permitting, though I would consider taking out Daisy—my horse—in a light spring rain." Rose reached for her sandwich and ate the meal with gusto. She closed her eyes on a sigh. "You've added provolone."

Aidan's mouth went slack. He swiftly averted his gaze to the young colts. "It's a favorite of mine," he professed.

"This is heavenly," announced Rose.

He stole a hesitant glance. "The food or coffee?"

Rose waved her hand about. "Both, including the view. As much as I love parts of a city, my heart is at peace when I enter any countryside. Wide open spaces, sprawling hills." She turned around and faced him. "Deep, lush forests filled with earthy scents and the sounds of nature. Those are my much loved spots to wander."

*As they are mine, Rose MacLaren.* "And not the ocean?"

She shook her head. "It's turbulent, fascinating, exciting, but I find contentment deep inside a forest. Shrouded and mystical—many secrets can be held within the trees. We have one member at the Society who takes a sabbatical four times a year into the Turlough Forest in Ireland. I begged her once to let me go with her, but she always rebuffs me. Tells me this is her *quiet time* away from the constant chatter of other females. Mind you, we all adore and love her. Her knowledge of plants, herbs, trees, and flowers is extraordinary."

Aidan almost choked on his food. His curiosity blatantly stoked the moment the lass mentioned the forest. Quickly recovering, he took a long swill from his cup. "Why does she choose to go to Ireland, instead of the deep forests here in Scotland?"

"It's where she's from. Have you heard of the forest?"

"Yes." He popped the last bit of bread into his mouth. Refilling the cup with more coffee, Aidan held it outward. "Turlough Forest borders my lands there. I know it well."

"Interesting. You own land in Ireland, too." Taking the cup, Rose took a sip. "How odd."

"Indeed. What is the woman's name?"

"Aelish, but I'm positive she would have remained hidden from anyone's view. She always returns refreshed, proclaiming peace and quiet away from other people is a tonic to her nerves."

Clenching his fists by his sides, Aidan cast his gaze outward in an attempt to temper the building fury and unrest of finding out the Master Fae Apothecary was also a member of the Society of the Thistle. Why didn't Loran mention this in his report? Was Aelish a guardian to one of the women? She did tend to those with special gifts of the land, so it was plausible. His mind reeled with the new information and what would be his next step.

*If you have remained hidden, you must explain yourself, Aelish.*

"Is something wrong?"

Rose's touch and voice focused him on the present.

Aidan rubbed a hand over his face. "No. Perhaps I can escort you back to the Society when you have completed your research."

Wariness reflected across her features. "Honestly, there's no need. I'll ring for someone to fetch me when I'm done. That's a long drive."

"Over 200 kilometers, I believe. Roughly, two and half hours or more, depending on the traffic. Your talks about the Society have intrigued me."

She did not look convinced.

Rose brushed the crumbs of her meal onto the ground. Placing the cup on top of the thermos, Rose held it out to him. "I'm sure we would bore you with what we do. And there's no need to *escort* me back. I'm a big girl who doesn't require a guard to whisk me back to my castle."

He would not be dismissed. Disregarding the thermos, he grasped her hand and tucked it in the crook of his arm. "Consider it part of the package for allowing you to peruse and study the archaeological dig."

"Seriously, there is no need," she protested feebly.

Aidan enjoyed seeing the heat bloom on her cheeks. When they reached the car, he opened the door gallantly. "Your carriage awaits, fair maiden."

She burst out in laughter. "Do you always get your way, Aidan?"

"Always, Rose."

"Hmm. I believe you've met your match. I am not easily swayed by good looks and charm."

This time, Aidan laughed with delight. *Time will tell, lovely Rose.*

\*\*\*\*

After strict rules were set forth by Professor

Linton, Aidan escorted Rose to the standing stones. Several other students were engaged in their own research on the outer standing stones. They gave them curious looks as they made their way to the altar stone. Two standing stones set as guardians on either side of the slab. He found it fascinating that the professor opposed the Society—the reason, he would delve into at a later time. Thankfully, Liam had persuaded the professor to let Rose conduct her research, but only if another from the university was present.

"How intriguing," Rose muttered, removing her satchel. Pulling forth a camera, she photographed not only the stone, but also the perimeter around the slab.

Aidan observed her motions as she continued to take pictures in all directions for quite some time. He settled himself against the base of a pine tree—content to watch her mind ponder in silence for a while. He noted the weak sunlight fighting to emerge from the dark clouds overhead and determined the lass had sufficient time to peruse her studies before the storm arrived.

After examining the stone, she approached him and dropped her satchel. Once she retrieved a notepad and pencil, Rose studied the eastern sky. Scribbling down some notes, she then went back to tapping the pencil against her mouth. As she bent down near the slab, Rose angled her head and then looked behind her.

"There were no pine trees at the time of the construction," she stated. Rising slowly, she pointed upward. "These trees are young, say a couple hundred years. The open sky was a vision for the ancient people."

"A speculation or conclusion?" asked Aidan.

Rose chuckled softly and moved around to view the slab. "First impressions are always a speculation. To make a conclusion would be foolish."

"Or there were other trees and they have since been removed," countered Aidan.

"True." She knelt in front of the slab, studying with intent for some time. When she stood, she frowned at him. "Are you not working on a project here? Or has the professor assigned you as my guard?"

Aidan picked up a fallen pinecone and rubbed it between his palms. "My input is needed for analyzing the data and artifacts from what is gathered by the students."

Pointing to the slab, she asked, "And your thoughts on all these symbols? They're fascinating and similar to the ones at the other dig in Glasgow."

Shrugging, he replied, "A sketchbook for those who visited and left their mark."

"Seriously? That's your best reasoning?"

His good humor vanished. "Then do share your thoughts, Rose."

She held her arms outward. "Look at the vastness of the area, say a couple thousand years ago. Yes, trees heavily surrounded the landscape, but I believe there's more. The arc of the standing stones is set behind this slab. Perhaps it was more elevated. We can't say for sure until the university inspects underneath."

Shrugging, Aidan responded, "They may decide not to destroy the land beneath the slab."

"What I saw on the tallest standing stone reflects a larger picture."

A chill of foreboding swept through him. In her short time of being among these standing stones, she'd obtained bits of knowledge no one else had come upon. "Continue," he encouraged softly.

Hugging her notebook against her chest, she went to the tallest stone in the center. "These symbols and images on the back mirror the three centered on the slab. In addition, they are all the same as the other site outside of Glasgow."

"They're merely circles," he admitted, keeping his voice steady. "The Celtic triskele symbol also decorates many other stone structures."

Her brow furrowed in obvious concentration as she disappeared around the back of the stone.

Tossing the pinecone aside, Aidan stood. His instincts screamed at him to do something to prevent her from further inspecting the stone. Only he knew the significance. And he now understood why he was sent here. In all his travels, not one human had documented his time among them. Or so he believed. Upon his arrival, he longed to pulverize the stones to shards of dust after viewing the back. The altar stone had remained buried under moss, dirt, and ivy. The same was true with the tallest stone at its base.

He fought against extending his hand outward and sinking the area a thousand feet underground. Making quick strides to Rose, he came to an abrupt halt. Her face was ashen as she knelt behind the stone, sketching an entire scene on her notepad. One side mirrored the stones, but on the opposite page, her hand drew an epic vista.

The blood pounded inside his head, and he dared to draw in a breath. With each stroke of her hand, an image came to life, and his greatest fear unfolded. Slowly, Aidan lifted his hand. The power built and traveled down his arm. He had to destroy the picture. Banish the past vision from her mind. Eradicate all knowledge of him. Seal the door to the past from the present.

*The truth must never be revealed.*

But when Rose lifted her gaze to meet his, Aidan's heart stopped. For the first time in his life, he was torn between duty and his own personal needs.

"I am sorry," he stated in a strangled voice.

Immediately, she dropped her notepad and stood. Rose cupped the side of his face with her small hand. "Are you all right?"

The energy swirled in a tempest around them and then slammed back within Aidan. With a flick of his wrist, thunder crashed over them, and the sky darkened. The first drops of rain splattered across her cheek. Aidan took his thumb and brushed away the moisture. "Yes," he whispered, though he barely recognized his voice.

Rose dropped her hand. She took a hesitant step back, searching his face.

Thunder once again resounded all around them, and this time, Rose stooped to gather her items. He watched as she stumbled across the dig to fetch her satchel.

She hurried out of the area until she disappeared into the trees.

Making no move to join her, Aidan went and stood behind the stone. Crouching down at the base, he traced a shaky hand over the etchings. "So long ago. What a fool I was to share a story of my home world to these ancient people."

He laughed at the absurdity and stood. Raking a

hand through his wet hair, he lifted his head to the torrential downpour. "What am I going to do with you, Rose MacLaren?"

Chapter Ten

*"A warrior's courage is akin to the red dragon stones on our home world of Taralyn. To waver is a sign of vulnerability."*

*~Edicts of the Fenian Warriors*

Rose stared out the car window, uncaring of the water dripping down her cheeks. Her hair was a sodden mess, since she did not attempt to throw her hood over her head when she fled from the standing stones. Protecting her drawings was foremost on her mind. "It was sunny. Not a cloud in the sky," she muttered. After wiping her nose on her sleeve, she rubbed her hands together to ward off the bite of chill in the air.

The other students were huddled under a tented enclosure. Were they waiting until the rain cleared? She noticed the professor speaking with Liam at the entrance. Lightning splintered the sky, along with another boom of thunder. She rummaged through her satchel and pulled out her pocket watch. Noting the time, Rose shook her head. The day was done. Nothing more could be accomplished in this weather. She prayed the rain would dissipate by tomorrow morning.

With a deep sigh, Rose leaned back against the headrest. Her nerves had gotten the best of her earlier, half expecting to go into a full-blown vision right in front of Aidan. Instead of observing more of the stone, she decided to draw her vision and compare it to the carvings from both the standing stones. Both sites were similar, but she was able to see more of the detailed carvings here.

When Aidan interrupted her, Rose thought the world had ended. He towered over her, though she did not fear him. His face had transformed to one of power, and his eyes glittered like stars. The man stirred emotions and curiosity inside her. She should have fled the moment his eyes shifted from lavender to silver. Yet, his gaze held her rooted to the ground. What was this fascination she had with Aidan Kerrigan?

"He's mysterious with interesting eyes, nothing more."

Though her sister would argue in favor of his looks. Raw magnetism oozed forth from the man and Rose was not oblivious. Regardless of his sexy appearance, the man was off-limits. "You probably have a woman in your bed once a week or possibly every night," she whispered.

She watched as Aidan finally emerged from the trees and made long strides to Liam. His friend met him part way, not letting the weather hamper their conversation or stance. Liam stole a glance in the direction of the vehicle, and Rose's face heated. Were they talking about her?

"Get a grip on your daft emotions, girl."

Aidan fisted his hands on his hips as he continued to speak with Liam. When his friend shrugged, Aidan pointed a finger at him. Rose became fascinated with the heated conversation. It was similar to watching a military man giving orders to a junior officer. Maybe Aidan no longer wanted her at the dig. Was she a hindrance? All she yearned to do was inspect the stones. Everyone, including the professor considered the Society an outsider without a proper education.

"You're assuming facts not yet presented," she complained.

Both men glanced sharply toward her.

"What? Do you have supersonic powers of hearing and observation?"

When Aidan arched a dark brow her way, Rose gasped. "Impossible," she declared, watching him intently.

His smile came slowly. A shiver coursed through Rose's body. "I'm freezing, so finish your conversation." She bit her lower lip and forced her awkward stare away from the alluring man.

She didn't have to wait long. Aidan arrived and entered the vehicle. "My apologies for keeping you." After starting the engine, he turned on the heater.

"Not a problem," she lied, holding her hands out to the blessed warmth.

Aidan maneuvered the car out of the area. "I was giving instructions to Liam for tomorrow's dig. He will be your guide. I have urgent business that requires my attention at Balleycove."

"Oh. Fine. Good to know." She turned away to hide her disappointment. *Why do you care if it's Liam or Aidan? Be content they're letting you examine the stones.*

Exhaling softly, Rose rested her arm on the edge of the door and watched the rivulets of rain splatter down the window glass.

Silence became their companion during the remainder of their journey back to the hotel. She sealed her foolish thoughts on the sexy man in the car and concentrated on what she had learned today. If she had uninterrupted time at the site tomorrow, she might be able to conclude her examinations. There would be no need for an additional escort. She could move to the area the Society was studying in Glasgow.

When the hotel loomed in the distance, the storm had all but abated. A light mist descended over the hills behind the tiny town, and she smiled. As soon as Aidan drove up to the front, Rose bundled all her items and exited the vehicle. Before closing the door, she glanced at him. "Thank you for your time today."

Not giving the man a chance to respond she slammed the door and made steady steps toward the hotel entrance.

"Rose."

Ignoring him, she kept on walking away. "It's better this way, Kerrigan," she muttered.

"Rose!"

His commanding tone halted her where she stood. She narrowed her eyes and glanced over her shoulder. "Yes?"

"Pick you up in one hour for dinner."

And without giving her time to refuse the offer, he sped off down the road.

She lifted her chin. "Maybe I won't show up!" Turning back around, she collided with a couple exiting the hotel. Making a swift apology, she entered the building and hastily registered and grabbed her key from the desk clerk.

Running up the stairs, she entered her room and unpacked her small bag. She grabbed her bag of toiletries and went into the bathroom. Gripping the sides of the sink, Rose studied herself in the mirror. "You should not go out tonight. You look a fright. Haggard. A sodden mess. You will gawk at the man. Make a fool of yourself." Indecision fought a battle within her mind. "He's an overbearing man. Dominating. Controlling. *Not* for you."

However, the more she tried to convince herself, the more her resolve melted away.

Smacking the porcelain, Rose shook her head. "This will be my parting meal with you, Aidan Kerrigan. Tomorrow is another day, and then we shall part."

Turning away from her reflection, Rose turned on the taps to the tub and stripped her clothes from her body.

****

Rose stood back and examined the outfits on her bed. One pair of jeans had streaks of dirt down the side. The other was still damp from the afternoon rain shower. A flowered lavender dress hung on a lone hanger in the closet, tempting her to yank it off the rack. What possessed her to toss in the garment at the last moment was a mystery.

She tapped her foot in irritation. "This is not a date, right? A final meal with a colleague. That's all this will be."

She straightened and went to the closet. Pulling the dress free, she slipped it on and zipped up the back. Reaching for her boots, she went to the bed and put them on. After inspecting her hair one last time, Rose grabbed her black jean jacket.

Hastily cleaning up the bedroom and clothes, she slipped her purse over her shoulder and opened the

Destiny of a Warrior

door.

She tried to mask her surprise and failed miserably.

Aidan stood leaning against the wall with his arms folded over his chest. He wore black jeans that molded his body to perfection, and the black long-sleeved T-shirt sculpted his muscular arms and torso. She noted evidence of tattoos on his wrists for the first time. Now she was eager to see what they were and how far they extended on his arms. Aidan Kerrigan was an altogether perfect male specimen.

His gaze traveled from her eyes down the length of her body. Heat pooled in places throughout her as if he had touched her intimately.

"*Lovely*, Rose," he stated, his tone sending ripples across her skin.

"Thank you," she acknowledged.

"May I?" he asked, pushing away from the wall. He took her jacket from her arms and placed it over her shoulders.

She nodded, unable to form any more words. Afterward, he reached behind her and closed the door to her room. His presence dominated the small hallway. When the brush of his arm touched her, Rose almost leaned against the man.

He took her hand and placed it on the bend of his elbow, leading her out of the hallway and down the stairs. Stepping outside, the blast of cold air slapped against her cheeks. Rose blinked and recovered her senses. "Beautiful evening," she declared, looking up at the sky filled with the first twinkling stars of the night.

"Most assuredly." He opened the door to his car and gestured her inside.

Once Aidan settled within the vehicle, he

maneuvered the car away from the main part of the town.

Rose frowned in confusion. "Are we not having dinner at the pub?"

"No."

"Then where?"

He kept his sight directed on the road. "I thought a quiet dinner at Balleycove would be nice. It's ladies' night at the local pub, and it tends to get boisterous, making it difficult to carry on a conversation."

Rose swallowed—hard. *Alone with the sexy, charming, mysterious Aidan Kerrigan? Not a good plan.* "Oh."

"Are you not keen at seeing the kitchens of a medieval castle?" inquired Aidan.

"Yes," she blurted out. "I'm just surprised."

A frown creased his brow. "If you would rather—"

"Goodness, no! You know my fascination with anything medieval and history." She clenched her hands in her lap. "I thought a quick meal would suffice, since you have business to attend to tomorrow."

He winked at her. "Trying to get rid of me?"

Now the man intrigued her with his teasing. "I don't understand your meaning," she lied. Why did he captivate her beyond reason? "If I may ask, why do you wear the dragon torc?"

He gave her a questioning glance. "Family heirloom."

"Umm…from what century?"

"Ancient."

"Evidently," she remarked dryly.

Aidan steered the car up a gravel path alongside a steep hill. The glow of the crescent moon slipped in and out of the trees as they traveled upward.

"I'm confident I can conclude my research tomorrow, so this will be a nice way to end my time here." She gestured outward. "My sister will be jealous." *And I do not want to be a burden to you or anyone else.*

When Aidan remained silent, Rose stole a glance at his rigid profile. A muscle flicked angrily in his jaw.

She swept her sight to the road in front of them, confused and wary. When the vista opened, Rose gaped at the mighty fortress. Two turrets flanked the sides of a massive stone structure. Aidan skillfully drove through what looked like a portcullis, and Rose swiveled in her seat to view it from behind. The gate tower loomed over them, and she half expected to see guards manning the post. Returning her gaze to the front, she noted torches flickering in soft waves near the main entrance of the castle. Vines of ivy twisted upward within the crevices of the stone and trailed a path over most of the main entrance of the castle.

"Impressive," she whispered. *Have I entered another time-period?*

Aidan parked the car off to the side near a group of tall pine trees. He quickly got out of the vehicle and came to her side. When she opened the door, he reached for her hand, bringing her to stand mere inches from him. "Welcome to Balleycove, Rose MacLaren."

"It's magnificent." Though she didn't know if her words were meant for the castle, or the man staring down at her making her senses tingle.

As he led her through the giant oak doors, she was drawn to the massive tapestry suspended high from a beam in the entryway. The dragon rose in a majestic arc from the water. Yet, what made her breath hitch was the depiction of three moons behind the dragon. Rose had seen those exact same moons in her vision. Was this a message from the Goddess? Had her journey led her here to discover something connected to the standing stones?

*But what did it all mean?*

She swallowed, fearing to ask the question. "What does this tapestry represent?"

"A tale told by the ancients."

Rose removed her hand from the warmth of Aidan's. "*Ancients*? To whom?" she asked, trying to recall all the stories of legends and mythology and not stare at the torc he wore around his massive neck.

"Tribes from long ago."

"You mean the Picts?"

Aidan clasped his hands behind his back. "Possibly."

Rose pointed to the tapestry. "I don't recall any *tales* regarding a dragon and three moons. Are you referencing mythology or something else?"

He gave her a skeptical look. "I assume your knowledge contains all the invasions pertaining to Ireland."

"The dragons of the *Tuatha Dé Danann*?" She gaped at him.

"Precisely." Aidan motioned her onward to the left. "*The Tuatha Dé*, to be exact."

"They entered Ireland, not Scotland," she protested, following alongside the man.

"Are you positive?"

"Did you have them made?" she asked, trying to keep up with the man.

"Many of what you see is extremely old. The tapestries were made for my home."

"Obviously your family believed in the legends."

Aidan cast a speculative glance her way. "Legends are based on some facts."

*Never once have I heard of a fact referencing dragons with the Irish.* Rose's steps slowed within the corridor, as she gazed upward at more tapestries. These were filled with glorious waterfalls and lush scenery. The colors teased her, and she ached to touch the flowers on one in passing.

The smell of bread lured her onward, and she followed Aidan. Upon entering the kitchens, she glanced around in all directions in awe of her surroundings. A giant hearth set in the back of the large room, dominating the entire wall. Copper glistened in the firelight on pegs near the hearth, and she observed a narrow passageway to the other part of the kitchens. Several tables graced the center of the room, one laden with baskets of herbs and one with loaves of bread.

Rose pinched herself. Yes, she was standing in a medieval kitchen.

"Are *ye* impressed, Rose?"

She giggled. "Ye could say that, *my Laird*. What's in the adjacent kitchen?"

Aidan laughed, the rich and warm sound filling her. "An area for drying herbs."

"No meat?"

"None," he remarked, observing her.

"Yes. I do recall you mentioning you didn't eat meat. I've never met a man who wasn't a carnivore." She walked to the hearth and bent over the pot near the flames. Inhaling deeply, she looked over her shoulder at

Aidan. "Pea soup?"

He nodded in acknowledgement. "I hope you favor the meal."

"Did you cook this?"

Aidan approached near her side. "Yes."

"I'm impressed."

The corners of his mouth twitched as he lifted a spoon off the hook attached to the stone wall. "That a man can prepare a meal?"

She shrugged in good humor. "Most of the men I've encountered resort to dining out or using a can opener for their meals. Furthermore, I find it fascinating to find you've heated the soup in a kettle over an open flame. Do you have a stove?"

"No." He dipped the spoon into the soup. Bringing it to his lips, Aidan blew across the hot liquid. "I am not like any man you have met." He held the spoon near her lips.

*On that we can agree, Aidan Kerrigan.* Opening her mouth, she devoured the tasty morsel of soup. She closed her eyes and savored the flavors. "Thyme, garlic, red pepper, but needs more salt."

When she opened her eyes, Rose noted the shift of color within the depths of Aidan's eyes. He took his thumb and swept the pad across her bottom lip. Heat blossomed in her face and her lips parted.

"You missed some," he uttered in a low voice.

"Oh…" She blinked and looked away.

Aidan dropped the spoon on a side table. "Would you be so kind as to take the bread into the Great Hall. It's through the door to the right of the entrance. I'll follow shortly with the soup."

"Of course." She hastily made her way to the table.

Reaching for a platter of bread and butter, her steps were unsteady as Rose made her way out of the kitchens and into the Great Hall.

If she thought the kitchens were spectacular, nothing prepared her for the expanse of the hall. More tapestries adorned the walls on either side of the room. Long wooden tables and benches were pushed against the walls, except for the lone large table near the giant blazing hearth. Candles inside iron holders were suspended from beams down the center of the hall. Their glow on the tables illuminated the wood's luster.

As Rose moved toward the table by the hearth, she tried to calm her racing heart. Her attraction to Aidan was clouding her ability to think clearly around the man. After setting the platter down, she wiped a hand across her brow. "Did you expect him to kiss you?" She laughed nervously, removing her jacket and draping it over a chair.

Rose took a deep breath in and released it slowly. Bracing her hands on the table, she almost missed the carved pattern near the platter. Shoving the food aside, her eyes widened in disbelief. The carvings were ones she recognized. Though she had not seen them on any table or book.

They were on the man in her dreams. Down his arms and across his back.

Her fingers shook as Rose reached outward. Trailing a path over the wood, she tried to bring back the vision. Images blurred inside her mind, sending her spiraling to another place. The man, three moons, and stars that blazed in a multitude of colors. Moonlight illuminated the man to perfection, and she yearned to see his face.

Her sister's words of warning echoed within her. "Help me to see," she whispered her plea to the Goddess.

"Whom do you wish to see, *Rose*?"

She turned so fast that her hand toppled two cups on the table to the floor. Aidan's eyes blazed like the starlight she'd witnessed, and she fought a wave of dizziness.

He stepped around her and placed the bowls of soup on the table. Grabbing her by the shoulders, Aidan drew her near him. Her instincts were to curl up in his arms. Safe, warm, and seductive.

Rose lifted her head and braved the storm she feared would come with what she would do. He ignited a firestorm just by looking at her. Standing on her tiptoes, she cupped his face and brought his full lips down upon hers.

Chapter Eleven

*"If a warrior enters the tempest of a storm, he must be equipped to steer a course through the skirmish, or let another lead the way."*
~Edicts of the Fenian Warriors

Aidan tried to throttle the dizzying current racing through him as the first brush of her lips touched his mouth. The heady sensation left him spiraling. His warrior instinct screamed at him to push her away. Spurn her advance and stop this insanity. Yet, he found himself eager and erratic as a summer storm on his home world. His whole being seemed to be waiting for this moment, and Aidan was lost in the euphoria of holding her in his arms. Her kiss was one of exploration—hesitant and unsure, and his calm resolve shattered with the hunger for more.

Grasping her firmly around the waist, Aidan crushed her body to his. Desire ripped through his veins. His tongue sought entry into her soft heat, and he inhaled her scent. Rose returned his kiss with reckless abandon. When she wrapped her arms around his neck, he groaned deep within her mouth.

He let loose the lustful beast demanding control and took possession of her.

Aidan lifted her with one arm, as their kisses became a frenzy of passion. Moving along the table, he came to a halt before the large chair. Shoving it around with one foot, he sat down and cradled Rose on his lap.

She twirled her fingers in his hair while he gazed into liquid pools of desire that mirrored his own. He trailed a path across her lower lip with the pad of his thumb and to the base of her throat where the pulse beat and swelled as though her heart had risen from its usual place.

He brushed away strands of silver blonde to cascade over her shoulder so he could bury his face against her neck. "You smell of spices and exotic flowers." Aidan felt her tremble under his touch as he trailed a path along the vein running up her throat with his tongue and then recaptured her lips, devouring their softness.

He drank in the sweetness and passion of the kiss, exploring, teasing, tempting him beyond all reason. Rose banished the darkness, and in its place there reigned starlight.

One kiss should have been enough. However, his soul cried out for more, and the Fae warrior became the man, yearning to experience what he had been denied.

Aidan banished all rational thought, except one. Conquer and possess the woman in his arms.

His hand cupped her full breast, pinching the taut nipple through the thin material of her dress. He ached to feast on her bounty, and removed his hand.

Rose let out a hiss of disapproval. "Don't stop," she pleaded.

He placed a finger against her lips to hush any further protest. And she responded by nipping tenderly on his flesh.

He found the zipper on her dress and tugged it

gently downward. Aidan waited in trepidation, fearing she would halt his desire to touch her skin. Her breathing hitched, but Rose's smile came slow and enticing, and he finished unzipping the dress. Pulling the material off her shoulders, Aidan feasted his eyes on what she presented him.

Trailing a finger over the lacy edges of her bra, he pulled out one ivory globe. The heat from her breast pooled in his hand, and Aidan bent his head to feast on her offering. Rose let out a guttural cry and tossed her head back. Not satisfied with only one breast to fondle, he yanked the material free and trailed a path between the valley of her breasts and to the other ivory globe.

She squirmed against his painfully swollen cock, and her moan of desire spurred him onward. Rose's hands fisted in his hair. The pleasure built and ached for release. Aidan brushed a hand along her thigh until he came to the flimsy material blocking his entrance to her most intimate area. He retook fierce possession of her mouth as his finger found and sought entry to her slick folds.

"Oh…" she gasped.

He found her center and rubbed his thumb over the sensitive core, watching the flame of her desire build within the depths of her eyes. With each flick of his finger, her body quivered two-fold from his touch. She breathed lightly between lips already swollen from his kisses. As he roused her passion, his own grew stronger.

Rose moved in an ancient rhythm of pleasure, and he gritted his teeth, longing to bury himself deep within her body. Her scent filled him. Mesmerized by the beauty in front of him, Aidan was swept into her own ecstasy of release.

Her cry echoed inside his mind as she collapsed fully against his chest. Aidan cradled her and gazed into the flames snapping within the hearth. His heart pounded erratically against his chest, trying to calm his raging desire to spread Rose out on the table and enter her swiftly.

When she lifted her head, her cool fingers grazed over his chin. "Take me to your bed, Aidan."

Did she not understand the control he battled? The lust he attempted to keep reined in?

He looked down at the woman he held.

"Claim all of me tonight," she uttered softly.

Aidan jerked as if he had been burned. "*Claim*?" he echoed, his voice sounding hoarse. She had no idea what the word meant. It was infinite. Forever. Soul to soul.

*How could a human contemplate?*

With shaking hands, he brought Rose to standing and held her away from him.

Utterly disheveled, she placed her hand against his chest. "I want you to be my first."

Aidan rubbed a hand over his slick brow and closed his eyes. "You're a virgin?"

When she didn't answer, he snapped open his eyes. Her grimace told him all he needed. She was indeed untouched.

And he was a Fenian Warrior. The revelation hit him solid, and he staggered back. Contempt and sorrow filled him.

He regretted the words before they tumbled free to pool in the silence. "No. Forgive me, but I deem it best I return you to the hotel."

Shock registered across her beautiful features. Rose quickly glanced down at herself. He reached out to help her dress, and she surprised him by slapping his hand away.

"Do not," she warned in a chilled tone. Turning her back on him, she quickly dressed.

Aidan fisted his hands by his side, hating himself more with each passing second. He yearned to take Rose back into his arms. Kiss away the hurt he had caused by his lustful intentions and make amends.

"I am sorry, Rose," he whispered, stunned he had spoken the words out loud.

When she turned around, though her eyes misted with unshed tears, he noted the fury and humiliation within. "I'm the one who should be apologizing. I kissed you first."

She walked around him and grabbed her jacket. Hastily putting it on, she marched out of the Great Hall, leaving him empty and alone.

****

Staring out the stained-glass window from his library, the sun-filled morning made Aidan nauseated. Birds chirped in greeting, and squirrels scampered from tree to tree foraging for food. A lone deer ambled toward the stream at the edge of his property, and he found no pleasure in the scenery.

By the time he had reached Rose's hotel last evening, the air between them waxed frosty and unsettled. Without a word, she departed the vehicle, and he watched her make hasty steps inside the building. His gut twisted with indecision and regrets. After he returned home, Aidan drank two bottles of single-malt to deaden his guilt and lust.

Sleep was elusive and when he finally succumbed, he drifted in and out of slumber.

He'd awakened with a throbbing headache and in a worse condition than the night before. His angst and guilt returned with a vengeance to add to the pain in his head. Rose had woven a thread of herself under his skin. Her scent lingered within his pores, and not even an early morning swim in the stream could douse the burning fire he felt for the lass.

Lowering his head, he blew out a frustrated breath. There was only one solution. Never set eyes on Rose MacLaren ever again. Liam would tend to her today. Did she not mention she only required one more day at the dig?

"Yes," he uttered with disgust and lifted his head. He folded his arms over his chest and leaned against his desk. "Situation handled. Task completed." He would survey the dig for a few more days until he was satisfied with their findings. If she came to any conclusions regarding legends and the Picts, he felt certain they would be contained within the Society.

Turning from the bucolic spring morning outside his window, Aidan sat down. Sorting out the daily ledger and accounts would keep his mind focused. When Liam returned, he would recruit him in the training list for further sparring. Exercise of the mind and body would rid him of this annoying emotion he had for the lass.

An hour later, Liam strolled into the library. Aidan's hand hovered above the open ledger. "Don't tell me Ms. MacLaren has finished her research?"

Liam gave him a passing glance as he pulled out a book from one of the shelves. He slumped down in an overstuffed chair by the hearth. "Did you two have a spat?"

Narrowing his eyes, Aidan resumed his work. He refused to acknowledge the irritating remark.

"I'm going to conclude you did, since you're ignoring my question and are referring to the lass in a *proper* manner." Liam continued to flip through the pages in a leisurely manner.

"Since when did your interests include Einstein's mathematical theories?" snapped Aidan.

"It was the first book that caught my attention when I entered." Liam held up the tome. "Interesting scholar, don't you agree?"

"As you know, I have met Professor Einstein many times and have acknowledged my admiration for the man. In conclusion, your question is irrelevant."

Liam slammed the book. "Then choose the topic of conversation, Aidan."

Perplexed by his attitude, Aidan dropped his quill. "As you can see, I have business matters that require my attention. Furthermore, I have nothing pertinent to discuss." He picked up the quill and resumed his task. "I can assume by your presence you are done escorting Ms. MacLaren. As soon as my duties are completed, I shall make my report to the Fae council and we both can return to the Brotherhood." He paused and scribbled a note in the side margin of the ledger. "Did she mention anything about her findings?"

Liam snorted and got up from his chair.

Raising his head from his work, Aidan watched the warrior return the book to its shelf. A niggling of unease prickled along the back of his neck. "What are you *not* saying, MacGregor?"

"You're assuming that I've met with *Ms. MacLaren*. You are incorrect."

Aidan rose slowly from his desk. "Were my orders not concise enough for you? I asked you to oversee the lass at the dig." He gestured outward. "Is she all alone there?"

"No."

"Explain."

Liam shifted his stance. "When I arrived to escort her to the dig, the desk clerk informed me she left on the last bus of the evening for Glasgow."

Aidan turned away from the warrior's questioning gaze. Isn't this what he'd wanted? To have her gone from this place and his life? Did it matter if she decided against researching further? He started to rake a hand through his hair and paused. Clenching his fist, he lowered his arm. "Good. Problem solved," he muttered.

"I wouldn't be so confident," professed Liam.

Aidan frowned and glanced over his shoulder. "Why?"

The warrior pulled out an envelope from his back pocket and tossed it on the desk. "This was left at the desk addressed to you."

Regarding the missive, Aidan contemplated throwing it into the hearth. His name in flowing script beckoned him to open the document, and he brushed his fingers across the writing. Picking up the envelope, he retrieved the note inside.

*Dear Mr. Kerrigan,*

Aidan winced, but continued to read her note.

*I've decided it best to return to the dig in Glasgow. It is my determination that both sites contain similar knowledge and should be researched concurrently.*

*Whether you consider my findings to be of use is entirely up to you and the university. However, I wouldn't dismiss the idea of another civilization assisting the Picts (or whomever) in the sharing of their wisdom. The evidence on the stones speaks for itself. If my observations are correct, the altar stone reflects a constellation. I will copy my findings to the university, but I doubt they will take me seriously.*

*Please inform the Professor there will be no need for a guide, since my studies and those of the Society, will be directed in the area away from the standing stones.*

*Sincerely,*

*Ms. Rose MacLaren*

Annoyed with the direction of his recent thoughts on the lovely lass, Aidan crumbled the note. And as he was unable to unleash his fury, he paced behind his desk.

"Grim news?" asked Liam, leaning against the other side of his desk.

"Apparently the lass has concluded that another civilization assisted the Picts and shared with them their knowledge."

"In just a short time? One day?" remarked Liam.

Aidan magically unfurled the letter and waved it over to Liam in the air. "Yes. In one bloody day, Rose MacLaren thinks she has unlocked the secret of the Picts being mentored by another group of people."

Liam snapped his gaze to the letter and then back to him. "You think it's us. The Fae."

"I noticed your statement is not a question," surmised Aidan.

"I am not going to ascertain the thought process of

the lass. Furthermore, she can't make a connection. There is no proof."

"Do not be so sure of Ms. MacLaren. She believes in others out there in the cosmos."

The warrior shrugged and placed the letter on the desk. "She cannot make the connection to us."

"Unless she has the gift of sight," argued Aidan.

Liam blinked. "Truly? How did you come upon this knowledge?"

Aidan had no desire to confess to the warrior what he witnessed last evening. Shock was not the emotion he recalled as she traced a finger over the carved symbol of his home world on the massive table. He was overcome with raw desire, as if she were touching the tattoo embedded in his chest. An aura of multi-colored lights swirled in a vortex around Rose, and he understood instantly their meaning. She was able to discern the past and possibly the future.

"Care to share what happened last evening? As per our last conversation, you were taking her back to her hotel."

"Plans change," snapped Aidan, wishing to end this current topic of conversation.

"By the hounds! Listen to yourself. You have not fully answered any one of my questions about *Ms. MacLaren.*"

Clasping his hands behind his back, Aidan glared at the man. "Because it's none of your business!"

Liam raised his hands in surrender. "Forgive me. I thought we were on a mission together. You are my leader, but I am duty-bound to point out my suspicions. Did you not profess this to all of us in our training? If two or more take up the mission together, one will lead, but the others *or* individual will be a conscience. Am I here to merely do your bidding?"

Aidan grimaced and closed the ledger book. "No. I do not require a slave. We had a quiet meal, and I returned her to the hotel. I informed her you would be her guide today, but apparently she reversed her decision to stay."

"Good." Liam sat down on the edge of the desk. "Anything else?"

Placing the quill back in its holder, Aidan could think of only one solution. An idea blossomed as surely as the river flowed into the sea. He saw no flaw in his plan. "I shall travel to the Society and squash any further thought process of another civilization. I will guide her in another direction and make sure the university does not receive her findings. You can remain here and help the students."

Giving him a skeptical look, Liam rose slowly. "Is Rose the link we must sever? Do you really deem this a wise course of action, Aidan?"

"Yes to both your questions. I shall return in a couple of days." As Aidan moved away from the desk to pack a few items of clothing, Liam's words made him pause.

"*Rose* MacLaren is a temptation. She's a luring siren, and you're blind if you don't see what she's doing to *you*."

Aidan kept his back to the warrior. "And as the leader of the Fenian Warriors, I know my boundaries." Clenching his jaw, he stormed out of his library, sealing all emotions for the alluring female.

Chapter Twelve

*"Gather the flower seeds on the first day of spring
and toss them out in a wide arc before the light of dawn
graces the ground. You will be rewarded with a carpet
of wildflowers come Midsummer."*

~*Society of the Thistle*

Splashing the cool water from the well onto her
face, Rose shivered and whispered a prayer. She shook
out her hands and then braced them on the stone ledge.
Looking inside, her image wavered in the watery
depths. "Help to banish his touch from my skin,
Brigid."

Minutes ticked by in agonizing silence. She waited
patiently for some sign the Goddess had heard her plea
and would remove his scent, face, touch from her
senses. Rose wanted the man gone from her thoughts. If
only she could wipe away the memory of being in his
arms. He had haunted her dreams after she'd returned to
the Society and when dawn arrived, Rose left the warm
comfort of her bed in search of spiritual meditation.

She laughed nervously. *"If only…"*

Turning away from the holy well, Rose wandered
to her favorite oak tree and settled herself against its
rough bark. "What a fool you were last night," she
mumbled and retrieved a small package inside the
pocket of her coat. "Foolish, brazen—a harlot. Ready to

give away your virginity to a stranger." Her shoulders slumped. "What were you thinking?"

She had not thought it through. Instead, she embraced the moment and desire to be with Aidan Kerrigan.

As she opened the material surrounding the scone, a squirrel scampered near her.

"Yes, I will share. But only a wee bite. Sugary treats are not always good to eat." Breaking off a piece, Rose tossed the bits of food outward.

She watched in quiet contemplation as the small animal gathered the morsel and dashed away. "You lead a simple life, my friend." Rose nibbled on the other portion of the scone, yet, the food did little to wipe away her foul mood and anguish.

Remorse settled around her like dark clouds. An unwanted companion, and Rose didn't know whether to scream or cry. The man had given her exquisite pleasure with his touch, and her face burned from the recollection.

"It's not fair!" she shouted, frightening a bird in a nearby tree. Crumbling the rest of the scone, she flung it to the side. She squeezed her eyes shut to stop the tears from falling once again. It was lunacy to weep over the situation. The man was gone forever from her life, and she prayed she'd never set eyes on him again.

After wiping her nose on her sleeve, she inhaled deeply and then released the breath slowly. "I'll never attend a class at the university. I'll have Lily or Maeve sit in on the meetings for the Society. Seclusion, studying nature, meditation, and taking care of the animals are my priorities." Silently ticking off other items of interest that would keep her far away from encountering Aidan lifted Rose's spirits somewhat.

Yet the niggling thorn of doubt returned with a vengeance, and she lowered her head onto her bent knees. She became someone else in his presence. He commanded the land, sun, and stars it seemed, and she yearned to explore more with him. "Time, Rose…give it time for the memories to fade."

"A thimble for your thoughts," announced Aelish coming up the path toward her.

"Nothing important," she mumbled, praying the woman would keep on walking past her. She hadn't even spoken to Lily when she came home last evening. Solitude was her only desire.

Aelish sat down next to her and patted the ground. "Bah. The energy around you swirls in a tempest from what you keep bottled inside."

Rose bit her tongue in an effort to keep from spouting a harsh retort.

"The land cannot accept this grieving and anger. The fresh buds will refuse to blossom forth," proclaimed Aelish. She lifted a dead leaf and waved it in front of Rose.

*I hate it when you talk in gibberish, Aelish.*

Lifting her head, Rose stared at the woman. "When I leave, the plants will return."

"Unless they wither and die."

She looked away. "It is the circle of life."

Aelish touched her arm, and Rose flinched. "Please do not."

"What causes this pain for you to lash out at the land *and* me?" urged the woman.

Hysterical laughter bubbled forth from Rose. For several moments, she let the tide of melancholy seep out in this manner. After regaining her wits, she wiped a hand over her face and once again leaned back against the tree. "I'm sorry, Aelish. It's only foolish nonsense. My regret over recent actions."

"Sweet Brigid. Did something happen at the dig site in Corridon? Is there a ban on the Society from entering near the area?"

"No. *No*. Nothing that serious."

The woman snorted and crumbled the dead leaf, discarding the tiny pieces. "What could possibly be worse?" She raised her hand. "The sun is shining, spring is abundant, and the Society is doing well."

Rose stood abruptly and brushed the crumbs and dirt from her clothing. "I misjudged a man."

When the woman remained quiet, Rose stole a glance at her. Aelish appeared to be in deep thought. She finally blinked and stood.

"I was unaware you were seeing anyone. The heart can be a fragile vessel."

"It's nothing like that, Aelish," she reassured. "I only met him recently. I made a grave assumption and it left me in a nasty mood." *More like a grave mistake.*

Aelish moved in front of her and tapped a finger to Rose's heart. "He made an impression on you."

"Definitely," Rose blurted out.

"Running does no good either."

She waved the woman off and moved away from the tree. "I have no desire to set eyes on the man again. I'll let Lily deal with him or his assistant."

"So he works for the university?" inquired Aelish.

"Yes. He was able to get permission for Lily and me to examine the standing stones here and those that are similar in Corridon."

The woman frowned. "But you are supposed to study the area *away* from the stones and take samples for botanical purposes."

She shrugged. "You know my curiosity with the ancient people who dwelt here and their writing, Aelish. I could not pass up this opportunity."

She studied Rose intently. "You had an attraction to this man."

"Over and done," acknowledged Rose and went to embrace Aelish. "I won't see him ever again. It was a silly lapse of judgment. I think I'll take Daisy for a ride."

The woman gave her a weak smile and started along the path back home.

Rose opened her arms wide, heading for the stables. "A good ride through the hills will wipe all traces of my encounter with this man." Though she doubted she would ever get rid of Aidan completely.

"You never mentioned his name!" shouted Aelish.

Rose's steps stilled, and she glanced over her shoulder. What did it matter if the woman knew his name? She would never divulge their conversation to anyone. One of the traits Rose admired in her friend.

"Aidan. His name is Aidan Kerrigan."

Fury flitted briefly across the woman's features, and then she quickly masked the emotion. "Good riddance," she hissed out and then stormed away, continuing with a litany of words Rose did not comprehend.

\*\*\*\*

When Rose entered the back entrance of the Society, her nerves had calmed. The ride with Daisy had been a soothing tonic on her frayed emotions, and the fresh air helped to clear her despondent thoughts. Maybe she was destined to be alone for the rest of her life. Her sister was correct. She craved men that were different. Elusive. Mysterious.

"Aidan Kerrigan," she whispered his name on the breeze.

She bent and picked up a branch and tossed it into the shrubs near the dense copse of trees. "Nope. Not even him."

Strolling through into the kitchen, she spied her sister. Lily raised her head from the current cookbook that had captured her interest these past few weeks. "Care to explain why you've returned home so soon from Corridon? And don't tell me you've been riding Daisy in a dress?"

Glancing down at herself, Rose fingered the material. "It's long enough, and I didn't want to trek back inside to put on jeans."

Lily closed the cookbook and folded her arms across her chest. "And the answer to my other question?"

Crossing the kitchen, Rose grabbed a mug and poured a hefty amount of coffee. "My work is done there. It was late, and I didn't want to bother anyone, so I hopped on the bus back home." She could feel her sister's skeptical glare against her back.

"Why didn't you wait until the morning? Maeve was heading to Arbroath. All you had to do was give a call."

Rose turned and took a sip of her coffee. The burning liquid mirrored the heat from her sister's eyes. "Does it really matter? I'm home."

"And Aidan?"

Rose moved to the table, wishing to halt any conversation pertaining to the man. "What about him? We're finished. I'll compare the notes I have and your pictures when you get them developed."

Her sister blew out a frustrated sigh and went to the sink. She remained quiet as she took to cleaning up the morning dishes. Rose pulled out a stool by the work island in the middle and perused the many cookbooks strewn about the counter. "Anything special you're preparing for us tonight?"

"I haven't decided. Maybe I'll go to the market and pick up some lamb chops."

Rose scowled. "Now you're being cruel."

"Just because you don't eat animals does not mean the rest of us have to abstain from all meat."

"Then I'll be content with the side dish of vegetables or potatoes," declared Rose, tapping her fingers against the side of her mug.

Her sister shrugged and continued with her chore.

"Who is at the dig here?" asked Rose, attempting to bring her sister into a normal discussion. She understood her rigid stance and clipped sentences. Lily was not satisfied with her answer about Aidan Kerrigan.

"Colleen," she responded, smacking the rag down.

"This is her day to be at the library," protested Rose, taking another sip of her coffee.

"Regardless, one of us had to be there or someone from the university would conclude our work was finished. Maeve is in Arbroath, which I stated, and Katie works at the pub on Tuesdays."

"Why is your tongue as sharp as stinging nettles?"

Lily gestured her hand outward. "Because as usual,

when it's too personal for you to talk about, you hide like a turtle."

"Aidan kissed me," confessed Rose.

Her sister whirled around. "What the heck?" She darted across the kitchen and pulled out a stool. "Tell me *everything*."

Rose didn't intend on blurting out her next admission. The words tumbled free, unable to contain within her box of protection. "He took me to dinner at Balleycove—"

"You got to see inside his *castle*? What was the meal like? Does he have servants? Any display of armory?"

Rose held up her hand, dizzy from the onslaught of questions. "Let me finish."

"Sorry," mumbled Lily, placing a finger against her lips to symbolize complete silence.

Staring into the inky murkiness of her coffee mug, Rose continued. "His kitchens are spectacular. He prefers to use the great hearth to cook his meals." She raised her head. "Did you know he's a vegetarian, too?"

Lily rolled her eyes, but waved her hand to continue.

"He made pea soup and—"

"Oh for the love of Brigid and all the Goddesses, tell me about the *kiss*," interrupted Lily.

Rose took a gulp of the coffee, letting the burning liquid be the reason for her heated face. "It was mind-blowing, intoxicating. He kisses with passion."

"*Kisses*?" echoed Lily.

Rose merely nodded.

"And?" squeaked her sister.

"Everything became heated and I offered myself to

him. Suggested he take me to his bed." Rose refused to tell her sister about the intimate details of what Aidan did to her body. It was exquisite—a memory she would cherish and bury.

"*And…*"

"He rejected me."

Her sister blinked once and sat back. Cupping a hand over her mouth, Lily tried to suppress the laughter and failed miserably.

Nudging her sister's leg with her foot, Rose lashed out, "You find this humorous?"

Lily nodded and then blurted out, "No, but parts, yes." Flipping her braid over her shoulder, she added, "You are really blind, my dear, sweet sister. You have *found* your chivalrous knight."

"I was humiliated! Totally embarrassed. One moment I'm tracing a pattern with my finger carved into his table in the Great Hall, and the next, he is…is plundering me on his lap."

"Ooo…I like the word *plunder*. And in the Great Hall? Fascinating…"

Rose longed to fling the mug across the kitchen. "Regardless, I was mortified and wanted to leave. He drove me back to the hotel in complete silence. I had no wish to set eyes on him in the morning, so I took a cab to the bus station. Fortunately, I was able to book the last one leaving." Standing, she added, "I never want to see the man again."

Lily gave her a skeptical look and went back to the sink. Retrieving the rag, she folded it and placed it in the dish drainer. "In all of your life, Rose, I've never seen you so rattled over a man. You should have stayed. If you don't take the leap, how will you ever experience the journey?"

Her sister's words rang true, but Rose would not make the admission to her. Not yet. Perhaps in ten years, or when they were old and gray. She didn't like not being in control of her emotions. They skidded and slid off into an unknown abyss whenever she was around the mysterious man. Besides, she behaved like a brazen hussy, letting him touch her in the most wonderful way.

"Well, I won't have to worry about him anymore." A twinge of sadness filled her, and she swiftly sealed the irritating emotion.

"Tsk, tsk," stated Lily, peering out the kitchen window. "Be careful the words you spout."

"I'm confident our paths will never cross again." *I'll make bloody sure they don't.*

"Really," drawled Lily. "Your chivalrous knight, *Aidan Kerrigan* just drove into the car park."

Rose dropped her mug, coffee splattering everywhere. "Blast! Hide me. Tell him I'm not here." She glanced in all directions, looking for the best escape route.

Her sister snickered and wandered slowly out of the kitchen. "Not on your life, Rose MacLaren. And don't you dare go running to your room, or I'll bring the man to your door."

Rose ran out into the hallway. "You're a horrid sister!"

"You'll thank me later."

Chapter Thirteen

*"There is one emotion a warrior strives to avoid. The beauty of love."*
*~Edicts of a Fenian Warrior*

Admiring the view of the front exterior of the Society of the Thistle, Aidan almost didn't see the mutt terrier until he responded with a loud bark. He bent and ruffled the fur on the animal's head, and then returned his gaze to the expanse of ivy and roses trailing a path around the entrance. His recollection of the Society was based on knowledge from a druid. The structure was given to five women in the year 1210 by a local chieftain. He believed in the old ways and sought to appease the Goddess. Yet, the new religion swept through with a mighty hammer, and he succumbed on his deathbed before he had a chance to see the dedication.

Thankfully, his sons sought to continue with the healing work the women were doing and expanded the building to include stables and other outbuildings. The Society thrived during religious battles, various kings, and wars. Never once did the women seek the assistance from the Fae. They honored the old and the new, and flourished. And their descendants continued with their work here today.

"What name have they given you, my friend?"

The animal gave a sharp yap.

"His name is Thor," responded Lily, stepping outside the entrance.

Aidan coughed in his hand to hide the mirth. "A fierce name for the wee animal."

"Don't let his size fool you. He's been known to chase larger dogs off the property."

Glancing down at the mangy mutt, Aidan smiled. "I shall endeavor not to cross paths with you."

The dog gave a low growl in understanding. And this time, Aidan laughed fully. "Splendid."

"Please come inside," suggested Lily, motioning him forward.

He nodded and proceeded to follow her. Stepping inside the dwelling, his attention was drawn to the large bouquet of flowers and herbs on a table in the entryway. The beautiful arrangement welcomed him with their light floral fragrance.

"Would you care for coffee? Tea?" asked Lily, standing before the sitting room to the left.

"Coffee…black. Please."

The woman's features betrayed an outward calm, but Aidan detected something else in her demeanor. "What brings you to the Society?"

"We have unfinished business. I am here to escort Rose to the Standing Stones of Bran," he replied.

"Our business is concluded," proclaimed Rose, coming down the staircase. She halted on the last step. "You can return to Corridon."

As their eyes met, a shock of delight shot through him.

"I'll get you that cup of coffee," replied Lily, hastily making her way down the corridor.

Words failed Aidan at the moment. He stood transfixed, staring at Rose. Her beauty filled him as surely as flowers on a spring day. Except Rose's scent was not only floral, but contained a fragrance of spices as well. Recalling his mission to her home, he clasped his hands behind his back, banishing the images of her in his arms last evening. "Do you not wish to inspect the stones further? And without others there?" *Say yes, lass.*

She angled her head at him. "What good would it do? No one takes me seriously. I sought to seek answers on the stones for my personal reasons. I regret not informing you of this fact from the beginning."

Aidan took a step near her. "Can you share your reasons?"

"This is a futile conversation. Please go back home, Aidan."

He was losing the battle of restraint.

Lily emerged with a tray. "I have coffee for both of you and food." She hurried into the sitting room and set the items down on a table.

"I'm not hungry or thirsty," announced Rose and then turned around to ascend the stairway.

"Don't be rude," scolded Lily. "At least you can make pleasant conversation with the man while I attend to some business calls. He did come all this way to see you."

Aidan watched in fascination the heated glances between the two women and determined it might be best to leave. The mission appeared to be in control, and no damage had been done with the connection to the Fae and the Picts. However, he found he wasn't completely convinced and crossed into the sitting room.

"Smells delicious," he stated, taking a seat on the sofa.

"Cinnamon rolls. Freshly made this morning," announced Lily, smiling.

Rose slowly made her way inside the room and sat in a chair opposite him.

Lily touched her sister's arm in passing. "Consider his offer," she uttered in a low tone.

When the doors closed, Rose reached for the pot of coffee and poured a hefty amount into each cup. Returning to her chair, she watched him over the rim of her cup, remaining silent.

Aidan snatched one of the cinnamon rolls off the tray. Taking a huge bite, he waited for her first question. Patience was not a quality he noted in the lovely emerald-eyed lass.

He devoured the tasty morsel in two bites. Licking his fingers, he reached for his cup of coffee and sipped the hot liquid.

Rose set her cup down abruptly and stood. "Now that you've finished your roll and had some coffee, you can leave."

By the hounds, he ached to trace his tongue over her pouty lips.

Carefully setting his cup down, Aidan stood. "Cinnamon, vanilla, *and* cloves."

She snorted. "Lily only puts cinnamon in her rolls"

Rubbing a hand over his chin, he stepped around the table, standing mere inches in front of her. "I meant *you*. Your scent is one filled with all of those spices."

Rose took a step backward, and Aidan advanced again.

"Why are you here?" she demanded.

Aidan thought he knew the reason when he ventured forth to her home. His mind was set. The plan indeed firm, and he was in control. Yet, emotion clashed with his rational, warrior instinct the instant he saw her descend the stairs.

Did he want to tame the luring call of the siren? Or did Aidan long for surrender?

Grasping her firmly around the waist, he cupped her chin and slammed the door on the shouting within his mind.

Aidan sought to have more kisses from the bewitching beauty.

Her luminous eyes widened in astonishment, and she gasped. Aidan did the unthinkable. He lowered his head and kissed her passionately. She stiffened and placed her hands against his chest in an attempt to push him away.

Breaking free from her mouth, he brushed a feather-like kiss over her cheek. "I have no regrets about last night, save one."

Her chest rose and fell with each breath. "Which is?"

His hand slid down to her bottom. "That I did not consider your offer fully and take you to my bed."

"Damn you," she muttered. "I've rescinded my offer." Though the lust in her eyes betrayed her words.

"Then I will have to convince you of the endless possibilities." His fingers gradually traveled back up along her spine. She trembled in his arms.

"Maybe we should take our time in getting to know each other," she suggested.

He arched a brow in amusement. "How much time do you believe it will take?"

"Unsure. I might become bored with your kisses."

Aidan nipped her lower lip. "Brazen lass."

"Only when I'm around you," she confessed.

Wrapping her arms around his neck, Rose reclaimed his mouth, igniting a firestorm within his blood with her powerful possession. Her tongue teased inside, and he groaned deep inside her. The warrior fled and the Fae man emerged, taking what she had to offer. The heady sensation of her lips on his had Aidan spiraling out of control.

Rose slowly withdrew her arms and lowered her head against his chest. "Did you really come back to take me to the stones?"

"Yes."

"Why?" she asked softly.

Aidan gazed out the window. Uncertainty clouded his thoughts. It remained a constant battle when he was with Rose. "You have not finished your research. This gives me another opportunity to see you."

She lifted her head and smiled. "Then let me go grab my items and change."

Taking in her appearance, he asked, "Why? I favor the dress."

"Coffee stains. Need to change." Giving him a kiss on his chin, she hurried out of the room.

Exhaling softly, Aidan wandered over to the large window. He rubbed a shaky hand down the back of his neck, hearing Liam's words once again within his mind.

*Rose MacLaren is a temptation.*

Never had anyone tempted him beyond his principles. She left him shaking, without words, and desperate to fill a void he never gave a damn about.

*To claim her—totally.*

The mere thought was blasphemy. Inconceivable. "*Forbidden*," he hissed out.

The door to the sitting room closed quietly, and Aidan turned around.

He stared at the diminutive Fae woman leaning against the door. "Aelish."

Sparks of fury glittered in her eyes like diamonds. "Fenian Warrior."

"Apparently you have forgotten my name, *Master Apothecary*."

"I know exactly who you are. Nevertheless, what I fail to understand is why you have entered into a dalliance with this human."

*Did the walls have ears?* "Are you her guardian?"

Wariness flickered over her features. "No. Another. Her sister. And you?"

"On a mission to thwart a connection to the work the Society is researching."

"Regardless, everyone within this home is under my protection."

"No, Aelish. Your reach extends to supervision and mentoring," Aidan corrected. "Does the Fae council know you are here *supervising* the Society?"

She looked aghast at him. Snapping her fingers, the door sealed magically shut. "I am not bound by their laws and rules. I take my orders from the King and High Seer."

"This mission was given to me personally by the High Seer," he admitted. "Knowledge of your presence should have been made privy to me." Aidan fought the urge to clench his hands and retained his calm façade. "Is there a reason you have sealed us inside this room?"

The Fae woman wandered to his side and glanced

out the window. "I have no wish for Rose to know we are acquainted. Do you?"

"No."

"Good. She'll be some time upstairs trying to choose the right garment to impress you. This shall give us time to have a conversation."

Aidan rolled his eyes and leaned against the desk.

"In truth, the High Seer has probably forgotten I'm here. I had orders for one year. When the time elapsed, I stayed on. The women are wonderful students and quick studies. Moreover, each possesses a unique inner gift—from healing, prophecy, and the ability to see into the past."

"Then you can understand why I am here," he countered.

Aelish tapped her fingers along the window ledge. "Rose's focus drifts to ancient writings, instead of concentrating on herbal lore. Her gifts are strong."

"You cannot direct their abilities," warned Aidan. "If the path beckons a human, you must step aside, or present another alternative."

The Fae turned her attention to him. "As I am aware, and Fenian Warriors are not supposed to have liaisons with their charges."

Aidan smiled slowly. "She is *not* my charge. Are you satisfied?"

"You have already broken a part of her spirit, Aidan."

*Impossible!* Though concern filled him. "How did you come upon this knowledge?"

"She told me earlier this morning, believing your paths wouldn't cross again. You are the leader of the Fenian Warriors and beyond these temptations and flirtations. I care for her—"

"What if my intentions were honorable?" Aidan admitted, stunned he spoke the declaration out loud.

Aelish smacked the wood. "For what possible purpose? To quench your sexual desires? Those are not honorable. Seek out the Pleasure Gardens and then return to complete your mission."

His anger snapped like the sting of a wasp. "*Never* tell me, the leader of the Fenian Warriors what to do! Your reach does not include governing me. In truth, I can order you to return to the Fae world, if you attempt to interfere."

The woman blanched and took a step back. "You would not dare...Besides, she is a human."

"Your point?"

"You play a dangerous game, Aidan."

He stiffened, his eyes narrowing at the woman. "I do not play games, Aelish."

"You were warned, Aidan Kerrigan. What you do from this moment forward will have consequences. Remember my words." With a flick of her wrist, Aelish vanished in a blur of soft colors and unsealed the doors on her exit.

Thankfully, the woman had not understood what he meant by honorable intentions. Sadly, nor did Aidan.

Glancing at the closed door, he realized he had two choices.

One, he could simply vanish and consider the case closed.

Two, he could let the Fates decree where the path wove. Why else would the High Seer suggest he take this mission?

"When did making a decision create mass

confusion?" Aidan barked out in laughter at the ironic twist of fate.

As a leader and warrior, the answer was simple. As a man, complicated.

He lifted his hand, preparing to leave, when Rose entered the room. Her radiance and serenity surrounded him—centering the conflict within. Aidan exhaled slowly and lowered his arm.

*See the mission through to fruition. Let the Fates determine if the threads are to be broken or looped together.*

"I'm sorry it took so long. No one has done any laundry, and I had to borrow something from Lily's wardrobe," she confessed quickly.

"No worries." *You could have worn rags and the essence of your beauty would have shone through.* Crossing the room, Aidan gestured her forward. "Before we leave, I'd like to see your horse."

"Daisy?" she asked in mystified tone.

"You spoke of her, and I have a fondness for the animals."

As they moved out of the sitting room and through the entryway, Rose remarked, "I must warn you, Daisy does not like men. So if she nips at you or stomps her hoof, do not take offense."

Aidan laughed. "Duly noted."

After following Rose around the back of the main house, they proceeded down a narrow path between a large garden filled with herbs and vegetables. He dipped under a trellis filled with flowering honeysuckle and the hum of bees. Onward they traveled through a cluster of apple and pear trees, their blossoms heady with the scent of the fruit they'd eventually bear. The area opened and curved to the right to reveal the stables and pasture.

The doors to the building were open as he stepped inside. He watched in awe as Rose reached for a small apple from a basket and handed it to him. "A peace offering."

"From what you've explained, the horse may take my fingers, *instead* of the fruit."

Rose burst out in laughter. Her entire face transformed, and Aidan was captivated. "Are you afraid?" she teased.

After taking the apple from her outstretched hand, Aidan rolled it casually within his palm. "Never of an animal."

Rose tapped him lightly on the chest. "We shall see. Follow me."

"Lead the way, fair maiden."

Rose led him down to the last stall. He came to an abrupt halt, assessing the large horse. "Daisy is a Clydesdale?"

Leaning against the gate, she nodded. "What did you expect? A Shetland pony?" Rose gave a soft clicking noise. The horse turned her head and trotted forth.

"Her name does not suit her," professed Aidan. "The flower is simple, not majestic like this animal." Gently, he reached out within the horse's mind, uttering soothing words.

"Sadly, I agree. The Society bought her at an auction for abandoned horses. She was a working animal and treated horribly. Our intention was to have horses to help with the land in the hills. We immediately changed our plans to include more fruit trees. Daisy was one of four we rescued. Their lives are simple: Wander the pasture, graze on food, and frequent rides through the hills."

He gently rubbed the horse's muzzle. Aidan removed a *sgian dubh* from his boot. "Greetings, Daisy. Would you care for an apple?"

Rose laughed, watching the interaction between him and the horse. "Do you always carry a knife?"

Slicing into the apple, he held it out for the animal. "Always. I have a fascination with blades."

"Impressive."

"The *sgian dubh* or that Daisy has taken a fancy to me?"

A cat jumped up along the stalls and made its way to Aidan. The feline sat down a few inches away, and proceeded to clean her paws.

Rose took a step back and stared at the scene. "Both," she answered softly. She pointed to the animals. "These two are the most stubborn and unfriendly here."

He brushed a hand over the back of the cat. The animal leaned against him and purred loudly.

"She *never* purrs," expressed a shocked Rose.

"Och, she required the gentle touch of a man. Correct, Mistress?"

The color faded from Rose's cheeks. "How do you know her name?"

Aidan angled his head at her. "Is she not the mistress of the stables?"

She swallowed. "You are a mysterious man, Aidan Kerrigan."

He winked at her. "Most assuredly, Rose MacLaren."

Holding out his arm, he added, "Let us retreat to the Standing Stones of Bran."

Chapter Fourteen

*"In the beginning of the Society, the eldest female made annual travels to all the Standing Stones in the surrounding hills. She returned with sage advice that included folklore wisdom from the ancients and historical lore."*

*~Society of the Thistle*

"Of course, I should have known it would rain," Rose protested feebly. Dark clouds threatened to invade the landscape where she'd settled in for some invaluable research on the altar stone. She narrowed her eyes. "I banish you until I am done here." Yet, she knew her words would do little to persuade the elements to halt their progress across the sky.

"Any chance you can command the storm to stay its course?" she asked in amusement.

Aidan's mouth twitched in humor, revealing more of the dimple she so admired. "Your wish is my command." He closed his eyes for a few seconds. Snapping them open, he announced, "Done."

"Be careful. You might have angered the God of the Sky."

He looked at her sternly. "I was not aware there was one."

"Teasing."

Continuing with her work, she concentrated on

sketching part of the slab, until a burst of sunlight illuminated the stone. Rose let out an audible gasp and lifted her head. Shielding her hand over her eyes, she burst out in laughter. "Amazing!"

The clouds had retreated to the north and far away from her position. Glancing in Aidan's direction, she gaped at the man as he reclined against one of the stones, eyes closed, and a smile that made her skin prickle. Even in his relaxed pose, Aidan commanded power and assurance.

Rose could study the man for hours, each nuance, each stance, and never become bored. When he'd stepped through the door at the Society and she heard his voice, her first instinct was to flee. Yet, the moment their gazes locked, she found herself glued to the staircase. She might have bit out harsh words at the man, yet, her heart had rejoiced in seeing him grace their entryway.

*He came back for you.* She smiled, the feeling warming her all over.

An idea took hold, and she flipped to a clean page in her sketch book and began drawing his face. Rose didn't know what propelled her to include his image with all the others, but if he left tomorrow, then she'd have something to remember. Aidan was the only one who ever seemed interested in her findings. He actually asked questions and didn't look at her like she was demented or not prone to knowledgeable opinions. So many others at the university discounted her work and those from the Society.

The warmth of the sunlight touched her shoulders as her fingers flew across the page. When she was satisfied with her work, she held it up and compared it to the live man sitting several feet away. "Perfection," she whispered.

Returning her attention to the slab, she got on her knees and brushed her hand over the entire stone. There was infinite beauty in these ancient carvings. And for a moment, she pondered if this might be a part of the dolmen stone, whereas there would be two or more supporting stones to the giant slab. She glanced at the surrounding area to see if any others from the university thought the same. However, the ground remained undisturbed. *What if there is a burial chamber underneath?*

Rose became giddy at the thought. Why didn't she think of this earlier? She dropped her sketch book. Placing both hands on the flat stone, she studied all the etched images, doing her best to discern the old etchings from graffiti.

Bright lights danced within her vision, and her stomach became queasy. Rose clutched her head. *No, please don't let this happen now.* She bit her lower lip so hard, blood oozed forth. *Stop, stop!* Her demands were futile against the inevitable.

The taste of iron filled her mouth, along with a deafening roar of the wind. Burning pain seized her lungs, and Rose fought to take in air. With a snap, everything ceased, and she tumbled onto the ground. Blackness engulfed her. Her fingers dug into the soft grass, and she blinked to focus on her surroundings.

There was that familiar voice. Strong, steady, and she tried to lift her head. After several moments, her strength returned. Rising from the ground, Rose turned in all directions. The standing stones were luminous in the bright moonlight. And when she halted, a man stood centered in front of the dolmen stone, with his arms raised. Except in this vision there was only one glorious moon, not the three she'd witnessed previously.

His voice carried with the breeze, caressing her cheek. The sharp scent of pine made her dizzy as she moved across the open landscape. Rose yearned to join him. Though his words made no sense, she understood this night to be special. He was there to teach—to share his wisdom with her.

As she approached, she lifted her hand to touch his back. A time to acknowledge and thank him for his gift to her people. "I am here," she announced and brushed her fingers over his back.

A blast of sizzling energy tossed her backward. The images blurred and tumbled away from her. Screaming, Rose fought to return to his side. She didn't want to leave him. There was so much more to learn. Strong arms encircled her, crushing her against a solid object, and Rose fought harder.

"Stop fighting," demanded Aidan. "Relax and let go, lass."

A battle between the murkiness of reality and visions kept its grip around Rose. She tried to fight— willing her mind to return, but Aidan's soothing touch and words calmed her.

Her eyes fluttered open, and then she squeezed them shut. "Let go," she pleaded in a hoarse voice. "Sick…"

Aidan turned her around, and Rose emptied everything in her stomach onto the ground. Embarrassed by her predicament, she scooted away from him. After taking in deep breaths, she wiped the back of her mouth on her sleeve.

Returning to her side, he handed her a flask. "Drink," he urged.

"Wh...*whisky*?" She pushed it away.

"Water," he said softly against her cheek, bringing the flask to her mouth.

Rose took a few sips and nodded her thanks. Her body trembled from the intensity of the vision. Hugging her arms around herself, Rose tried to stop the quaking in her limbs. When the brush of Aidan's fingers touched her shoulders, she cringed, but Rose allowed him to continue. Heat invaded her pores, filling her. Bending her head forward, she sighed as he massaged her neck and shoulders.

She squeezed her eyes shut to fight the tears from streaming down her face. Never before had she hated her gift until this moment. Did she have violent spasms in front of him? *You bloody fool, you know you did.*

"Can you share what happened, Rose?"

Shaking her head, pain was her reward, and she placed a cool palm over her forehead.

"A simple *no* would have sufficed."

Rose let out a frustrated breath and attempted to stand. Aidan wrapped a strong arm around her waist. Averting her gaze from the questioning look she knew covered his features, Rose concentrated on the tree branches swaying gently in the breeze.

"An intense vision?"

Stunned, she swept her gaze back at him. "How did you know?"

"My sister has...*a gift* of foresight," he admitted.

Rose swallowed. "Tell me more."

"Nuala—"

"What a unique name." She blushed and then

157

added, "Sorry, do continue…"

Aidan chuckled low. "Yes, *Nuala*, acquired the rare talent from our family. I perceived you did as well by certain actions when you are in a trance."

"I'm totally embarrassed," she gushed out. "I've never experienced the intensity of a vision, especially the same recurring one. And in front of you." She waved her hand dismissively around the area. "It is all centered on these two digs. I don't fully understand the purpose. Perhaps I'm only to gather the wisdom left behind and not share it with anyone else? Others might suspect I'm ready for a mental institution. It's difficult to explain to those who don't believe. Sometimes I see the past when I touch an object. Other times, they simply come upon me without warning. I usually can sense when they're about to happen by having auras, being nauseated, or the sensation of floating away."

Tipping her chin up with his finger, Aidan kissed her nose. "Then I am happy it was me and not a stranger who witnessed this display of your gift."

Rose studied the man. "Who are you, Aidan?"

Wariness reflected briefly in his eyes. "A friend."

Leaning her cheek against his chest, Rose watched the sun slip behind the gray clouds. "Rain is coming, I fear. I'm done here."

Gently, Aidan held her back. "Are you positive?"

Emotions clouded her logical, rational side. "I can't continue to do research until I figure out why I'm having these visions." Rose tugged on his jacket. "Why don't you introduce me to your sister? Does she live nearby?"

"Sorry. Her home is in Ireland."

Her mood brightened. "Perfect. I'm leaving in a

few days to oversee a new site for the Society outside of Dublin. If you don't mind, I'd like to meet her and discuss our similarities."

Aidan released her. "Nuala is away on business."

The warmth fled her bones and a chill descended. Why did she not believe him? Without saying anything else, Rose retrieved her sketch book and went to grab her other items. Digging through her satchel, she pulled out some mints. She popped one into her mouth and contemplated the man who was a complex layer of mixed puzzle pieces. He owned a castle in Scotland, has mesmerizing eyes, is a scholar, animal whisperer, and now lays claim to a sister who shared a similar gift.

*Are you seriously considering an attachment? If not, then you shouldn't meet his sister or any other member of his family. Who are you kidding? You have a serious crush on Aidan.*

"If you'd like company, I can go with you to Ireland. I have business matters that require my attention there at my other home."

Halting her progress, she gawked at the man. "Another castle?"

He reached for her satchel, and Rose willingly surrendered it to him. "A much smaller version of my home here in Scotland."

"A castle is a castle, regardless of the size," she stated emphatically. *And the list of puzzle pieces keeps growing.* "Anything else you'd like to share about your background?"

Aidan braced a hand above her on the tree, trapping her with one look. "If I divulged everything about me, you might become bored and leave."

"My intuition tells me I'd never get tired of you.

159

Do you have deep dark secrets?"

"Only one," he admitted, smiling.

Rose placed a hand against his chest. "You now know my dark secret. Surely you can share yours?"

Aidan grasped her hand and placed a kiss along the vein in her wrist. Her heart beat rapidly when he gazed into her eyes. "Let me take you to dinner, and we can discuss our trip to Ireland."

Tugging her hand out of his grasp, she pushed away from him. "I haven't agreed to let you come with me."

He caught up with her in two strides. "Then we can discuss terms at dinner."

Rose slowed her pace and held back the protest she wanted to fling at the man. In spite of his annoyed self-assurance, she enjoyed the view of his lovely ass as he made his way to the car. As always, Aidan Kerrigan managed to have the last word.

****

Rose surveyed the interior of the pub, noting a quiet booth away from all the chatter of regular customers at the bar. A favorite among the young and old, The Raven attracted many with its fine selection of single-malts and ales. She waved at the barkeep and darted between tables to reach the booth. After removing her coat, she placed it on a nearby peg and settled onto the soft leather cushions.

"Where are the other lovely ladies this evening?" inquired Bill, slapping down a few coasters.

Rose smiled at the young man. "Just me and a friend."

He scratched his chin. "Male or female?"

"Male," announced Aidan, striding forth.

Bill nodded slowly and gestured for Aidan to take a seat. He returned his attention to Rose. "The usual? Pale ale?"

Rubbing her hands together to ward off the chill, she replied, "I think I'll take an Irish stout tonight, and the potato leek soup."

Giving her a wink, Bill then turned to Aidan. "And you?"

"The same."

"Good. I'll return shortly with your drinks." The man swiftly departed, dodging between several more customers.

"Give me your hands," ordered Aidan.

She glanced sharply at him. "What?"

"Your hands. Put them on the table."

"They're cold," she complained. "I'm trying to warm them up."

Aidan leaned across the table and held out his hands.

"Oh for the love of…" Rose complied and heat seared across her palms, up her arms, and throughout her body. She all but melted from his touch. "Wonderful," she mumbled, suddenly recalling how his fingers were in other parts of her body recently.

"Warm?"

"Huh? Yes. Definitely. Thank you, Aidan."

The smile he gave her speared a path to her heart. He slowly released his powerful hold and sat back against the cushioned booth. Rose wished she was a mind-reader, so she could determine what his thoughts were at the moment.

"Have you recovered from your episode out at the dig?" he asked, spreading his large hands on the wooden table.

"Yes. Only a mild headache."

"A good meal and pint will help to banish the remainder of your pain."

Rose tried to keep her focus on the conversation, instead of the man's mouth, eyes, hands, *and* body. She cleared her throat. "Agreed."

Bill returned with their drinks. "Food will be up momentarily."

She nodded her thanks and reached for her glass. Rose guzzled deeply, enjoying the drink.

"They call this the food of the Gods," remarked Aidan, taking a sip of his pint.

"Not here, but in Ireland." She drummed her fingers on the table. "And I've often wondered who started that falsehood about this particular Irish stout."

Aidan laughed. "Perhaps it was someone who had intimate knowledge of one of the Gods." He took another sip and then placed his glass down.

"Or one who had far too many pints," she snickered, recalling past memories.

Leaning back, Aidan folded his arms over his chest. "Are we in agreement with me accompanying you to Ireland? Or shall we discuss terms?"

"Goodness, Aidan. You are so formal." Rose stared at the man. "I won't ravish you, if that's what you're thinking." *Maybe one more kiss?*

He arched a brow seductively. "And here I believed you thought I would take advantage of you."

Thankfully, Bill arrived carrying a large tray with their meal. After setting down the soup bowls and basket of bread, he pointed to the empty glasses. "Care for another round?"

"Yes," responded Aidan.

Rose waved off the gesture. "No. I'm leaving early on the ferry."

The man gave a curt nod and departed.

Rose tried to steady her nerves and placed her hands in her lap. "If I do decide to allow you to come with me, will you show me your other castle?"

"How much time do you have?" he asked, keeping his gaze centered on hers.

"Plenty. Where is this other home of yours?" she asked, fearing he'd spout the northern end of Ireland or one of the remote islands.

"Cuilcagh Mountains, near the mouth of the Shannon River." He picked up his spoon and proceeded to eat his meal.

Stunned, Rose gaped at the man. Recovering her wits, she leaned across the table. "Where the faeries built one of the entrances to their realm?"

Aidan's hand hovered above his bowl. "Would this be a problem, lass?"

Embarrassed in front of the scholar over her silly question, Rose plucked the spoon from the table and bent her head. "No," she mumbled. *You probably don't believe in the Good Folk, and now I've admitted another secret of mine.* She quickly took a mouthful of soup, and the liquid scalded her tongue. She chose to remain silent during her painful episode and continued to cautiously eat her meal.

After several minutes ticked by in agonizing silence, Aidan confessed, "The Fae have given their blessing over the land and my home."

Rose dropped the spoon into her soup, the liquid splattering everywhere. "Not everyone believes the area to be sacred." She hastily reached for her napkin, attempting to clean the mess she'd made on herself.

"True. Only those who have lived a long time on the land can fully understand its history."

Rose's heart beat rapidly. Had she encountered a kindred spirit? Could this be the reason for her fascination with Aidan? Their connection seemed more than physical, and she yearned to know the truth. "You believe?"

The warmth of his smile echoed in his voice. "*Absolutely.*"

Chapter Fifteen

*"A Fae law can bend, twist, curve along the loom of Fate of an individual. If broken, chaos shall engulf the warrior."*
~Edicts of the Fenian Warriors

Aidan refused to acknowledge the warrior. Liam's grim expression when he entered his home told him everything. Mounting the stairs two at a time, he went into his chambers and pulled out a leather bag. Every rational thought had vanished from his mind as he prepared to leave for Ireland.

"You've been ordered to appear before the Fae council," stated Liam quietly, entering the room.

Pulling forth several T-shirts, jeans, and a sweater, Aidan stuffed them into the bag. "When I have completed the mission."

His conversation with Aelish must have reached the members' hearing. Part of him hoped she'd hold off from interfering, but obviously, she'd fled to the Fae realm to give her report. "Who sent the message?"

"I had a visit from Ronan this evening."

Aidan half-expected one of the council guards. "How is my friend?" He was grateful it was one of his finest warriors who came to deliver the order and not the puppets who did the bidding of the council.

"Unhappy he came with the news. Troubled with

the council's interfering practices."

He glanced over his shoulder. "I'm departing for Ireland in the morning. After I've concluded my business, I will make my report."

Liam eyed him warily. "And Rose?"

Aidan dropped the packed bag by the entrance. "Coming with me to attend to Society business in Dublin."

"Damn," hissed Liam and moved away from him. "You court trouble with a capital T!"

Shrugging, he rubbed a hand over his chin. "Must see the mission to completion." But did Aidan truly understand the repercussions? No. He traveled along a path between justice and the unknown abyss. And grew weary from the constant battle.

"Can you stay and finish the work at the dig in Corridon?"

Liam sighed heavily. "Yes. Anything else?"

Aidan approached the warrior and clamped a hand on his shoulder. "Send a missive to Ronan, alerting the council members I have unfinished business in Ireland. When completed, I shall return home. For now, I have to check on flights to Dublin. The ferry will take too long, and Rose is set on traveling across the sea. I will have to convince her."

"Is there anything else you'd like to share?" Liam studied him like a hawk.

Turning from the intensity of the warrior's gaze, Aidan went to his wooden cabinet and pulled out a black leather jacket. Indecision rattled him on what to say.

"You never mentioned why you took this mission. Usually, another warrior is chosen."

After dumping the jacket on his bag, Aidan went to the window. A light rain shower blanketed the land. Beyond the river, sunlight danced in glittering jewels between the gray clouds. When did he notice the colors? His sister spoke of him only seeing black and white, but now, his world consisted of colors. Before he encountered Rose, unrest had hounded him.

*Rose was a colorful beacon of warmth and light, and somehow I stepped into her radiance.*

Aidan turned around. He'd chosen Liam to accompany him for his keen insight on archaeological digs and history. Had he initially intended on informing the warrior of the particulars of the mission? No. Not in the beginning. Leaning against the stone wall, he replied, "I was ordered by the king *and* High Seer."

Lines of concentration deepened along Liam's brow. "I had thought the king sent you, since this entire excavation and findings were based on the Fae visiting the Picts. Obviously, this entire mission is a delicate one, pertaining to *you*. Otherwise, the High Seer would not have requested you."

Aidan nodded reluctantly.

"You could have shared this knowledge in the beginning," protested Liam.

Pushing away from the wall, Aidan slashed the air with his hand. "Share what? A mission was given to me, and as yet, I am unable to discern the messages. I seek closure, Liam. In truth, I did argue against coming to the human world. I asked Loran to send another warrior. Regardless, this is my destiny. Each decision I make will be mine alone. You need not worry. The Fates have set in motion their plan." Aidan smiled ruefully. "Yet, the threads on the loom can be rewoven in another direction, and *I* will decide."

Liam sighed. "This sounds like a personal quest."

"Not my initial intent. But I have ignored recent signs in my life and now must follow this through. No matter the conclusion."

"You are the leader of the Fenian Warriors, a Fae—"

"I do not need a reminder *or* lecture," interrupted Aidan, not wanting to discuss his personal reasons for this quest or Rose any further. The battle of restraint belonged to Aidan and not the warrior.

Liam fisted his hand over his heart in reverence. "Then go with Mother Danu and finish this quest. I shall await your further orders."

Aidan gave him a curt nod and watched as Liam vanished in a sliver of light.

****

Surveying the lush rolling hills bordering the potential site of the Society outside of Dublin, Aidan breathed in the crisp late morning air. Not only had he successfully argued his case to Rose about flying, instead of taking the Irish ferry, but he had insisted on paying for everything. He had no intention of being trapped on a boat for hours, considering the Fae council was demanding his return.

"What do you think now that you've inspected the place?" asked Rose, giving him a nudge and smiling. "Suitable structure for another Society of the Thistle?"

He spread his arms wide. "Stunning vista, rich land, and a stream that flows west. I deem you have found an excellent location."

Crestfallen, her smile faded. "So you don't believe a little paint and minor repairs can fix the sagging structure?"

Aidan angled his head to the side. "Two columns are slanting and they're the main posts holding up the front veranda. Plumbing needs an overhaul, along with the electricity." He pointed upward. "There is damage on the second floor due to flooding from the hole in the roof, so you might want to consider replacing walls, especially if there is rot inside. Hardwood floors on the first floor need to have animal dung removed and cleaned, since that area of the house appears to have been used by wild animals."

Rose cut him off with a wave of her hand. "Stop. You've made your point."

"*Several* valuable points, I might add."

"Yes, yes." She bit her lower lip and then tugged on his jacket. "Can you not see beyond the possibilities? I was hoping the repairs were minor. The surrounding area is beautiful, peaceful, and a perfect site."

He glanced down at her tiny hand. "After the monetary ones? Of course, I can envision a lovely home for the Society."

Folding her arms over her luscious breasts, Rose huffed out a frustrated breath. "The Society does not have tons of money stashed away. There is some money from grants we receive, but it gets invested back into the work we do. We thought with the income we bring in from lectures and selling our wares at the local markets—from soaps, candles, and herbal salves, we might be able to get a loan for another house."

Aidan hesitated briefly and then wrapped an arm around her shoulders. "You did not need to confess your financial status."

Rose lifted her head and gazed into his eyes. "Yet, I wanted to. You have been extremely generous of your time and knowledge. I appreciate your honesty."

"You're welcome."

She laughed, and Aidan felt the tension leave her body.

"I was not aware of giving you thanks," she stated, all previous humor vanishing as she cast her sight once again on the aging structure.

Aidan took charge, desiring to uplift her sagging spirits. "Is there not another building on your list to inspect?"

Giving him a dubious look, Rose moved away from his embrace. "Only this property. We'd heard glowing reports from a friend of one of the girls at the Society. At the pub one evening, he painted a picture of a grand home. Even offered to sell it to us at a cheap price." She laughed nervously. "If it wasn't for Lily interceding, I believe the deal would have consisted of a handshake between Colleen and the man."

"Colleen is another member?"

"Yes. She fancies Ireland, and the man's brogue was thick with the Irish, along with his charm."

Aidan burst out laughing. "A slick charmer."

Rose flashed him a steely look that would harden any of his warriors. "Wait until I tell her what a bunch of rot he tried to pass off on her—us!"

He admired her fierce determination. "I'd like to witness the tongue-lashing from the lass when she finds out."

Wagging a finger in front of him, she countered, "Colleen is the most sweet-natured out of all of us. She never raises her voice, or refuses to see the worst in others. This is why I am here and not her. She'd look beyond the mess to find the gem underneath and then cut the man loose."

"A passive individual."

"An optimist," Rose corrected. "What a waste of time to come out here." Turning away from the crumbling house, she made her way back to the jeep.

Flexing his fingers, Aidan yearned to bring some light into the dreary situation. Rose's rigid stance against the vehicle spoke volumes. While her back was turned, he magically brought forth a red rose. Striding across the muddy terrain, he presented the flower over her shoulder.

Her indrawn breath at his gift resonated within him. "How lovely, Aidan. I don't recall seeing any roses on the property." She grasped the flower, but winced. "Ouch."

Stepping around in front of her, Aidan removed the rose from her delicate fingers and placed it on the roof of the vehicle. Droplets of blood oozed from the damage done by the thorn. Without thinking of the consequences, Aidan brought her injured finger to his lips. Instantly, the taste of her blood ignited a war in his veins. Passion so intense slammed into his body. As he released her hand, his gaze roamed over her features.

Rose was his land—his home. A part of him fractured with the realization. When did his world tilt off its axis? There was no firm compass anymore. No sure direction, save one. *Rose.*

The roar of desire hummed into his being, and Aidan crushed her to his chest. His hand took her face and held it gently. He covered her mouth hungrily, seeking entry into her velvet softness with his tongue.

When her moan slid inside of him, Aidan groaned. Her scent consumed him.

Emotions within him whirled and skidded. Unable to control the flood of so many, he swayed and broke free from the kiss. These feelings were foreign to him, but he no longer feared them.

Aidan breathed heavily, keeping her at arm's length. The sensuous flame of desire reflected back within her sparkling emerald eyes. "Forgive me?"

"Not for the kiss, Aidan," her tone low and sultry.

Slowly, he took hold of her hand and kissed her finger, which was now healed from his touch. "I meant the thorn."

Her tongue darted out along her bottom lip, enticing him further. "Not for the thorn, either," she admitted, plucking the rose off the top of the vehicle. "Isn't it time you showed me your other castle, Aidan?"

"*Croí Dragon.* That is the name of my keep."

Rose placed her hand on his chest. "*Dragon Heart.*"

"Yes," he confirmed. Aidan reached behind her and opened the door.

She turned and slid inside the vehicle.

When the rumble of thunder vibrated across the land, Aidan ignored the first warning sign. His last rational thread of defense tried to make one final stand. Yet, he banished it with a single thought. In all of his lifetime, he'd never strayed from the loyalty due his people.

*Not until he fell in love.* It seemed as if, even if he'd not known it, he'd been waiting for this moment for all eternity.

And in a sudden flash of clarity, Aidan broke the

chains around his warrior heart and allowed emotion to flow within.

His hands shook with the knowledge of a new road. Exhilarating and frightening at the same time.

Lightning splintered the sky all around him. A second warning.

The air vibrated with energy from the Guardians of the night sky—the dragons that had silently ascended to the cosmos. Did it matter if they opposed or approved? Was this not his choice?

He slowly lifted his head, half-expecting the ancient giants to descend and end his life with a breath of fire. Waiting for several heart-beats, he walked around to the driver's side.

As Aidan entered the vehicle, he glanced sideways at Rose. Her gaze never wavered from his. Strong, focused, and filled with passion.

When she smiled and placed a firm hand on his arm, the sun broke out in a glorious arc of light, filling Aidan with the reassurance this was their destiny.

The power of this new-found emotion grew and deepened within him.

Chapter Sixteen

*"Once a seed is planted, growth will eventually break free. What the new life requires is sunlight, water, love, and honesty."*

~Society of the Thistle

Rose beamed, glancing upward at the stone fortress. Though it was smaller than Balleycove, this castle had a moat surrounding the entire stone structure. Geese flew overhead, and she shielded her eyes from the sun to take in their flight. The land here reflected a serenity—one vastly different from Aidan's home in Scotland. Power and strength resided at Balleycove, much like the man in front of her. Here, she sensed an ancient hum of old souls and mystical charm.

In addition, the presence of the Fae surrounded this home, and Rose smiled.

Making a grand gesture with his hand, Aidan proclaimed, "Welcome to *Croí Dragon*, fair maiden."

Dipping a curtsy, Rose crossed the pebbled lane into the keep. Once inside, she took in the tapestries. Her attention was drawn to the giant wooden statue of a dragon set in the middle of the entryway. Standing at least twelve feet tall, the dragon cast its sight outward, as if in welcome. The luster of the polished wood gleamed in the sunlight streaming in through the front doors.

Trailing her finger over the etchings of Celtic symbols, Rose wandered slowly around the statue. As she came to a halt in the front, Rose's attention was drawn to the writings etched down the center of the dragon.

Recognition flared brightly within her mind. Her heart raced at the knowledge. She had seen them before in her visions. "What do these mean?" Her question barely a whisper.

Aidan brushed his hand over the symbols. "Of a land beyond the stars."

"Are you teasing me?"

His features softened. "Never, Rose."

She pointed to the carvings, fear holding her back from touching the wood any further. "How do you know?"

"Writings that have been studied, catalogued, and researched by my family."

Taking a step back, she regarded him slowly. They had this conversation before, but not to this extent. "Then you believe others have come from distant worlds to share their knowledge with certain tribes. Have you shared your findings with the university?"

Aidan grasped her elbow and steered her away from the dragon. "Without proof, it's only an opinion. Many have speculated the same but have been rebuffed."

Rose halted their progress. "Why didn't you tell me this earlier?"

"Tell you what exactly?"

She gestured her arm outward. "That we are not alone in this grand universe."

"It would be egotistical of humans to believe they

are the only ones occupying the cosmos." He moved across the entryway and proceeded to open two double-doors. Aidan beckoned her inside.

As Rose entered, she took in the vastness of the room. The library was extensive, and her fingers itched to explore the many volumes of books resting on shelves. A large table was positioned in front of the stained-glass window—a window depicting a dragon. She gave her host a sly glance. "The Welsh and Scots have their dragons, and now the mighty Aidan Kerrigan. Or as you have proclaimed the dragons of Ireland came with the *Tuatha*—"

She paused, gathering her knowledge of the myths and legend. "The Fae," she whispered.

Leaning near her ear, he murmured, "Precisely," and then quickly added, "I shall return momentarily."

When he straightened, she noted there was no trace of humor in his features. The man truly believed. Unable to say anything, Rose gave him a jerky nod.

After Aidan departed, she wandered around the room, taking in the massive fireplace at the opposite side of the room. Two oversized chairs flanked either side, luring her to curl up on their velvety softness. A unique collection of swords was displayed above the stone mantel. Approaching them, she stood on her tiptoes to get a better view. "Outstanding."

Rose continued her exploration of the library. She brushed her hand over the spines of several books on Shakespeare, Homer, and others she didn't have a clue as to their language. Aidan's library spoke volumes about the man—educated, masculine, and mysterious. When she drew near his desk, she became fascinated by the stone and crystal collection on a tray off to the side.

Her hand hovered briefly over them. Their energy vibrated, especially from the large reddish quartz. She'd never witnessed one with this particular hue. Sunlight danced in a prism around the stone, luring her to brush her fingers over the raw edges.

"Would you like to see more of my home?"

Rose clasped her hand to her chest and twirled around. "You have a beautiful collection."

His smile was enticing. "Books?"

"Everything," she confessed.

He held out his hand. "Allow me to give you a tour. Let me show you the rest."

Smiling, she hurried to his side. He placed her hand in the crook of his arm, escorting her to the kitchens, herb room, a small sitting room, a banquet hall, office, and then to the bedrooms upstairs. Three rooms were located on the second level and two more bedrooms on the third floor. Recalling the tour of Balleycove, or what she'd gotten to see, she paused to consider his home there was considerably more extensive than the one they were in.

When they traveled the length of the corridor, Aidan released her hand and opened two massive oak doors. "These are my chambers."

Heat blossomed in Rose's neck as she peered inside. Everything was huge—from the fireplace, armoire, desk, and the cushioned bench by the window arch. As she cast her gaze upon his bed, she fought the urge to place her cool hands over her burning cheeks. Aidan Kerrigan's bed was by far the biggest one she'd ever seen. The wooden four-poster structure had Celtic knotwork and foliage carved into the dark grain of the headboard. His chambers reminded her of a forest.

Deep rich colors of the earth filled this room—gold, green, brown, and amber.

And when she noted the three images on the carved headboard, she became dizzy. They rose in an arc over all the carvings. *Three moons.*

Rose stole a glance at the man, fearing to speak. He was leaning against one of the doors with his hands clasped behind his back. Nevertheless, it was those eyes that scalded a path into her heart and soul. She desired Aidan like no other, and this frightened Rose. He was not a man she yearned to have for one night. There was more within her heart than she cared to acknowledge and even more to this mysterious man that she refused to admit.

The air was too warm inside his chamber. She couldn't breathe. A battle of uncertainty took root, and Rose fled the room. Bolting down the stairs, she barely heard him calling out her name. Her feet propelled her swiftly out the front doors, and she kept on running, darting along a path to the left. She went in the direction of the setting sun, letting her instincts guide her. Ducking under a trellis of ivy and jasmine, the heady floral aroma teased her as she sprinted farther down the path.

The pathway split, and she once more sprinted to the left until she came to a cluster of giant oak trees. Peaceful serenity entered her body when she stepped inside. Rose slowed her pace, allowing her breathing to return to normal. Though the air was chilled, she needed to remove her coat. Dropping it over a fallen log, she walked to one of the tallest trees. Tears stung her eyes as she placed her palms on the tree. The last remnant of light slipped over the horizon, leaving her in darkness.

"Impossible," she muttered, squeezing her eyes shut. *Cannot be true. Must try and find the logic. It's all wrong, or is it?*

"What is wrong, *leannan*?"

Did she hear him correctly? Did he actually call her sweetheart? She swallowed, trying to force down the emotions that were lodged in her throat. Lifting her chin, Rose turned and faced him. "I ask you again. Who are you, Aidan?"

He closed the distance between them. Power radiated off the man. "What are you afraid of?"

Her mind and heart were not functioning. Emotions and logic raged a war inside of her. "I asked you a question."

Aidan placed his hands on the tree, trapping her against the rough bark. "If I tell you, will you flee? Will it alter your feelings?"

"I don't even understand my *feelings*," she blurted out, aching to wrap her arms around his neck. Instead, she clenched her fists so tight, her nails bit into her palms.

He brushed a kiss along her neck. "Share them with me, *leannan*."

She melted into a muddle of mush with the soft burr of his voice. Some aspect of sanity looped its way into her thoughts. "*Who* are *you*?"

Nudging her thighs apart with his knee, Aidan rubbed her intimately. "Say what your heart is burning to release, and then I shall tell you."

Desire slammed into her, hot and powerful. Rose cupped his face. "I…believe—"

"*Believe*?" he echoed, pinning her with those

179

mesmerizing eyes.

"I love you, Aidan." The words tumbled free, escaping from the hold she tried desperately to rein in. Brushing a lock of hair away from his eye, she added, "I can't explain how or why. It's too soon—so *sudden*." She tapped her chest. "But it's there wedged inside my heart."

With a feral growl, he took her mouth in a firestorm that sent her spiraling. Rose surrendered to the passion. A pulse of need drummed between her legs, and she groaned deep within him. Their tongues clashed in an erotic dance. Her hands yanked on his shirt, needing to feel his skin against her.

His breathing was ragged as he ripped the material over his head and tossed it to the ground. "This is who I am, *mo ghrá*."

Rose's heart constricted with his admission of the endearing words he spoke to her. She gazed upon all the tattoos across his chest and forearms, as if she had known all along what they represented.

Taking her hand, he placed it centered to his chest. Cupping her chin, he forced her to meet his gaze, compelling and magnetic. "This is my name, which is emblazed over my heart. The markings denote my rank among my people."

"And the three shall rise in unison," she blurted out, confusion straining her thoughts. "Three moons?"

"You have unlocked the secret, my love." Aidan's hand skimmed across her collar bone, and she trembled from his touch.

"What secret?" she asked in a low whisper.

He grasped her hips, bringing her closer to his body. The warmth of his fingers burned through the material of her dress. "You have seen me before, have you not? In another dimension?"

Flashes of another time spiraled within Rose's mind, and she blinked in an attempt to focus. "I'm…unsure."

Releasing his hold, he took a step back. She watched in a haze as he removed his boots, sinking his feet into the soft earth. "Accept or reject, Rose. I give you the proof of your visions. Wait here."

Slowly, Aidan turned around and walked away from her. He went to the clearing and waited. Rose could barely make out the outline of his form between the trees. She clutched her hands to her chest, unable to control the shaking within her body. The minutes ticked by in agonizing torture, but Rose held on, leaning against the aging giant for support.

An owl hooted in a nearby tree as the first moonbeam graced the evening sky. Rose held her breath as the light of illumination radiated through her. Snapping her gaze to where Aidan stood, she watched in awe while he lifted his arms wide, greeting the full moon. When moonlight dusted his features, Rose pushed away from the tree. The blood pounded in her ears, and she feared this was another vision.

Yet, when her hand touched Aidan's back, she let out a gasp. Warm, solid, and very real. The same tattoos she had visualized in her visions etched his back. Even though the man in her vision had longer hair, she knew they were one and the same. Lights spiraled in an arc around Aidan, and he glanced over his shoulder.

"You are not from here." Rose pointed upward. "Your home is…out there?"

"Taralyn," he proclaimed in a hoarse voice.

Rose removed her boots, aching to feel the land on her skin as well as the man before her. She moved around to face him. While tracing a finger over his chest, she lifted her gaze to meet his. "You are ancient?"

"Yes."

"Powerful?"

"Extremely."

"Dragons, Celtic tattoos, legends—"

"I am from the tribe of Mother Danu, the *Tuatha Dé Danann*," he admitted.

His eyes shimmered with the light of a thousand stars as she placed her hands against his warm skin. Some part of her had always known who he was. "You are a Fae."

Aidan skimmed his hands down her arms. "Are you afraid?"

"Of you?" She smiled fully. "No. But of my love for you? *Yes*."

"Then that makes two of us. For I love you, *leannan*." He looked away, watching as the moon rose in all her glory. "Never in my lifetime have I ached to possess or love another. I have fought the battle since I held you in my arms that morn."

Heat poured off his body, and Rose leaned her head against his chest. Inhaling deeply, her head spun from the intoxicating scent of the man. A wave of desire shot through her, making her want him more than anything. She could feel the length of his desire against her body. Rose leaned away from Aidan, studying his raw profile. He was all hard lines and muscular strength—from his chiseled jaw and broad chest to the soles of his bare feet. It did not matter if he was human or Fae. She remained steady to the truth in her heart. "Take me here, Aidan. Make love to me."

Returning his gaze to hers, he cupped her chin and brushed his thumb over her bottom lip. "Once I make love to you, Rose, you will be mine. *Forever*. There shall be no regrets. Can you give me your soul, along with your body?"

She smiled seductively and moved a step back. Unzipping the back of her dress, she slipped the material off her shoulders and let it slide down her body. After stepping free of the garment, she held his bold gaze. "A vision was shown to me, Aidan. It set me on a path to you. I do not understand its purpose, except one. *Love*. I will have no regrets."

Aidan reached for her, crushing her to his chest. His hand shook as he brushed the back of his fingers over her cheek. "I deem I have waited an eternity for you, Rose."

His mouth covered hers hungrily. The kiss sent new spirals of ecstasy through her. He tugged on the snaps of her bra, freeing her breasts. Lowering her arms, the lacy material fell to the ground. At the first touch of his hand on her breast, Rose moaned.

"You are beauty beyond anything." He breathed the words against her neck.

When his tongue trailed a path between her breasts, she let out a hiss of pleasure. She watched in a passion-filled haze as he continued to fondle and lavish them. It was an erotic scene, making her tingle all the way to her toes. When he nipped on her nipple, she cried out in exquisite pleasure.

His lips recaptured hers, more demanding this time. Heat smoldered between her thighs, and Rose ached to have him touch her down there. She rubbed against his huge erection, needing him inside her. She let out a soft hiss when he broke free from the kiss.

With slow movements, Aidan removed his jeans. His thick cock sprang free, and she marveled at the Fae standing in front of her. "You are magnificent." She lifted her hand out to him. "May I?"

Aidan gave her a smile that sent her pulse racing more. He took her hands, encouraging her to explore his body. She traced the contours of his erection, soft and hard. A small trace of fluid graced the opening, so she swiped a gentle finger over the top and heard his sharp indrawn breath.

"No more," he demanded in a guttural cry.

Not giving her time to utter a protest, he ravaged her mouth with a soul-searing kiss. The fever built within Rose as his hand slipped between the fabric of her underwear, touching her again in the most glorious way. With a snap of his hand, he tore the flimsy material from her body. Hypnotized by his touch, she tingled under his fingertips. "Aidan," she whimpered, trying to grasp the elusive spark that continued to spread within her body.

"Yes, *mo ghrá*. I am here, giving you pleasure." He nipped a path along her neck. "Your scent of desire fills me. I long to taste you, tease you with my lips. I *hunger* for you."

Her breathing became ragged, and her legs wobbled. When his finger delved inside her, Rose began to tremble, and she surrendered to his masterful seduction of her body. She wanted to yield to the burning sweetness that held her captive. When Rose thought she couldn't take anymore, she abandoned herself to the whirlwind of pleasure and shattered into a million pieces of ecstasy.

Screaming his name, Rose was lifted into Aidan's arms. He gently laid her down on the cool, lush grass, murmuring words of endearment over her face as his hands skimmed over her body.

Opening her eyes, she gazed at him. The moon illuminated behind him created an intoxicating vision. "You came from the stars. You are mine."

Aidan grabbed a strand of her hair and wove it around his finger. Bringing it to his lips, he kissed the lock and then let it slip free. "You are a daughter of the land and mine."

"Do not torment me, Aidan," she pleaded, reaching for him.

His hands skimmed over her thighs, nudging them farther apart. When the she felt the heat of his hardness enter her, Rose hissed. Pain and pleasure battled each other, and she tensed, closing her eyes.

"Relax," he encouraged, inching slowly into her.

She let out a whimper, and Aidan stilled. "Look at me, *mo ghrá*."

When she opened her eyes, love reflected back from his. He leaned down and brushed his lips against her mouth. The spark of desire from that one sensual and unforgettable kiss removed the ache. Tremors of excitement swept across her skin, and she arched under him, taking him fully into her body.

He let out a groan and then pulled back out.

"*No…*" she gasped.

And then he entered her swiftly. It was a heady sensation, and she soon found a rhythm.

The turbulence of his passion swirled around them

in a multitude of dazzling colors as he continued to thrust into her. His lips seared a path over her face, finding their way to her mouth. As his thrusts became urgent, more demanding, beads of sweat broke out along his brow.

While the hot tide of fervor raged through both of them, the fire grew between her legs.

"Body to soul, I claim you, Rose. You are *mine* until the last star fades from the cosmos," he murmured against her cheek.

She gasped in sweet agony, raking her fingernails down his back. Aidan's own guttural cry of release echoed within the trees, lifting her higher. The ground rumbled beneath her and for a moment, Rose thought the stars descended around them.

After several moments, Aidan rolled onto his back, bringing her sated body against his chest. Contentment and peace flowed between them, until the night sky flashed with lightning and the clap of thunder boomed overhead.

Chapter Seventeen

*"Love is a powerful emotion for a Fae and a blade
to a Fenian Warrior's heart."*
~*Edicts of the Fenian Warriors*

Scanning the sky, Aidan held his breath. When the first arc of lightning sliced through the sky, he had no strength left to battle any foes. He'd surrendered his body and soul to Rose, leaving him in a weakened state. If the mighty dragons dared to renounce their watch among the stars to strike a blow against him, Aidan's only regret would be in not fully protecting his beloved.

*Rose.*

Each time he said her name within his mind, his heart burst with joy. Never had he been so sure of a path. Even despite knowing and understanding the impending ramifications. Swiftly closing the door on distressing thoughts, he returned his attention to the beauty in his arms.

He brought a lock of her hair to the moonlight. "Yours is a moonbeam of colors. Rare and cherished among my people," he uttered softly.

Rose lifted her head, giving him the most glorious smile. "Tell me about them."

He laughed uneasily, allowing the silken strand to slip from his fingers. "Where does one begin to explain a race of people who are older than your planet?"

Her eyebrows shot up in surprise. "Amazing." Her features quickly turned to confusion. "Then all the legends about the invasions of Ireland are true?"

"Every legend has its roots based in facts," he acknowledged, brushing a hand over her soft curves.

She nodded slowly. "So the Fae live side by side with…us?"

"No. Our race is not permitted to be above ground. Only an elite group of warriors is allowed to travel among the humans."

"Why?" she asked softly.

"The Fenian Warriors have assisted humans for thousands of years. Many kings have sought our counsel—those who believed in the Fae. Of course, with the new religion, we became lesser known. Our knowledge proved to be insignificant. We continue to aid humans, but we also observe. There are times when a mission needs to be swayed, *encouraged* in another direction."

"Really." Rose swallowed and scooted off him. She kept her back to him. "Was I one of those missions? Did I see something on the stones relating to your people?"

Distressed at the loss of her warmth, Aidan sat up and brought her body against his chest. Cradling her softly, he replied, "Yes."

She gave him a stern look. "Please share how you were going to *sway* or *encourage* me in another direction?"

Aidan grimaced slightly. "Discourage your findings."

"But you really didn't dissuade me. In fact, you listened and observed."

He shrugged. "I grew curious."

"And if you found you were unable to sway me in another direction? What then?"

"Destroy all the evidence with magic." Though he knew the process might not be successful.

A look of horror passed over her features. "Not fair," she scolded. "When you told me you were powerful, I thought you were referring to brute strength. Definitely not magical."

He blew out a frustrated sigh. Patting the ground with his hand, he said, "Where do you think all this lush grass came from? Or the flowers that border the area? Or the rainstorm at the dig?" With a snap of his fingers, Aidan produced a floral bouquet filled with jasmine, roses, honeysuckle, sweet peas, and violets.

Rose gasped, her eyes growing wide.

"Do not fear me," pleaded Aidan, fear welling up inside him. He could take anything at this moment, but not her rejection of him.

"Oh, Aidan." She took the flowers from his hands and clutched them to her breasts. Cupping a hand against his cheek, her lips trembled. "I don't fear you. But I am shocked by the magic. It's…beautiful, as are you."

His heart hammered inside his chest. Him a hardened warrior brought low by mere words. Lovely words. She was his rising moonbeam and the setting sun. The range of so many emotions made him dizzy.

He lowered his mouth against her warm palm and placed a kiss along the skin. "I shall cherish you always, beloved."

"It's as if I've known you for so long," she professed, leaning into him.

When thunder rolled over them, followed by the first drop of rain, Aidan lifted her off of him and stood.

"Is this your doing?" Rose asked, holding out her hand to him. "Rain to spoil our evening?"

Aidan's brow furrowed. "No." Helping her to stand, he cradled her head against his chest. "I fear I have angered the night guardians."

Slowly, Rose lifted her head. "What have you done, Aidan?"

Sweeping her into his arms, Aidan strode with intent back to his home. By the time he entered the front doors, the rain had turned into a colossal thunderstorm. Still carrying Rose, he mounted the stairs two at time. He placed her gently on his bed and with a wave of his hand closed the doors on his chambers. Ignoring her slight gasp, he went to the fireplace and snapped his fingers. A blaze ignited the wood and kindling, and he blew across the flames, fanning the fire.

When he turned around to face her, Aidan saw love reflected in her eyes, and something else.

*Endearing trust.*

"Your vision was of me standing on my own world of Taralyn," he began. "What you saw at the Standing Stones of Bran and Óg are etchings—carvings of *me* on my world. In fact, you sketched a partial drawing at one of the sites."

"Your hair was much longer in my vision."

Aidan rubbed a hand over his chin in thought. So long ago, he had forgotten. "Yes. In my early years, I wore it long. As did many other warriors."

He moved to her side and sat down next to her. "Somehow, one of the Picts determined it was

190

important for them to make it known about the Fae. Thousands of years ago, I shared a story of the rising of our three moons in various hues of moonlight with them. I recited a bardic poem on the night of their full moon. It resonated deeply with the Picts, but I never deemed they would make an account in this fashion. Nor did I understand why you would be shown these images."

Rose reached for his hand and interlaced her fingers with his. "Regardless, I had my recurring visions, which I never have, *before* I witnessed the standing stones."

Aidan glanced at his carved headboard. "A path destined. The three moons. My story told to one of your ancient civilizations." Returning his gaze to her, he added, "Nevertheless, it is a union forbidden."

She tugged on his hand. "Now you're scaring me, Aidan."

He kept a firm hold on her hand. "Do not be, beloved. I will always protect you. But I fear I have damned myself."

"For loving me?" asked Rose tersely.

"A joining between your people and a Fae, especially one who is the leader of the Fenian Warriors, is strictly forbidden."

Rose shivered, and he wrapped a protective arm around her body. "You are their *leader*?"

Exhaling slowly, he nodded. "Yes."

"What will happen?"

"Unsure."

Lifting her chin, she cupped his face with both hands. "They cannot take away the love I carry within my soul for you, Aidan. Even when this world ceases to exist, I will forever love you."

His heart swelled at her declaration. Nevertheless, his beloved had no idea the wrath of the Fae. His life might very well be forfeit. Rules, edicts, hundreds of years training and obeying his people had taken a blow the moment he confessed his love to Rose.

As he grasped her hands and placed a kiss along her knuckles, Aidan was sure of only one emotion. Rose was an elixir, as potent as any from the Pleasure Gardens, and he became spellbound under her enchantment. Partly from taking her body and the other—simply because he loved Rose.

His sister spoke of two paths of destruction, and now Aidan understood. Either road led to a path of sorrow. If he stayed with Rose, they would strip him of everything and possibly end his life. If he left Rose to return home…the blood pounded in his ears.

*Never!* This was the destiny he chose.

Placing her hands on his chest, he brushed the back of his hand over her cheek. "My love for you consumes me. Understand this, my beloved; though the journey may be fraught with pitfalls, boulders, and an unsteady future, no one can take away the love I bear for you."

"No matter what, I shall never leave your side," she confirmed.

Shoving aside the further turmoil of negative thoughts, Aidan lowered her against the soft cushions. He pressed his lips to hers, caressing her mouth more than kissing it. "You are my compass when the shadows descend."

"And you are my home, Aidan. A mighty fortress of strength and love." She breathed a kiss along the vein in his neck, and he let out a growl.

Clasping her hands above her head, Aidan reclaimed her mouth in a slow, drugging kiss. This time, he would take his time in a seductive exploration of her body. After breaking free, he trailed lingering kisses below the soft spot of her ear, the pulsing hollow at the base of her throat, and the valley between her breasts before taking her pert nipple into his mouth.

Rose clutched the coverings on a moan.

Firmly cupping her ivory breasts, he inhaled deeply. "You are *intoxicating*, beloved." Suckling each breast lightly, he released them and moved down her body.

His tongue teased a path to her intimate area, and he spread her thighs farther apart. He placed a feather-like kiss on the inside of her thigh, her scent filling him. Taking his finger, he parted her delicate folds and blew across her soft nest of curls.

"Not there," she protested feebly.

"I long to feast on every inch of your lovely body," he asserted in a hoarse tone. He slid one hand slowly down the side of her leg and then back up to her hip.

Her eyes grew wider as Aidan stroked a finger over her sensitive core. "I want to give you pleasure, *mo ghrá*. Will you open for me?"

Desire flamed in her emerald depths. Taking that as a sign of confirmation to proceed, Aidan lowered his head and lavished the beauty under him. Aidan teased and nipped, feasting on her seductive nectar. She uttered a guttural moan and squirmed beneath him. Soft pants escaped from her luscious lips, only inciting Aidan more. His cock swelled painfully, aching to sink deep within her heat.

When her whimpers and pleas turned to a cry of

release, Aidan could no longer contain his ferocious need. He raised himself over her and thrust into her body in one swift movement. They both cried out in unison at the heady sensation. Allowing his fiery passion to consume him, Aidan took possession of the primal dance of their mating. With each kiss, touch of his hand across her taut nipples, and words of endearments nipped along her neck, her desire built. His thrusts became wild and urgent, and he found the tide of control ebbing away. When she wrapped her leg around his waist, he growled and captured her mouth with his. Arching fervently against him, Rose moaned deep with him.

Unable to hold back, Aidan shook as his pleasure exploded and vibrated all around them. His roar of release echoed off the stone. The residual passion rippled across his skin as he rolled over onto the cushions, bringing Rose against his chest. His heart hammered as he cradled his beloved.

The storm continued its relentless pursuit over the land, but Aidan paid no heed. The elements could rage a battle of epic proportions as far as he was concerned. Lifting his hand, he magically brought the coverings over their bodies.

"I had no idea love making could be so exquisite," she uttered softly against his chest.

He grinned, stroking her back with his fingers. "Intense? Too sharp?"

She lifted her head. "Beautiful. Lovely. *Wonderful*."

"Then I have not scared you? My tastes can be demanding. You have sampled only the beginning of what I like to do." He took in her flushed cheeks, pouty full lips, and desire hummed within his veins once again.

"Will you teach me?"

His cock swelled at the invitation. "With pleasure."

"Where shall I begin?" she asked in a throaty whisper.

A wave of guilt swept through him for wanting to take her again so soon. "Tomorrow. Your body needs to rest."

Giving him a scowl, Rose slipped her hand beneath the covers. His jaw clenched when her fingers seized his partially swollen cock. "I am firmly aware of what my body needs, *Warrior*."

His seductive temptress had him breathing heavily. "If you continue to fondle me in that manner, I shall spill my seed in your hand."

Rose cupped his balls, and he hissed at the heady sensation. "Can I not give you pleasure the same as you did to me?" Her tone was one of teasing, and she lowered her head. "Am I doing something wrong?"

"On the contrary. You are a swift learner."

By the hounds, the mere thought of her taking him between her luscious lips had him throbbing with need. Her eager response was immediately aggressive and feeding his lust-filled desires. Yet, he had other plans for the enticing vixen.

Pushing her aside, he swept his feet over the bed and went into his inner chamber. Waving his hand over the enormous copper tub, warm, scented water materialized inside. Returning to the entrance, Aidan leaned against the door.

Her pout of displeasure did not sway him. He held out his hand. "Come here."

In defiance, Rose patted the bed. "I'm not finished."

His roar of laughter reverberated throughout the chambers. How he loved her. Free spirited, seductive, and full of passion. He grabbed a hold of his cock and squeezed. Loving the way her mouth dropped open in awe, he continued to play with himself. "If you don't join me in the water, I'll see to my own pleasure, imagining your tongue over my cock and balls."

Turning around, Aidan strolled into the chamber and stepped into the warm water.

The echo of her scampering across the wooden floors made his heart race. She bolted inside and halted near the tub. Long hair flowed down past her breasts—a vision of perfection.

He placed his hands on his hips. "Care to join me?"

"My goodness, Aidan. The tub is huge," she exclaimed.

"Like me."

Rose blushed. "Obviously."

Gazing all around her, she stood fixed to the floor. In fact, Aidan didn't mind the delay. It gave him a chance to cool the raging desire to take her rapidly in the water.

"It's like a forest in here with all the plants and flowers." She pointed behind him. "Is that a pine tree? And look at all those crystals at the base of the trunk."

"Yes."

She snapped her gaze back to him. "In here?"

"The special chamber was built around the tree. I prefer nature around me while I'm bathing."

"It's striking. Perfect."

Aidan moved to the edge of the tub and held out

his hand. "Come here."

Complying with his order, Rose took his hand and let him help her into the tub. She let out a pleasurable sigh, sinking into the water.

Aidan grabbed a soft washcloth on a nearby table along with lavender-scented soap and a bottle of oil. Sloshing his way over to Rose, he pointed to the side. "There's a bench here, if you'd like to sit."

Her face lit up. "Do you also have jets in the tub?"

He lathered the wet cloth with the soap. "No need." He set the bottle on the edge of the tub. Dipping his other hand into the water, he moved his fingers in a circular pattern. Soon the water began to churn and froth.

"So lovely." She sighed and scooted over to the bench.

Her breasts bobbed gently above the water, and Aidan fought back the tide of passion. Coming near her, he took his time in massaging her skin with the cloth. She leaned her head against his chest as he took his time with her back. When he was done, he spread her legs apart and cupped the cloth over her intimate area.

"Feels good," she mumbled, resting her head on the back of the tub and closing her eyes.

As he roused her passion, his intensified. He whispered words of love over her breasts, on her shoulders, and across her rosy cheeks. When he halted his ministrations, Rose let out a weak cry of protest.

Reaching for the vial of oil, he removed the stopper. "Sit up on the upper bench.

Rose's eyes fluttered open. "What is it?"

He poured some in his hand. "A soothing oil. It will help in the healing from where I entered your body."

Disappointment flared across her features, but she complied and scooted to the higher bench within the tub.

He stood between her legs, letting the water lap against them. Without saying a word, Aidan fondled her breasts, eliciting soft moans from her.

"Smells divine," she admitted.

He nuzzled her neck, preparing for his next task. "Rose, lavender, and a special herb from the Fae realm." Reaching again for the bottle, he instructed, "Spread your legs, *mo ghrá*."

Her eyes darkened with desire as she slid her legs farther apart for him. Slowly, Aidan dripped the oil over her intimate area. Placing the bottle on the edge of the tub, he massaged the oil between her delicate folds.

Rose's pleasurable sigh traveled across his skin.

"You have the most amazing tou...*touch*," she uttered softly.

"And you are a temptress," he confirmed.

Her body began to move in an erotic dance. When her breathing turned to short gasps, Aidan removed his hand and entered her in one thrust. The combination of water, oil, and Rose had him spiraling out of control. His need so fierce, he yearned for more.

"Wrap your legs around me," he demanded.

On a whimper, she did so, and Aidan cupped her bottom, sinking deeper inside her sweet body.

"Oh, Aidan, *more...*" she growled into his ear.

The blood pounded in his body as he fought the tide of passion, wishing Rose to claim hers first. Taking her mouth with savage intensity, he felt the tremors of her release vibrate around his cock.

He shuddered, unable to hold back. "*Rose*," he cried out her name, emptying everything he had into the woman he loved.

When the last wave of euphoria swept from him, Aidan lifted her quaking body from the water and to a quartz bench. Reaching for the soft towel behind her, he gently dried her off.

She trailed a finger over his cheek. "I adore this dimple."

Capturing her hand, he placed a kiss along the vein in her wrist. "I love you beyond words."

Aidan stood and cradled her into his arms. Taking her back into the main chamber, he tucked them both under the covers. Her sigh resonated deeply, and she closed her eyes on a smile.

Contentment filled Aidan for the first time in his life. His love for Rose had taken over the void and emptiness inside his heart as he stared at her sleeping form.

Regardless, a part of his heart grew heavy with the knowledge that his peace would shatter a kingdom.

Chapter Eighteen

*"There are many healing herbs for wounds, though
none for the pain within a heart."*
~*Society of the Thistle*

Fragments of a delicious and sensual dream flitted
within Rose's mind. Her hand sought the warmth, yet,
coldness greeted her. Blinking in an effort to vanish the
last remnants of sleep, she glanced across the bed
covers to find the space empty and bleak as the gray
light filtering in through the stained-glass window.

She bolted upright and immediately regretted the
action. Wincing from the twinge of pain between her
legs, Rose rested back against the soft pillows. The past
twenty-four hours had changed them both. What did the
future hold? Aidan spoke of rules forbidding the Fae to
be with humans, but he didn't specify the ramifications.

Shoving the covers off, Rose rolled to the side of
the bed and dangled her feet over the edge. "A cruel
people, if you ask me. What's so wrong with us? What
will my sister think?" She cupped a hand over her
mouth, trying to squelch the hysterical laughter which
threatened to spill out.

Shaking her head, she glanced around the room.
Rose had no intention of lying in bed without Aidan
one second longer. But there was the problem of her
clothing. They had been discarded in the forest, and her

bag was somewhere in another room. She shivered, recalling their lovemaking. Certain places still tingled with pleasure.

"Where are you, Aidan?"

Glancing over her shoulder at his giant armoire, Rose stared in disbelief at the pale green nightgown draped over one of the chairs. Crossing the room, she fingered the silken material. However, doubt crept in, casting its shadow over her feelings. Did this gown belong to another woman? She bunched the material in her hand. Yes, he was skilled in seduction and lovemaking. Rose was not his first, but to have female clothing in his room was a bit much.

The green-eyed monster wove a thread inside Rose, and she swiftly cast it aside. It did no good to make assumptions. A lesson her mother had taught both her daughters. Loosening her hold on the gown, Rose sighed.

Lifting the gown from the chair, she held it outward. "You need to find your bags." Slipping the garment over her head, she went to the giant mirror. The reflection of a woman who had been loved stared back at her. Touching her red, swollen lips, she gazed at herself. "Is this what being loved does to one's skin? I'm positively glowing."

Rose shivered. Casting her sight once more around the room, she noted a plaid wrap on a chair by the giant hearth. Quickly retrieving the covering, she draped it over her shoulders and wandered out of the room.

Silence surrounded her as she descended the stone circular stairs. When she reached the last step, smells of food drifted by, enticing her to go into the kitchen. As Rose pushed open the door, she smiled at the scene within the warm place. She stepped quietly inside, admiring the view of Aidan humming a tune by the hearth. He wore nothing but black sweatpants that barely covered his firm ass.

"Good morn, *leannan*," he crooned, keeping his back to her.

She rolled her eyes. "Let me guess—special Fae hearing?"

"Assuredly."

"What smells so good?" asked Rose, stepping fully into the kitchen.

"Spices for a meal. Here in the pot over the flame is—" He turned around, holding a wooden spoon.

"Yes?" She moved slowly toward him.

Visibly swallowing, he replied in a low voice, "You are ravishing. I may take you here on the table."

Rose leaned to the side, trying to hide her mirth. "What's in the kettle?"

"Vegetable soup." Tossing the spoon onto the table, he closed the distance between them. His hands skimmed down her arms and to her waist, gripping her firmly. "You steal the breath from my lungs, beloved."

Trailing a finger over his chest, she asked demurely, "And who was the previous owner of this lovely gown?"

"No one."

She looked at him in surprise. "But where?"

He gave her a wink. "Magic."

Feeling utterly foolish at her previous thoughts, she bit her lower lip. Would she ever not be surprised by Aidan's actions or powers?

"Do you truly think me that shallow?" he asked softly.

"No," she blurted out, further embarrassed. "But you must understand my thoughts tend to travel in a linear human direction. I don't have a clue as to how far your powers extend."

His laughter rumbled through her as Aidan wrapped his arms around her. "Were you jealous?"

His question only infuriated Rose, and she glared up at him. "Let's turn the tables for a moment, shall we? What if you woke and found me missing. Furthermore, the only item I left for you was a pair of men's pants?"

"I'd find out who the bastard was and slice off his balls."

Horrified, Rose pinched him. "Thankfully, you don't have to worry about any previous men taking me to their beds."

Aidan growled. "And there shall be none in the future, either."

Wanting to direct the conversation elsewhere, she glanced at the items near the Aga. "Is there something I can do to help?"

"No."

Rose squeaked as he lifted her into his arms, silencing her with a passionate kiss. After breaking free, he strolled to a nearby chair and settled her on its cushioned seat.

"I'm preparing you a meal to break your fast," he announced. "The soup is for later."

"Medieval man," she spouted in good humor.

"Nae. Ancient," he corrected, giving her a wink.

"What culinary delight are you preparing?"

Aidan reached for the bowl and a ladle. "Pancakes."

"My favorite food!" Rose almost jumped out of the chair in glee. "How did you know?"

"I asked your sister when I called her earlier."

"Damn!" She rubbed a hand over her forehead. "I totally forgot to check in with her last evening."

"Before you make any assumptions, I merely told her you were staying on here at *Croí Dragon,* instead of the hotel. You were gathering some research nearby."

Rose laughed nervously. "You don't know my sister. She'll be praying to all the Gods and Goddesses that you have taken me to your bed."

Aidan stirred the batter while he arched a brow. "Truth?"

"Oh, yes. She was positively giddy to know you were coming with me to Ireland."

"I am happy to hear she approves of me," drawled Aidan.

Rose removed the plaid from her shoulders and dropped it over the back of a chair. "She was infatuated the first time she saw you."

"After our meal, you can use the phone in my library to give her a call." He paused to ladle out scoops of batter onto the griddle. When he finished, he wiped his hands and went to her. "Have I overstepped?"

Rose placed her hands on his warm chest. "The great Aidan Kerrigan overstep?" She stood on her tiptoes and gave him a kiss on the chin. "No." She closed her eyes and inhaled deeply. "What is that wonderful smell?"

"Vanilla bean from the Fae realm, and rum for the pancake batter."

"Goodness, Aidan." She opened her eyes in surprise.

He shrugged. "And for the whipped cream."

"I'm swooning."

"Here I thought it was my body that caused you to become dizzy." He pressed intimately against her.

"That's an entirely different feeling."

"Good," he murmured against her cheek and then returned to the stove.

Rose leaned against the table for support. The man moved with power even in the kitchen. A yearning to know more about this Fae took root in her.

She wandered by his side, studying him. "Tell me about your life in your world. You spoke of a sister, Nuala, correct?"

Aidan's hand stilled. "The Queen of the Fae."

"For real?" Her question barely a whisper.

He nodded and flipped the pancakes. "She is married to King Ansgar."

"Any other siblings?"

"Yes."

When he remained quiet for several seconds, Rose feared there was more. A muscle twitched in his jaw, and his movements slowed. "If you don't want to talk about this, I'll understand." She placed a gentle hand on his arm.

His face tight with strain, he dropped the utensil and grabbed Rose around the waist, lifting her into the air. Setting her on the counter next to the giant Aga, he braced his hands on either side of the marble. Keeping his head bent, he said, "One other brother, Eógan. He was the second son born to the Royal House of Óg . He died in the last battle between our people and the *Milesians*." When he lifted his head, Aidan's eyes had turned to shards of silver. "I have never spoken of his death with anyone. It cleaved mine and Nuala's heart in two. After today, I shall speak no more of the great warrior. He has returned home to the cosmos to be with our parents."

His confession and pain sliced into Rose's heart. She cupped his face and kissed him tenderly. "And he watches over you."

Aidan snorted and wiped a hand over his face. "Not likely. Once a Fae dies, his soul returns to the land of forever, *Tir na nÓg .*" He waved his hand outward. "The night guardians—dragons—guide us. They are the only ones permitted to watch over us."

Rose watched him silently flip the pancakes. She regretted asking him about his family. In addition, all the mythological references were burning a hole in her brain. Her knowledge was extensive, and she knew the *Milesians* were part of the invasions of Ireland. After they won the great battle between the *Tuatha Dé Danann*, they remained above ground, banishing the Fae race to live beneath the land in Ireland.

Brushing her hands down the front of her gown, she looked away. An alcove was tucked off the entrance to the kitchen. Leaning forward, she could make out drying herbs on pegs. It would be an area to explore later. Recalling what Aidan said earlier, she longed to ask him more.

*Don't cause him any further pain. Perhaps another time.*

"I smell flowers, yet, there are none in here."

"The lemon tree in the other room is blossoming. At this time of year and in autumn, the heavy floral scent fills the kitchen."

She dangled her feet, itching to go and explore the

other room.

"What is your question?" inquired Aidan quietly.

Rose pointed a finger at herself. "Me? Why do you think I have a question?"

Giving her a glorious smile, he added more batter to the griddle. "Because you're fidgeting."

*You know me too well, Aidan Kerrigan.* She nodded in the direction of the alcove. "Is that a drying room for herbs?"

Scooping out a dollop of whipped cream from a bowl, Aidan plopped it on a stack of pancakes. "Yes. There are two rooms—one to dry and the other to cultivate herbs, along with the lemon tree. Now tell me your *real* question?"

"That was a real question," she stated emphatically. "Did you build the room around the tree?"

Aidan took a fork and sliced into the pancakes. "No. Now ask me anything."

Blowing out a frustrated breath, she replied, "You mentioned the Royal House of Óg. Any correlation between the name and the Standing Stones of Óg?"

"Open your mouth," he ordered, stepping near her.

When the first bite entered her mouth, Rose let out a pleasurable moan. The savory combination of vanilla and rum was heady. "Great Goddess, this is good."

Aidan bent and kissed the corner of her mouth. "Missed a bite."

Pinpricks of desire trickled down her body, settling in the most wonderful area.

He leaned back and took a bite for himself and then presented her with another forkful. "Yes, there is a connection to the Standing Stones and my royal house. We are under the lineage of Angus Óg as well."

Rose choked on the revelation, causing her food to lodge in her throat. *Goodness.* Her thought after first meeting him had been correct. He did resemble this particular Celtic God.

Aidan dropped the plate on the counter and filled a glass with water. Returning to her side, he handed it to her. "Drink," he encouraged.

Even the small sip of water made her sputter. When she finally recovered, Aidan wiped a napkin over her lips and face. "Too much information?" he teased, mirth dancing within his gorgeous eyes.

"Definitely," she muttered, drawing her hair over her shoulders with her hand. Settling back on the counter, she regarded him. "God of Love?"

Aidan chuckled and took another bite of food. "Also a musician—a lover of the harp. I can show you mine later."

"Well his skills have not diminished with his descendants."

"Shh…be careful. He might hear you," he scoffed playfully.

Rose glanced in all directions. "Seriously? Would he actually show up here?"

Presenting another morsel of pancakes in front of her mouth, Aidan responded, "No. The Gods and Goddesses made a vow to never return to Earth after the last battle. They live with the dragons among the stars."

Rose opened her mouth, silently accepting the bite of food. She had no words. Her mind reeled with this latest declaration.

Aidan continued to feed Rose in this leisurely fashion until she held up her hand. "Why are you feeding me?"

He nudged her legs apart, giving her a dazzling smile. "Part of my seduction. After I am through, I'm going to lick some of this decadent cream off certain parts of your skin.

Rose edged closer to him and swiped at a dollop of whipped cream from the plate. "Only if I can return the pleasure."

He smiled sensuously as he lowered the plate to the counter. Reaching for her hand, Aidan slowly bent and sucked the cream from her finger in slow movements. After he was finished, he slid the straps of her gown over her shoulders, allowing her breasts to spill forth.

Leaning closer, Aidan brushed his face against her cheek. His soft whiskers sent tremors of desire throughout her body. "What part of my body would you like to lick the cream from?"

Her pulse skittered, knowing exactly where she yearned to taste the man. Reaching between them, Rose slipped her hand inside his pants. Aidan's hot erection seared a path up her arm and she squeezed the solid length. "Here."

Closing his eyes on a pleasurable sigh, he whispered, "Take me, Rose. I'm all yours."

Chapter Nineteen

*"When doubt slithers in to challenge a warrior, he must seek the counsel of only one. Himself."*
~*Edicts of the Fenian Warriors*

In an effort to contain his laughter, Aidan lowered his head on his knees. He refused to watch the bantering of his beloved with one of the feral cats trapped in a tree. Rose coaxed, pleaded, and attempted to climb the limbs of the birch tree, but to no avail. The feline ignored, hissed, and even took a swipe at her with its claws extended. In truth, the animal wanted to be left alone. Content to forage for food on her own, the cat had no desire to become a pet.

Aidan tried to tell Rose this admission, but she cut him off with a steely glare. An hour later, with her cheeks red, and her hair blowing in the gentle breeze, her pleas turned pathetic.

"Please, sweet kitty, I can promise you some cream," she begged.

He snapped his head up. Images of Rose taking him fully with her succulent mouth in the kitchen several mornings ago made him hard. Desire roiled within him, and he stood.

"Enough!" he demanded, snapping his fingers at the cat. "Get down, or I shall do the honors."

The feline hissed at Aidan, but promptly did as she

was ordered. Scampering down the trunk of the tree, the animal darted off along the river's edge.

Rose gaped at him for several seconds. Waving a hand in the direction of the cat, she asked, "That's it? How in the heck did you manage to get her out of the tree? Or was it sheer terror that made the cat flee?"

Plucking a daisy from the ground, he held it outward. "Did I not say the animal wished to be left alone?"

"Yes, but…" Wariness reflected within her eyes.

He tucked the daisy in the valley between her luscious breasts, which were barely contained in the flowing gown she wore. "I can communicate with all animals," he confessed.

"Sweet Brigid and all the Goddesses." Removing the flower, she turned and walked away from him, muttering more complaints about her lack of knowing all of his powers.

Content to watch her backside as Rose sauntered away from him, Aidan smiled. He had to consider how this must all seem to her—a human female. In time, she would accept everything about him. If not, then he had seriously misjudged his beloved.

A tremor of power slipped over him, and Aidan turned abruptly.

"What devious games are you playing here?" demanded Flynn.

Unprepared to answer his friend, he glanced away. Tempering his fury, Aidan moved to the water's edge. "This is not your concern. Return to the Brotherhood."

"Yes, it is," argued Flynn, coming to stand in front of him. "The kingdom has sensed a rift and *you* are at the center."

*So the reckoning has begun.* Aidan tilted his head to the side. "Are you here as a warrior or friend?"

"If I was here as a warrior, you'd be in cuffs."

He arched a brow at the Fae. "Leave, Flynn."

"Have you not considered what will happen, once the Fae council realizes what has occurred here?"

All Aidan wanted was to be left alone. Regardless, the time of facing his actions was drawing near. "I require a few more days. Until then, return and keep silent."

Flynn grabbed his arm. "This is madness. What is it you seek here?"

"You cannot fully comprehend."

Releasing his hold of Aidan, he stepped back. "Then tell me. I am your oldest friend. At least share with me the truth, for I have no wish to hear it elsewhere."

Aidan fisted his hands on his hip. He owed the truth to Flynn, along with one final decision. "I have joined with Rose. I am in love with her."

Flynn gaped at him in shock. "Is she a witch? Did she cast an enchantment over you?"

"Do not be ludicrous. Our fates were decreed. Why else was I the one chosen to take on this mission?"

"You're thinking with your cock, instead of your brain and heart."

"*Wrong*," warned Aidan, pounding his chest. "My heart has fallen in love, and I listened."

"As a warrior trained to seal off emotional involvement with human females, I find this weakness in you a sickness. You are the leader of the Fenian Warriors. Above this flippant behavior."

It took all of Aidan's control not to level a fist to

his friend's jaw, but he understood the warrior's anger. He'd expect nothing less.

Striding away, Aidan went to the river. "There were two roads on this path, each leading to the same conclusion. Destruction. The mission was not one of silencing the information, but illuminating a new direction for me. Sadly, the Fae council, and the king will see it as an act of betrayal."

Flynn approached by his side. "Then you have been preparing for the inevitable the entire time?"

Aidan released his breath slowly and glanced at his friend. "Since the moment I took Rose into my soul. The ramifications will be vast."

"Then I cannot sway you in another direction?" Flynn asked.

"From loving her?" Aidan shielded his hand over his eyes, searching for his beloved wandering along the edge of the river bank. Upon seeing her, he smiled. "No."

In a gentler tone, Flynn added, "Is Rose prepared for the aftermath of your consequences?"

An ache settled like a lodestone over his heart, and Aidan placed the heel of his palm over his chest. "Unfortunately, she's continuing to come to terms with finding out the man she loves is a Fae with magical powers and descended from the God, Angus Óg. I have yet to share anything more."

"You don't have much time, Aidan."

Nodding slowly, he returned his gaze to his friend. "There is one more decision I must make before you take your leave."

"Shield you from the wrath of the Fae council?" chided Flynn. "Though she is a radiant vision and one who possesses a valuable gift of sight. I can see her aura from here."

With a wave of his hand, Aidan brought forth the ceremonial crystal dagger. Clutching it firmly, he ordered, "Kneel, Flynn Brodie, from the Royal House of Camue."

The warrior snapped his attention to Aidan in shock. "What are you doing?"

The emotions swirled within Aidan as he held the dagger high. "There is no other to take my place as leader, save one. Kneel, Fenian Warrior."

"No, Aidan. I cannot take your place as leader. There is so much yet to learn."

Aidan shook his head slowly. "You are ready. Another warrior is destined to come forth, but he is not ready. His time is in the future. *You* must guide them all."

Flynn fisted his hand over his heart in reverence. "Don't do this," he pleaded. "We can think of another solution."

"It is my right and within my power. Once they strip me of my leadership, the decision will be in the hands of the Fae council. I say again, *kneel*, Fenian Warrior!"

Flynn dropped to his knees, but kept his gaze fixed on Aidan. "In my heart, you shall *always* be my leader, mentor, *and* friend."

Unable to hold back the tide of emotions, Aidan let the power he held in check swirl forth in a blue haze from the dagger. Swiftly tapping the blade on both Flynn's shoulders, he released the energy. The air hummed with residual power, followed by a loud snap. Aidan staggered back from the blow.

Recovering quickly, he tried to focus. His hands shook while he held the dagger outward. "From the past to the present. From the old to the new. I, Aidan Kerrigan, from the Royal House of Óg step back into the mists and relinquish all rights as the leader of the Fenian Warriors."

Accepting the dagger, Flynn tucked the blade within the belt at his side and stood. "I shall hold the council guards back for as long as possible."

Aidan clamped a hand on Flynn's shoulder. "Thank you. I require time to put everything in order."

Flynn nodded and embraced him. "Farewell, my friend."

"Long life to you, as well."

In a blazing shaft of light, Flynn vanished.

Breathing deeply, Aidan swept his gaze across the River Shannon. There were two items to conclude. One required his immediate attention. And the other…

His heart beat rapidly at having to tell his beloved that when they came for him, they might be parted for a long time.

****

Waiting for the first star to grace the evening sky over Loch Ness, Aidan leaned against the pine tree and folded his arms over his chest. He fought the temptation to glance upward. He would not beg the guardians for their approval. They were merely the timekeepers, not rulers over affairs of the heart.

Nonetheless, they did rumble their disapproval on several occasions.

After his friend had departed, Aidan sought out Rose, explaining his need to have a conversation with an ancient being.

When her shock subsided at his news that Nessie was indeed a dragon living within the depths of Loch Ness, she sent him away with her blessing. Additionally, she made him promise to bring her here after they were married.

He laughed at the memory. To him they were already married. Regardless, he'd grant her the moon and stars to keep her happy and always smiling. And he agreed to a formal celebration with her sister and those from the Society.

When the first whisper of an ancient power brushed against his thoughts, Aidan stepped forth from the shadows of the trees. Reaching the water's edge, the mists retreated from the loch, and he knelt on one knee. "Greetings, Great Dragon."

*"Why are you here, Fenian Warrior?"*

Aidan sensed a thread of anger and prepared for her rejection. "To seek counsel and your wisdom."

*"For a decision you have already made?"*

"No," he clipped out, losing his control. "What I have done is follow the path of my heart. But what about the love I bear for those I shall leave behind?"

*"Love is more powerful than any power you covet, Fenian Warrior. Your path was ordained in the stars long ago. Your destiny forged on the loom of Fate and within the crystal caverns on our home world. Will you not always love your people?"*

Confused, Aidan rubbed a hand over his brow. "Until my last breath. But how do I reconcile both—my new-found love and the pain it will bring to others?"

*"Uncertainty cannot guide you. If even a thread of doubt exist, then you are not fully prepared. Is this new path sure and steady?"*

"Yes," he affirmed with conviction.

*"With love comes pain, regardless of the great joy. You are divided in your logic. Remove the Fenian Warrior and think and feel as a Fae. If your love is pure and true, your family will understand."*

"These emotions are foreign to me."

*"And if you do not reconcile them, I fear you shall surround your heart in a lorica and be unable to find the answers you seek."*

"As a Fenian Warrior, I contained my heart in a breastplate. The moment Rose MacLaren entered my arms, her essence cracked the exterior."

*"Have you since removed the breastplate?"*

"Yes," he acknowledged.

*"Rise, Aidan Kerrigan, from the Royal House of Óg, descended from Angus. You no longer need my counsel. Love continues to guide our people, even during difficult times. Your ancestor is proud."*

Rising slowly, Aidan glanced upward. The air warmed considerably as the mists swirled around him. "Thank you," he uttered softly.

After retreating back to the trees, Aidan waved his hand outward and vanished in a shimmer of soft lights.

As he emerged from the trees bordering *Croí Dragon*, he smiled. The stars glittered like diamonds against the inky blackness. With no threat of rain on the horizon, Aidan paused to consider an evening spent under the stars. Or he could open the window to his chamber, allowing the starlight to fill the room.

Quickly crossing the gate, Aidan's steps hastened. By the time he dashed through the doors to his home, he was taking three steps at a time up the stairs. Excitement flared within him, and so did the yearning to hold Rose within his arms.

His conversation with the Great Dragon had left him with inner peace.

When he approached his chambers, he almost used his power to open the door. Pausing, he exhaled slowly. *Even if they strip all my powers from me, they can never take the love I have centered in my soul for this woman. Power is fleeting. Love is everlasting.*

Aidan's heart soared as he pushed open the doors to his chamber.

Rose bounded from the bench by the window arch and into his arms. He buried his face into her hair, inhaling deeply. *I am home.*

"Did she approve?" asked Rose softly.

"Wholeheartedly."

When Rose began to tremble in his arms, Aidan pulled back. "Why do you weep, *mo ghrá*?"

"Would you have left if she had protested this match?"

His smile came slowly, and he wiped away the lone tear that had trickled down her cheek. "No."

She hugged him fiercely. "Good. Because I was prepared to show the Fae my anger."

Curious about her confession, he cupped her warm chin and lifted her head. "Explain how you would demonstrate your anger?"

Eyes that sparkled with determination and strength gazed back at him. "There is an old oak on the Hill of Tara. Some whisper it is the entrance into the Fae world. Many drape ribbons and leave gifts with their prayer requests to the Fae. Is this correct?"

"Yes," he confirmed hesitantly.

"What do you think would happen if I took one of

your swords and leveled a blade to the trunk? Or stripped the gifts from the base?"

A sense of foreboding slithered down Aidan's spine. *It is time.*

Lifting Rose into his arms, he walked across to the window. Placing her on the bench, he leaned forward and opened the huge stained-glass window. This was not how he wanted to spend this evening with his beloved.

Taking a seat beside her, he brought her hands to his chest. "I have not shared everything with you, *leannan*. Before I speak about this knowledge, you must give me your solemn promise you will stay away from the Tree of Life on the Hill of Tara."

"I don't understand." She tried to tug her hands free from his grasp. "Why would you ask this of me, unless—"

"You must give me your vow, Rose," he ordered with more force than he intended.

Her expression turned to horrified shock. "They are coming for you?"

"Soon, I believe."

"No, *no*! I will not let them!"

"You cannot stop them, *mo ghrá*."

Rose stiffened. "Release me, Aidan."

Surrendering, Aidan let her hands free. "What I have done cannot go unpunished."

Even after turning her back on him, he could feel the fury, hurt, and confusion fall off of her in waves. "So is this your parting goodbye, Aidan Kerrigan?"

"*Rose*," he pleaded, reaching his hand out to her. His fingers ached to pull her back into his arms.

She took a step away and faced him. "All this talk

of forever, claiming me as your own, is now null and void?" Lifting her arms outward, she added, "Why even fall in love, when you *knew* this would happen?"

In one swift movement, Aidan grasped her around the waist. "For love, Rose. I am merely preparing you that I have to return, most likely under guard." She started to protest, and he placed a finger over her lips. "Once I stand trial, I shall profess my desire to leave the Fae realm forever and then return to you."

Confusion marred her brow, but she did not try and pull away from him. "But you're the leader of the Fenian Warriors."

"I surrendered my power to another earlier today."

"Oh, *Aidan*." Placing her hands on his chest, she continued in a somber tone, "What about your family? Your *sister*?"

Aidan glanced at the starry night. "Forever we shall be linked. Forever I will love Nuala." Returning his attention to Rose, he stated with conviction, "Nevertheless, my heart and soul belong with only one—*you*. If I lose you…"

He held his breath, fearing her objections. Or worse, her rejection.

Rose wrapped her arms around his neck. Warm and strong. "Remember, no regrets, my love—my *Fae* warrior. We walk this road together."

"Leannan, *leannan*," he breathed the words against her soft cheek. "Let us not waste another moment discussing trials and tribulations."

"Only happy thoughts," she encouraged.

He nuzzled her neck, eliciting a soft purr from her lips. "I intend on worshipping more of your delectable body."

Her breath came in long surrendering moans, and Aidan captured her mouth with a fiery kiss.

Chapter Twenty

*"The sole directive of the Society of the Thistle is to establish or restore a natural habitat of the historical site, similar to its beginnings."*
*~Society of the Thistle*

Bees swarmed in the distance and birds chirped in the warm spring air. Contentment filled Aidan as he watched Rose gather some wildflowers near the bank of the river. Each time she plucked some, he encouraged more to blossom. Her sound of delight at finding a new flower filled him with joy.

Rose's light followed her, and he found himself continually smiling.

For several blissful weeks, they talked, took long walks, rode his horses, and made love passionately. Briefly, he pondered why the Fae council was taking so long in ordering his return. Even considering that the time moved vastly slower in the realm, he assumed the guards would have been here by now. His guarded look eased slightly, and he quickly dismissed the thought. Instead, he'd focused on loving Rose.

Each moment was a treasure not to be wasted.

As she sauntered back to his side, she dumped all her flowers into a basket. With her cheeks flushed from the sun and other recent pleasurable activities, she straddled his thighs. "If you think I don't know you're responsible for all these glorious flowers, you're mistaken."

Chuckling lightly, he brushed a lock over her shoulder. "You have found out my secret."

"Goodness, I thought I had discovered all of them."

"I believe there are a few left," he teased.

Rubbing against him provocatively, she leaned near his ear. "Did you know tomorrow is Beltaine?"

"The festivals are in my blood," he murmured, skimming his hands under her dress and along her thighs.

"Speaking of festivals, I hear there is one in the local village. When the last ray slips over the horizon, they're going to light a bonfire."

"Would you like to dance around the fire?" he asked, slipping a finger into her heated flesh.

Gasping, Rose responded to the seduction of his passion by placing her hands on his shoulders. "Nothing would make me happier."

"Your wish is my command. A night under the stars dancing with you. I will do anything to make you content. Besides, we have yet to dance with one another."

She leaned her forehead against his. "Why do I fear this happiness is only temporary?"

Aidan paused in his seductive foreplay and withdrew his hands. Gathering her into his arms, he held her snugly. "You sense it, too?"

"*Yes*. It's like a dark cloud following us."

"Banish the darkness, for it has yet to happen," he reassured Rose, though he doubted his own words.

Resting his chin on the top of her head, Aidan glanced outward. When Rose remained quiet, he cast his sight to all the flowers. Releasing his hold, he plucked another from the ground, attempting to dispel any further negative discussion. "Tell me again the Latin name for this." Aidan twirled the delicate flower between his fingers.

Rose lifted her head and regarded him with a speculative gaze. Her fingers brushed over his as she took the flower from his hand. "*Ranunculus acris* for Buttercup."

"*Fearbán féir* for the Irish translation," he added.

A smile tugged on the corners of her mouth. "Correct."

Aidan reached for another flower. "And this lovely primrose?"

Brushing her fingers over the delicate petals, she replied, "*Primula vulgaris*."

"*Sabhaircín* for the Irish."

"Ahh…I believe I found one of your favorites." Reaching behind her, he brought forth a handful of flowers.

She gasped in delight. "I don't recall seeing any Forget-me-knots."

Letting them fall into her lap, he asked, "*Lus mínola goirt* for the Irish. And the Latin?"

"*Myosotis arvensis*." She drew them against her breasts, her smile filling him. "You're wonderful, Aidan."

So for the next hour, the conversation consisted of Latin, Irish, and a few Fae names of the many flowers that surrounded his beloved. When Rose attempted to correct him on a certain flower not native to Ireland, he listened in rapt attention. Aelish was wrong. She had another avid pupil in Rose.

"Where are your thoughts, Aidan?" she asked, tapping him on the temple with her finger.

"Merely considering what an astute teacher you are. Worthy of any in the Fae realm."

She sighed and leaned back. "Tell me the special flowers only grown in your world."

"Happily," he agreed. "Shall I refresh your memory on the walk back?"

"I am getting hungry," confessed Rose, glancing around. "Look at all the flowers."

Aidan helped her off his lap and stretched. Standing, he reached for her hand and helped her up. "For each one we plucked, I planted a hundred more with magic."

The warmth of her smile echoed in her voice. "I love you so much."

He brushed a feather-like kiss across her lips. "As I love you, *leannan*."

Aidan bent and retrieved her sandals. "Let me assist you, fair maiden."

Rose giggled and waved off his gesture. "I enjoy the feel of the land beneath my bare feet."

"That makes two of us."

As they ambled along the path back to the castle, Aidan's thoughts returned to their vague future. His silent prayer to Mother Danu was that his trial would be swift, and they would banish him from the kingdom.

He returned his attention to telling Rose about the vanilla scented orchids that were as big as his hand. And cherry blossoms that were speckled with gold, so they could mirror the sunlight.

Reaching the front entrance, Aidan pushed open the massive doors and swept his hand forward for Rose to enter.

"What culinary delight do you favor tonight, *mo ghrá*?"

Entering the kitchen, Rose went and retrieved the kettle. "Nothing fancy. I'll be happy with eggs and toast."

Grumbling a protest, Aidan responded, "I'll make you an omelet."

"Although I'm curious."

Arching a brow, Aidan went to the fridge. "About?"

She gestured outward. "Why don't you use magic to whip something up to eat?"

"It's simple," he stated, pulling out eggs, cheese, peppers, and wild onions. "Cooking gives me pleasure. I have always prepared my meals in this fashion, unless I was deep on a mission. During those times, warriors barely manage to eat. And contrary to what you may believe, the Fae do prepare their meals. Magic is not the solution for everything we do in the kingdom."

Moving to the sink, Rose filled the kettle and then returned to the stove. "The only difference between you and the military is that you're a Fae with magical powers."

"Seems incredulous, right?" Aidan deposited the food items on the counter.

Rose snorted, leaning against the wall. "More like mind-blowing." She tilted her head to the side. "Will you miss the missions? Traveling back and forth through time?"

Aidan sighed heavily. "Have we not already gone down this road of conversation?"

"Yes," she uttered in dismay and walked away.

Going to the window, she kept her back to him. "There are times when my knowledge and life cannot compare to yours. What in the world did you see in me?"

Stunned by her admission, Aidan immediately went to her side. Grasping her by the shoulders, he forced her around to face him. He scanned her lovely face, seeing wariness reflected. "*Never* discount the woman you are, Rose MacLaren. *Ever*. I saw beauty inside the depth of your soul. Your intelligence would rival any Fae in the herbal gardens, and you possess a wisdom that sparks from a desire to learn more. You challenge me, *leannan*. Do not ever think yourself beneath me."

Nodding slowly, she said, "Then we will teach each other."

"A grand idea," he affirmed.

A twinkle of mischief replaced uncertainty in her eyes. "Though I do love being under you at specific times."

Desire rolled through him, and Aidan let out a groan. His mouth captured hers hungrily, sealing any further words from his beloved with a searing kiss.

\*\*\*\*

Watching as the setting sun bled into the sky on its way to the golden dusk of twilight, Rose reached for Aidan's hand. She laced her fingers, drawing him to her side. Anticipation danced like butterflies in her stomach as they waited for the bonfire to be lit. Children could be heard in the distance singing songs in delight of the faeries that would join with them at this Beltaine celebration. Little did they know that a large Fae had been with them all day.

Aidan laughed, feasted, and appeared carefree. It

seemed like he belonged here. A part of the village and the people who lived there.

She stole a glance at Aidan. His relaxed stance and profile made her heart sing. She had never been so happy in all of her life. Each time he entered a room, her heart leapt in joy. He stole the breath from her lungs and made her tremble with a single touch.

Rose loved the warrior with unbridled passion.

"Are you admiring the view, *leannan*?" His deep husky brogue swept over her skin in a soft caress.

Embarrassed, she nudged him playfully. "Was I that obvious?"

He wrapped a warm arm around her shoulders and bent near her ear. "I can *feel* your heated gaze."

"Let me guess. Special Fae senses?"

"Precisely." Aidan chuckled and placed a kiss on her cheek.

Rose nuzzled against him. "You smell good."

"It's the cinnamon in the apple pastry I purchased from a vendor earlier."

"You forget I had the strawberry scone."

Aidan released his hold. "Wait here. I'll return shortly."

"But they're about to light the bonfire," she protested.

He tweaked her nose. "Not yet."

Rose watched as her warrior strolled through the crowd of people to the stall of vendors. Humming a tune, she swayed back and forth. Contentment and peace centered her. She curled her toes into the lush grass, eager for the dancing to begin.

True to his word, Aidan returned quickly, presenting her with an apple pastry. He dipped a slight bow. "For the fair maiden."

"So gallant, my warrior. Thank you." Taking the offering, she savored the delectable confection.

After she finished the last morsel, Aidan reached for her hands. "Now for my treat."

When his mouth touched her fingers, heat blossomed within her. Taking his time, he licked and nipped across her skin, devouring the sticky leftovers. Desire unfurled within her body in the most intimate places.

She stepped closer. "You are the most seductive man ever."

Lowering his head, he trailed his tongue over the bottom of her lip. "And you are a siren that makes my blood burn."

Rose let out a moan and wrapped her arms around his neck, taking his kiss with reckless abandon. When the first rousing cheer surrounded them, she drew back. The bonfire had been lit, and the merriment had begun.

Aidan took her hand, giving her a dazzling smile. "Shall we dance around the fire once, before departing for somewhere more private?"

"A wonderful plan."

Gaiety filled her as they rushed with the others to dance around the huge blaze. The air hummed with good energy as the flames snapped and flared into the night sky.

Aidan held her hand firm within his grasp, his voice ringing loud in song. "One more turn?" he shouted.

"Yes!"

Onward they went in laughter and song, enjoying the moment. After a third time around the bonfire,

Aidan pulled her away from the crowd. They ran across the open meadow and into the forest. A shard of moonlight dusted the ground as their steps slowed.

Aidan pulled her deep within and backed her against one of the pine trees. His eyes flashed silver as she melted into his arms.

His kiss was demanding, and Rose surrendered, giving him all she had.

A thunderous explosion shook the ground, shattering their peaceful interlude. Aidan drew back suddenly and turned around abruptly. Mists crept along the forest floor, snaking their way to them.

"What's wrong?" she whispered in a shaky voice.

The agony of his silence ripped through her, and an ache settled within her chest. Their blissful time had come to an end. Her shoulders sagged with the realization. "The Fae are here for you."

"Yes."

Rose reached for his hand. Her pounding heart grew stronger. "I cannot leave you, Aidan."

Bringing their joined hands to his chest, he cupped her chin firmly. "Whatever happens, do not interfere, *mo ghrá*. Do you understand? Promise me no matter what you witness, you will not come forth."

She wanted to scream at him. How could he ask her to remain docile and compliant? Though she longed to argue her case, she simply nodded in agreement. "I promise," she stated weakly.

In one swift move, he grasped her around the waist and crushed his mouth against hers. Breathing heavily, he released her. "*Never* forget my love for you, Rose. Remember, time moves slowly in the Fae realm."

"What are you saying? Days, weeks, until you

come back?" she asked.

"Possibly months for the council to make their assessment."

Rose grasped his hands tightly. "I don't care how long I have to wait, Aidan Kerrigan. You are mine, body and soul. Return to *me*." Her voice choked on the emotions.

He nodded behind her. "Go stand against one of the larger trees farther down. Do not move from there."

Tears stung her eyes, but she refused to be weak in front of him. He needed her strength now. Her breathing became shallow and the air thick. "I *love* you," she blurted out.

"Och, *leannan*." After taking her mouth one more time in a fiery kiss, he released her and pushed her away. "Go."

Rose staggered away, her feet dragging over leaves and twigs. Her heart cried out to return to his side, but she had given him her promise. When she reached the tree, Rose turned around and let the tears fall down her cheeks.

Chapter Twenty-One

*"A Fenian Warrior takes his shield of honor with him to his death."*

*~Edicts of the Fenian Warriors*

Aidan fisted his hands and waited. The power coiled around him, evidence that the guards from the Fae council had arrived. Another trickle of energy washed over him, alerting him to the presence of Fenian Warriors as well. Were they working together? He dared not open his mind and risk finding the glaring truth. No. He'd wait for them to make the first move.

As the first guard appeared out of the mists, Aidan gave him a curt nod. "Tadhg."

Silently, others emerged and stood around Tadhg. Each warrior withdrew their swords in a show of power.

"Does the Fae consider me such a threat that they've sent ten of their guards?" asked Aidan.

Tadhg stepped forward. "As leader of the Fenian Warriors, your power is vast. You are under arrest, *Fenian Warrior* and have been summoned to appear before the Fae council to account for your heinous crime."

The burning rage Aidan fought to keep in control threatened to unleash. "The name is Aidan Kerrigan. Do not insult me, *Tadhg.*"

The guard snarled. "Your time has come to an end." Holding out a pair of crystal cuffs, he tossed them onto the ground. "Put them on."

He heard Rose's gasp from within the trees. When the other guards looked beyond him, Aidan took a step back. Any attack on his beloved and he was prepared to kill them all.

"Your disrespect for our leader is unfathomable," stated a familiar voice.

Aidan glanced to his left, seeing Liam MacGregor and five other Fenian Warriors approach his side. His ire only ignited further. "What are you doing here?"

Liam kept his gaze fixed on Tadhg. "Giving you a proper escort back into the kingdom. If these Fae guards wish to accompany us, I see no issue with denying them." He returned his attention to Aidan. "Do you?"

"I am no longer your leader," grumbled Aidan.

"Since Flynn is not here, we will consider this our last act with you."

Aidan nodded slowly. He turned to Tadhg. "I shall go willingly, as long as you accept the escort of the Fenian Warriors."

Tadhg spat out a curse, but relented. He pointed a warning finger at Liam. "I hold you responsible if this warrior slips from our grasp."

"Do not insult me again," warned Aidan.

Tadhg turned his back on Aidan and spoke quietly with one of the guards.

Aidan faced his friend. "I have one final request."

Liam arched a brow, but remained quiet.

Clamping a firm hold on the warrior's shoulder, Aidan said, "From this moment forward, I charge you as the guardian to Rose MacLaren."

"By the hounds," hissed out Liam, raking a hand through his hair.

"There shall be no argument. I require your solemn vow."

"Now? Can't it wait until after we take you back?"

Aidan's voice tightened with emotion. "No. Furthermore, return here and make sure she is safely concealed at *Croí Dragon*." Indecision battled across Liam's features. "Until you swear your oath as a Fenian Warrior to me, I cannot leave here. At present, Rose is witnessing all deep within the trees."

Letting out a groan of protest, he uttered quietly, "As my allegiance to the Brotherhood and as a Fenian Warrior, I give my pledge to you, my leader, that I will protect, guide, and give my sword to Rose MacLaren."

A bright shaft of light pierced the night sky, sealing the bargain Liam had made with Aidan.

Relief washed over Aidan. His beloved was now safe. With a sigh, Aidan released his hold. "Thank you. I am ready to depart."

Aidan gave one parting glance over his shoulder to the woman who held his heart. *Love you, mo ghrá. I promise to return.*

In a sliver of light, he vanished, along with all the other warriors.

Instead of arriving within the Fae council chamber, he stood on the steps outside the Crystal Cathedral. Aidan lifted his head and viewed the council members standing under an awning before the entrance. As he glanced around, he noted the absence of the other Fenian Warriors. Surrounded by an entire garrison of Fae and royal guards, Aidan allowed the gentle spring breeze to cool his burning temper.

Fae council member, Seneca, stepped forward. "Aidan Kerrigan, Leader of the Fenian Warriors, from the Royal House of Óg , you are hereby—"

"Forgive the interruption, but why am I treated to a mockery of a trial *outside* the Fae council chamber?" demanded Aidan.

"It was by my order," stated King Ansgar, emerging from the shadows of a column.

Aidan regarded his king and once friend coolly.

"All must be a witness to your crime within the human world," continued the king.

Slowly, Aidan looked over his shoulder. Did the entire kingdom come forward to observe his public trial? Returning his attention beyond the king, he searched for the one familiar face he knew he'd brought hurt and shame to the most. *Nuala.*

Instantly, Aidan severed the mental link to his sister. He could not allow her to suffer any more pain. If she was not present, then she did not wish to watch or feel his pain.

King Ansgar descended the stairs. As he drew near, he leaned near Aidan. "Tell me I am wrong. Give me something to lessen your punishment. Was it merely a dalliance with the human female?"

"I cannot lie to protect myself. And you know the truth already. I am in love with Rose MacLaren, a human. I have since claimed her."

A blow of power slammed against Aidan's chest, and he slumped to the ground. The crowd gasped behind him. Unable to stand by himself, Aidan had no choice but to allow the two guards to pull him up.

Aidan glared at the king, seeing the rage flashing

within his eyes. "Banish me and be done with this," he rasped out.

The king's voice hardened ruthlessly. "You deem it that simple? Banishment for your crime? No, Aidan Kerrigan. What you have done is violate one of our most important laws since we descended underground. All power granted to you as the leader shall be removed. Afterwards, your body will undergo a transformation to eradicate any longevity. I cannot remove the blood of your heritage, but I can shorten your life strings."

A tendril of fear snaked inside his body. Why would he inflict such a harsh punishment? Only one thought illuminated. *To be made an example for the entire kingdom by giving me extreme torture, so that another avoids the same mistake.*

The king stood back. "Strip his shirt," he ordered.

"King Ansgar, should you not let another?" asked Seneca, her eyes growing wide.

He silenced her with a flick of his wrist and motioned to the guards.

Aidan's gaze never wavered from Ansgar. When his shirt was ripped from his body, Aidan held his arms outward. "Do what must be done."

The king drew forth a silver dagger and placed it over Aidan's chest. Blinding hot pain seared across his skin, removing all his Fenian markings and power. He clenched his jaw so tight, Aidan feared it would snap. Minutes ticked by in agonizing torture as he fought the bile heaving from his stomach. Beads of sweat broke out along his brow, and he blinked in an attempt to thwart the dizziness. As the last blue marking vanished, he drew in a sharp hiss. His breathing came out in short gasps, but Aidan refused to show any weakness.

"Aidan Kerrigan, *former* leader of the Fenian Warriors, from the Royal House of Óg, you are hereby renounced of all power, rights, and honor associated with your name! Once your final punishment is concluded, your banishment will be swift. You will be exiled from the Fae realm, if death does not claim you first." The king gestured toward the guards. "Remove him to the underground chamber."

Shards of pain throbbed behind his temples as they vanished in a vortex of lights. Emerging inside the chamber, Aidan continued to fight the waves of nausea. Each wrist was shackled in a crystal cuff against a black jasper and onyx wall. With no light above and the ground covered in the same stone, Aidan had to rely on his own inner strength. He knew all about this room and its horrifying affects.

Complete and utter solitude in a chamber that would alter him totally.

His rage intensified and a great roar escaped from his very soul. "Fools, all of you! Love is the greatest power!"

The air swirled in a tempest around Aidan, making it difficult to breathe. Clenching and unclenching his hands, he waited for the first slice of excruciating pain to enter his body. When it did, he vomited everything he had in his stomach onto the ground.

****

Swarms of vipers ate away at his flesh, reminding him of dragon fire and other battles from long ago. Where was his sword? Or the others to help him defeat these monsters? He shook his head, but the pain only intensified. He'd dared not utter a scream, or they would strike out more viciously than before.

Onward they dug their claws into his body, causing him to slam his head back against the wall. Only once did he crave for death's blessed blow. And when he called out for her hand, another reached forward. Her silver-blonde tresses graced a lovely body as she approached. Cupping his face, she whispered soothing words, and he breathed in the soft scents of flowers and spices. In that briefest of moments, Aidan recalled his promise to his beloved.

"*Rose*," he uttered in a garbled voice and lowered his head, trying to bring forth her image once again.

Golden light spilled inside the chamber and Aidan cried out in pain, closing his eyes at the intensity.

Soft fingers brushed across his temple, forcing the pain to recede. "It is only temporary, Aidan, but use this time we have together wisely to regain some strength."

He blinked, trying to focus. "Too bright," he complained and closed his eyes again.

"You're speaking as a Fae and not as a warrior, *my brother*."

"Nuala," he croaked out, opening his eyes. When his vision cleared, he sighed heavily. "You should not be here."

She snorted in disgust and wiped away the matted hair from his face. "As if they could keep me away."

"Is the king aware you're down here in this pit of horrors?"

"Yes," she stated with conviction. "It was a parting gift for both of us. After today—" She swallowed and looked away.

"I am sorry," he uttered softly.

She glanced sharply at him and placed a palm upon

his chest. "Do not be, Aidan. Remember, each path led to destruction."

"Or change," he countered.

"True." Smiling weakly, she added, "But love has found you, no matter who she is."

He nodded slowly. "Yes. But I do not agree with this form of slow methodical punishment to purge my body."

A tear trickled down her cheek. "Nor I. At present, I am not speaking with Ansgar. I argued fiercely against this barbaric form of punishment. The Fae council regarded your life as forfeit and wanted the guards to end your life above. This was the only alternative form of punishment they'd considered. Regardless, I can share that your actions have fulfilled a promising prophecy. In time, I pray you come to terms with how this was done."

Aidan laughed and immediately regretted the action. Great spasms wracked his body, and he coughed up blood. Again, Nuala placed cool fingers across his brow.

"It is almost over," she whispered.

"How long have I been here?"

"Two weeks, one day."

"Over a month in the human world," he admitted gravely.

"If she loves you, Aidan, she will wait."

"Rose's love extends within this chamber. I have felt her essence."

Nuala cupped his cheeks. "Then her love is honorable and steadfast. She has my love—always." Stepping back, Nuala held out a small vial and removed the stopper. "Drink this, Aidan. It will diminish part of the pain, allowing this procedure to hasten to completion."

An inner strength of power seemed to grow inside Aidan. Doing his best to straighten from the wall, he shook his head slowly. "No. If I become weaker, I might succumb to the alluring temptation to call forth the barge to *Tir na nÓg*, ending my life."

"But the elixir will only lessen your pain, enabling you to continue," she pleaded, resealing the vial.

Aidan fisted his hands. His spark of anger gave him inner fortitude. "I want to be fully conscious when the last remnant of power is stripped from my body."

Gazing upward, Nuala leaned her head to the side as if listening to another. "My time here has ended," she whispered.

Grief and despair flooded Aidan. He gazed upon his beautiful sister one last time. "Your beauty and wisdom are a boon to our people. I shall miss you and our conversations."

Nuala lowered her head, her eyes blazing like a trillion stars as she stared at him. "If ever you should need me, seek out the well near Balleycove. Wild violets are sprinkled around the stone in protection. Call out my name and I will hear your words, dear brother."

Stunned, he asked, "How do you know about my home?"

Her smile was one filled with sadness. "I gathered my information well about your life above. Never shall we be parted. No matter who rules the kingdom, our blood ties are more powerful. Remember, Aidan, all that you've been taught prior to becoming a Fenian Warrior. This room may alter the very fabric of you, but not your blood. You are a Fae, descended from the

Royal House of Óg. Your deeds and name shall be *remembered*."

On a choked sob, Nuala embraced Aidan and placed a kiss on his cheek. "I will love you forever. Be well—live the life you yearn to have with Rose."

In a soft blur of multi-colors, his sister vanished, leaving him to his misery and torture.

Chapter Twenty-Two

*"Even a beautiful flower possesses the ability to bring about death."*

~*Society of the Thistle*

Rose paced furiously around the giant oak on the Hill of Tara, surveying its bark for any signs of decay or weak areas. She scanned high and low, but found no evidence of flaws in the massive giant. Picking up a fallen tree limb, she smacked the branch against the rough bark.

"Give me your blade, Lily."

"For the tenth time, I will not have you engage in a destructive manner against the tree. Did you not tell me you made a promise not to harm this ancient oak?" Her sister huddled beneath a plaid on the ground. Pulling forth a thermos, Lily proceeded to pour some hot liquid into a cup. "Here, drink some tea to help calm your nerves."

Rose gave the tree a passing glance as she went to her sister's side. Slumping down on the blanket next to her, she draped part of the plaid wrap around her shoulders. "Bloody cold day for summer," she muttered, taking the offered cup.

"We should not be out here," complained Lily, replacing the lid on the thermos. "How many days have you visited this spot?"

Rose sipped the warm liquid, letting it settle within her body. "Two months."

"What do you expect to accomplish?"

Glancing at her sister, Rose saw the skepticism across her features. "Still having doubts about who Aidan Kerrigan is?"

Lily hugged her knees to her chest. "No. I fully believe everything you've shared. I told you there was something different about the man the first time I shook his hand. I want to know how being out here will help to bring him back. Since this is a sacred tree to the Fae, I don't think it's wise to do it harm. Furthermore, why do you believe Aidan will come through here from his world?"

Rose held the warm cup to her chest and gazed outward. "I can't explain it, Lily. I actually feel closer to him when I'm here." She swallowed and let out a sigh. "I need to be here when he returns."

"From what you've shared, it may be many months. What if they don't let him back into our world? What if his punishment is to remain forever locked below?"

The tea left a bitter taste in her mouth, and Rose tossed the remainder in her cup onto the ground. "I *refuse* to think on those scenarios."

"You always were the stubborn one in the family," scoffed Lily, lifting the cup from Rose's hand.

Lowering her head, Rose fought the wave of emotions. Each day, she battled the onslaught of tears—going from wracking sobs to quiet sniffling. Her eyes were constantly red and puffy. Food no longer tempted her. On the contrary, she had trouble keeping anything down. "Please Lily, only positive thoughts and prayers."

Her sister placed a comforting hand on her head. "Then let us offer up another prayer to Mother Danu and Brigid for his safe return to us."

Rose exhaled softly and raised her head. "Yes—thank you."

Her sister's voice lifted in a melodic lit. "Our beloved Brigid of the triple flame and daughter of the Mother, hear our heartfelt prayer to watch over Aidan Kerrigan. Ease his suffering and comfort him in his time of darkness." She nodded to Rose.

"Permit my love to enter his heart and keep him strong. Remind him of our bond during his long days and nights. Comfort him…" Rose trailed off, choking back the words. Wiping a hand over her eyes, she quickly added, "Until he returns to me. We thank you for your healing and wisdom."

Lily smiled. "Good. I'm sorry, but I can only stay one more day, and then I must return home."

Reaching for her sister's hand, Rose squeezed it lightly. "You have no idea how grateful I am that you halted *everything* these past few weeks to be here with me."

She nudged Rose. "A sister's bond is powerful, too."

"Have you shared anything about Aidan with the others?"

"Only Maeve. I think it's best if we keep a tight circle around the true Aidan Kerrigan. Even though we all believe in the old ways, this might be too much for some of them."

Stretching her legs out, Rose nodded and removed the plaid covering. Securing it more firmly over her sister's shoulders, she focused her attention on the tree. "He will come back to me. He must. And then we'll have a proper wedding ceremony."

"We'll include a handfasting," suggested Lily. "We'll hold it at the Society or wherever you want."

"Yes." Images of their lovemaking and words of love they declared to one another came back in a rush. Rose clasped a hand over her heart. "However, in our hearts and souls, we are wed. Forever."

"When you do return to his home, start making lists of everything for the ceremony. This will help to keep your mind from wondering what's happening." Lily huddled more under the covering. "I never did ask, but how is his home managed without staff or anyone to care for the horses?"

"His castle," corrected Rose. "All done with magic. The animals have a never-ending supply of food and water."

Lily chuckled. "And the man has *two* castles. Is he rich?"

Snapping her attention to her sister, Rose gaped at her in astonishment. "I don't know," she mumbled.

"Then let him pay for everything."

Rose narrowed her eyes. "You're wicked."

"Aren't we both?"

"Of course not." Rose winked and embraced her sister. "Thanks, sis, again. I love you."

"And I love you." When Lily drew back, she frowned. "Please don't spend the entire day out here. Come every other day and only for a few hours. This is draining you."

Rose bit her lip and looked away. A squirrel scurried around the base of the tree, and she watched its playful antics until it dashed up the trunk.

"Promise me, Rose," demanded Lily sternly.

"I promise." She may have said the words out loud to her sister, but Rose knew in her heart, she could not make the commitment to stay away.

Never from the Fae who held her heart.

****

Thunder crashed over the rolling hills, inching its way across the sky toward the Hill of Tara. Rose huddled against the base of the giant oak, bringing her bent knees to her chest. Her sister's words from a week ago came slamming back into her.

The moment Lily's car had been packed, and she gave her tearful farewells, Rose found the keys to Aidan's jeep and returned to Dublin. Quickly securing a hostel, she traveled to the site daily. She no longer concerned herself with making the long arduous trek back to *Croí Dragon*.

Now with the threat of an approaching storm, Lily's words of caution about daily visits became her conscience.

Rose leaned her chin on her bent knees. "Sorry, sis. But I cannot leave him."

An ache of longing filled her. "Can you hear me, Aidan? How I have missed you." She placed her palms on the ground. "Sense my heartbeat. Feel my love. Come home to me."

The wind lashed across her face, mocking her. Or was it the Fae?

Shoving a fist into the air, she shouted, "Our love is real. Powerful! I used to love the Fae. Now I despise you for what you've done to us."

Her despair turned to anger, matching the thunder,

and Rose stood. She brushed the leaves and dirt from her clothes. Rubbing a hand over her forehead, she tried to ease the dull pain behind her eyes. Lack of sleep and little food were ebbing away at her patience. She wanted to scream at these people. Confront them in their own world. Regardless of their vast power and knowledge, her respect for them had diminished.

Turning abruptly on the tree, Rose pounded her fists against the rough bark. "Does *anyone* hear my pleas? Do you sit on your mighty thrones and laugh at us humans? What have you done with the Fae who I love?"

The deafening roar of thunder silenced her shouts, and she glanced over her shoulder. Ominous dark clouds spiraled above her. She swallowed as she slowly moved away from the shelter of the tree.

The wind grew fierce, howling like a banshee. Her braids whipped across her face, and Rose pulled the hood of her coat over her head. Lightning flashed all around her, leaving her skin prickling from the energy. Clenching her fists by her side, she stood in defiance of the approaching storm.

Had the Fae heard her rants? Steadily moving forward, she stared at the darkening sky and halted. Her love for Aidan held her rooted to the ground, daring anyone to cast her aside.

With a thunderous boom, the ground beneath her shook violently. Rose stumbled forward, landing on her knees. Fury took over her senses and she quickly stood. "How dare you!"

When the first drop of rain splattered across her cheek, Rose shook her head. "You can unleash the mightiest storm, but I'm not leaving!"

"Cease bellowing at the Fae and help me!" demanded a familiar male voice behind her.

Turning abruptly, Rose gasped. Liam MacGregor was going through her belongings, but it was the man at the base of the tree who caught her attention.

"Aidan!" she screamed, running to his twisted form. Slumping to the ground beside him, she feared to touch him. His battered body was mottled with bruises, and his hair matted against his face.

"Where are your car keys?" shouted Liam.

She barely registered the man's voice. "What?"

"Keys," he demanded.

Digging into her coat pocket, she fumbled for them. "Here."

After snatching them from her, he sprinted away.

Rose placed a hand on Aidan's forehead. Heat flared into her skin. "I'm here, my love." Swallowing the lump in her throat, she swiftly gathered her items. Removing the plaid blanket from her bag, she wrapped it over Aidan to protect him from the torrential downpour.

Her fingers trembled as she pushed away the ebony locks from his face. Shoving a fist into her mouth to stifle her cry of protest, Rose fought the bile in her stomach from heaving onto the ground. His features were drawn and ashen. Gone was the mighty warrior she knew. It was as if he had aged tremendously the last few months.

And her heart grew heavy with guilt. "They did this all because you loved me."

The sound of an approaching vehicle snapped Rose out of her anguish. Liam had somehow managed to bring the vehicle up the hill. When he appeared in a flash in front of her, she blinked. He firmly gripped her shoulders. "No questions, Rose. Not until we get him back to the *Croí Dragon*. We have to get away from here."

She gave him a curt nod and stood. After Liam had secured Aidan in the vehicle, Rose dumped everything in the back and got in the passenger side. Her hands shook as he maneuvered the car away from the giant oak. Several times, lightning seared across their path, challenging their mad exodus. Yet, the farther they traveled, the more the storm lessened. Glancing out the side mirror, the entire Hill of Tara seemed to bear the brunt of the tempest.

When the first tear slipped down her cheek, Rose promptly brushed it away. There would be none. Not in front of Liam. No, she would not let the man she loved hear her weeping. Rose would harbor no weakness. She would become Aidan's strength and help to heal him.

For the next several hours, Rose made a mental list of all the supplies—from healing herbs, teas, broths, and any bandages she might need for Aidan. And when the gates of *Croí Dragon* appeared, she had steeled her nerves.

Liam drove the vehicle up to the front entrance. They both hastily exited, and Rose pulled out the keys to the castle. She watched as he lifted Aidan from the car as if he weighed nothing.

Once inside, Liam ascended the stairs. Dumping her bag in the entryway, Rose followed him to Aidan's chambers. She swiftly removed her coat and shoes.

After he had settled Aidan back against the pillows, Liam stood back.

Rose scanned his body. "Are there any wounds that

need tending to?" Her voice betrayed her turbulent emotions.

"No."

Unable to hold back the tide of questions, she turned on Liam. "What did they do to him? Where are the tattoos on his chest and back?"

Liam visibly swallowed. "They altered him."

"*Altered*?" she hissed. "In what way?"

Liam's eyes flashed with fury. "Sadistic and agonizing torture. He no longer is the Fae he used to be. What's left is his soul and blood. They stripped him of everything. The only visible signs left are the markings on his arms. Those denote his *former* royal house."

Rose clutched her stomach. *No weakness. Not now.* She stiffened in an attempt to hold back the tears. "Remove his pants and help me to get him under the covers."

Without a word, Liam assisted her.

Brushing his hair back, Rose placed a kiss on his forehead. "Rest, my love." She lowered herself next to him on the bed. Taking his hand within hers, she willed the love she bore for the Fae into his body. *Feel my touch. Hear my words. Let my love heal you.*

Rising slowly, she turned to face Liam. "I need you to do me a huge favor."

"By Fae law I am not allowed to be here."

Rose pointed to the door. "Then leave us! I'm sick to death of hearing about your damn laws."

Blowing out a frustrated breath, Liam shifted his stance. "What do you need?"

"I don't care how you manage to get there, but I require the healing knowledge of one of the members of the Society."

"There is no cure, Rose," he admitted hesitantly. "I'm shocked he's still alive. No Fae has ever survived."

Fisting her hands on her hips, she glared at Liam. "Then let Aidan be the first Fae to survive. Because he will."

He glanced at Aidan's lifeless body. "Whom do you need?"

"There is a woman by the name of Aelish. I require her skills—"

"No," he stated emphatically. "Not possible."

Her lips thinned with irritation. Liam held his hand up, halting the biting words she was about to fling at him.

"The woman, Aelish, is a Fae. Her title is Master Apothecary. Furthermore, I believe she was responsible for informing the Fae council about his *liaison* with you."

"Liaison," she echoed tersely.

Crossing the room, Rose leaned her head on the cool glass. Her mind was dizzy with the new information. "Betrayal even among my friends," she mumbled, unable to fathom that one of their dearest women was not who she portrayed herself to be.

"I pray one day you can forgive me," uttered Aelish softly.

Stunned to hear the woman's voice, Rose turned around slowly. Anger replaced sorrow. "You lived with us. Ate at our table. Held our quaking bodies during sorrowful times. *Why*?"

Aelish clasped her hands in front of her, but made no attempt to enter the room. "It was not my intention to bring about this destruction. I merely stated my concerns to an elder. The knowledge was sent to the council."

Confusion marred Liam's features. "You did not seek out the Fae council?"

Sorrow reflected within Aelish's eyes. "No. I admit to being angry with Aidan and saying harsh words, but I did not wish to cause him harm."

Rose moved away from the window. "This does not explain why you lived with us. For what purpose, Aelish?"

"My duties are to guide those with certain gifts. Your sister, Lily, has a powerful connection to the land. One which extends to you. Regardless, I am Lily's guardian. In truth, I have come to love all the women at the Society." Aelish approached. "If you will permit me, I can assist you in Aidan's healing."

"You cannot," warned Liam, stepping in front of Aidan's bed.

Aelish jabbed a finger into the warrior's chest. "Might I remind you that you've already broken a law by removing him from the Tree of Life?"

Liam grimaced. "Rose would have been caught in the fury of the storm's path."

Crossing her arms over her chest, Aelish tilted her head to the side. "Am I correct in believing you are now Rose's guardian?"

Liam nodded slowly, and Rose gasped.

"My last solemn vow given to my leader before they led him away," he confessed.

Rose's mind throbbed with all this new information. She had no time to consider everything. All energy had to be spent in saving the man she loved.

Going to Aidan's bedside, she stared at him. If his

injuries were internal, what could they do? Reaching for his hand, Rose brought it to her chest. "What can we do, Aelish?"

"I have brought herbs from the Fae realm and those from Aidan's garden. We can tend to his body, but I fear his mind is where the battle is ongoing."

Glancing sharply at the woman, Rose feared to ask the question. "*Battle*?"

"The one between life and death. Aidan will either accept this new transformation or succumb to the *Land of Forever*."

Chapter Twenty-Three

*"A warrior can train and hone his body as sharp as his sword. Yet, his mind must be far more superior."*
*~Edicts of the Fenian Warriors*

"As the lush rolling vista spread out in a carpet of emerald green, I ran barefoot across the heady bouquet of floral scents, which filled my being." Rose closed the large book and shoved it across the bed. "What a nauseating scene, right? Would you prefer a story on an epic war battle? Swords slashing, guns blazing? Taking out the enemy and rescuing the fair maiden?"

Rose huffed out a breath and removed her reading glasses. Stretching out alongside Aidan, she placed her hand on his chest, allowing the rhythm of his heartbeat to soothe her inner turmoil.

"Two weeks is long enough, my love. You have not budged, cried out, twitched—*nothing*." Her voice caught, and she rolled over onto her back.

Fatigue, worry, and pure exhaustion had become her companions. Each day, Rose fought the wave of emotions. Battling against hope and doubt, she and Aelish continued to care for Aidan. Liam returned daily at dusk, asking the same question about his friend. And the answer remained the same. No change.

If not for the warmth of his skin, Rose would have believed him to be a corpse. Even his breathing was barely notable. Nevertheless, defeat was not an option, and she breathed the very words across Aidan's face every day.

Rose rolled over and caressed the dark shadow of his beard, which now required daily shaving. "I do not mind this new look, Aidan. You're sinfully seductive, reminding me of a pirate. You may have to keep this look when you awake." After placing a soft kiss on his lips, she left the bed and wandered over to the window arch.

She traced a path over the stained glass. "Did you know it's summer? You missed the Midsummer festival, but no worries, we shall attend next year."

Opening the window, Rose inhaled deeply. The air was warm, and no threat of rain was in the forecast. Shielding her eyes, she glanced in front of the trees that bordered the front of Aidan's castle.

"What the bloody hell?" She leaned forward and let out a small gasp. As far as she could see, Fae stood with their fists clenched over their hearts. She lost count after twenty.

Quickly dashing out of the chamber, Rose almost collided with Aelish. "Sorry. Do you know those men outside?"

"Yes."

"Are they here to take Aidan away?"

Fear seized Rose's heart. Without giving a chance for the woman to answer her, she ran down the stairs and out into the courtyard. As she came to a halt at the end of the gates, she fisted her hands on her hips. There were so many of them and only one of her. Her courage and determination were like a rock inside her.

"You can't have him! Leave this place!" Her

resolve unwavering, she took a step forward. "You are not welcome."

"Rose, they are not here to take him away," uttered Liam, coming alongside her.

She glanced sharply at the man and gestured outward with her hand. "Then why are they here? And so *many*?"

Sadness reflected within his eyes. "These Fenian Warriors are waiting to *escort* him to *Tir na nÓg*."

Lights blurred Rose's vision. Wiping a trembling hand across her forehead, she refused to acknowledge this was happening. Taking a deep breath in, she released it slowly and straightened. "No," she declared. "He will not go. He will not die!"

The pain was far too great to shed tears in front of all these men. On a choked sob, Rose fled down through a rough path sloping toward the river. The sting of branches slapped against her face, but she gave no care. Onward she traveled, stumbling over tree roots until she came to the edge of the water.

Letting out an anguished cry of grief, Rose bent her head and collapsed to the ground.

"There is nothing you can do." Liam knelt down beside her.

"There is always a plan," she mumbled, refusing to believe the man she loved with all her soul would die. For if he did, Rose feared she'd be unable to handle the pain of his loss.

"The land here is powerful to our people. He is too connected in Ireland and his spirit longs to be free," protested Liam, reaching for her hand.

She drew back, realizing he was correct. Recalling everything Aidan had told her about the Fae and

Ireland, an idea blossomed and grew. No wonder he wasn't able to heal here.

Rose lifted her head and wiped a shaky hand over her brow. "You can tell the other Fae to say their parting words of farewell and then leave. Aidan Kerrigan will not require an escort."

"*Rose*," pleaded Liam.

Pointing a warning finger at him, she ordered, "You may stay, since I need your aid in this next plan to save Aidan's life." Standing on shaking limbs, Rose retreated back along the path.

Liam groaned and stood. Running alongside her, he asked, "What is this plan of yours?"

As they entered the castle, Rose glanced up at the dragon statue with a renewed sense of hope. "We must *remove* him from Ireland to his other home in Scotland."

Liam rubbed a hand over his chin in thought. "I never thought of this solution."

Rose laid a gentle hand on his arm. "We must try. I refuse to give up. Aidan would expect nothing less from us and not this defeatist attitude, right?"

Smiling, Liam nodded. "You are a mighty warrior, Rose MacLaren."

"Rose *Kerrigan*," she corrected.

Aelish stood at the top of the stairs. "It is a grand idea, and I shall prepare everything if we are departing for Scotland."

"Let me pack my belongings and book a passage on the ferry. I'm assuming you'll transport him magically to Balleycove?" asked Rose.

"Wrong," countered Liam. "You are coming with us as well."

257

Her eyes grew wide. "With magic?"

"Of course. The only link to this world keeping Aidan alive is you, Rose. Anything can keep you from making the journey—from weather to traffic."

The thought of traveling magically in a matter of seconds made her queasy. She clutched her stomach. "I think I'm going to be ill."

Aelish descended the stairs and took her arm. "I will give you something to calm you before we depart."

"No. I'll keep my eyes closed."

The woman clucked her tongue in disapproval. "Do you not trust me?"

"Most definitely," Rose blurted out. "But I'd rather keep my wits."

Within an hour, they were all huddled in Aidan's chambers. Rose took a sweeping glance around. Everything in the castle had been secured. Sadness filled her at having to leave their beautiful home—a place where they had made love countless times and which brought them both so much joy.

"Did you forget something?" asked Aelish, placing a comforting hand on her shoulder.

"Why do I sense we'll never return to Ireland and *Croí Dragon*," muttered Rose, staring at Aidan's limp body on the bed.

"Does your gift of sight extend to the future?"

"It never has before," admitted Rose. Going to Aidan's side, she brushed her fingers over his brow. "Nevertheless, I firmly believe we're doing what's best for him by leaving."

"I concur. Ready?" asked Liam, approaching the bed.

Rose nodded.

Liam lifted Aidan's body into his arms and for a brief moment, Rose ached to see any response from him.

"Clutch my arm," stated Aelish.

Rose took a hold of the woman's arm and closed her eyes.

"Remember to breathe, Rose."

"I will."

Dizziness swept through Rose as the ground beneath her floated away. She dared not open her eyes for fear she'd faint. In seconds, her feet touched the ground.

Aelish squeezed her fingers. "We are at Balleycove."

"Great Goddess! How amazing. And we're inside the castle." Rose glanced in all directions within Aidan's chambers, marveling at how swiftly they got to Scotland.

Aelish chuckled as she deposited her bag by the table.

After Liam settled Aidan into his bed, he went to Rose and grasped her hands. "I must return to the Fae realm. If you need anything, have Aelish send for me."

Rose swallowed. "Thank you so much. Will you offer prayers for him in your world?"

He smiled fully. "Most assuredly." Releasing her hands, Liam inclined his head toward Aelish. In a whisper of light, he vanished.

Rose shivered. "I swear it doesn't matter how many times I've seen him disappear, I will never get used to this form of magic."

Shrugging, the woman moved toward the door. "Magic for us is as simple as breathing. We carry it within us as you do certain parts inside your body."

Rose went and sat next to Aidan. She gripped his hand, placing it against her cheek. "How will you deal with this loss, my love?"

"Aidan is one of the strongest Fae I've ever known," confessed Aelish. "His love was strong enough to get him this far, so anything else will not be so difficult for him to deal with when he awakens."

"But if what you stated is true about magic and the Fae…" Rose paused and placed a kiss in his palm. After lowering his hand over his chest, she stood.

"Do not allow the black cloud of death to linger in this room."

She knew the woman was correct. Rose had to focus on the positive, even though the weight of the past several months were beginning to take a toll on her body and mind. "Would you like some tea? Food?" offered Rose.

Smiling, Aelish wandered to her side. "Let me go prepare you a meal."

Rose took the woman's hand. "I think I can manage a simple task."

The woman cupped her cheek. "Slip into something more comfortable, and I'll bring a tray up to you. In the morn, you can fix your own meal. When a human is transported it is vastly different than for a Fae. It can weaken you for a time."

"Thank you."

As soon as Aelish departed the room, Rose rummaged through her clothing and pulled out a short sleeveless nightgown. She stripped off all her clothing and slipped the silky garment over her head. Letting out a sigh, Rose went to the window. Unlatching the clasp, she pushed it outward.

"Bonny Scotland…We are home, Aidan. Here there is a rugged beauty."

After saying a silent prayer to the Goddess, she crawled into bed beside him.

"I love you, my husband," she murmured on a yawn.

Within seconds, Rose slid into the abyss of deep slumber.

\*\*\*\*

Tapping the pen to her chin, Rose contemplated what else she could add to her growing list of what she wanted for her handfasting to Aidan. It had become her morning ritual for the past several weeks. Afterwards, she wandered Balleycove, surveying all nineteen rooms, a massive library, enclosed nursery, kitchen gardens, orchard, stables, and what looked like a sparring camp. What she found fascinating was the grand room containing a huge collection of armory— from swords, shields, axes, a variety of bows, equipped with arrows, and other unique blades. Some were studded with precious gems, but the ones Rose admired greatly were the giant claymores.

"I want you to teach me archery, Aidan. Then you can show me how to handle a blade." She pursed her lips in concentration. "I've never mentioned that I have this fascination with ancient weaponry." Smiling faintly, she added, "Yes. Another *fascination*."

Rose looked over her shoulder at Aidan. "You missed the feast day on the first of August."

Dropping her pen, she stretched her arms over her head and stood. "It really is a lovely day, my love. Won't you wake up?"

She scooted away from the desk and went to Aidan's side. In recent days, his coloring had faded. It was as if he remained in a cocoon of suspended time, unable to break free from whatever hell he was experiencing. Yet, even after all this time, he maintained his massive physique. Aelish told her it would be the last to diminish, when or if he passed over to the realm of forever.

Sitting down on the bed next to him, she blew out a frustrated breath and pinched the bridge of her nose. Her grief was becoming a lodestone on her chest. Tears stung her eyes, and she blinked. Her resolve to remain strong was failing miserably. She even thought about calling her sister to come and assist her when they first arrived, but she swiftly banished the idea. Rose didn't want the others to know about Aidan's condition, and Aelish was in agreement.

Time was slipping away as surely as the mists over the hills behind Balleycove.

Rose reached for his hand and placed it over her abdomen. Unable to hold back the tide of emotions, she let the tears fall freely. "I'm tired, Aidan. Really, *really* tired. I need you to come back to me. It's important." She paused, biting her lower lip, uncertainly filling her. "This is not how I wanted to share my beautiful news with you. But I refuse to let you go without knowing what you'll be leaving. We are going to have a daughter, Aidan Kerrigan. I have seen her in a vision. In a beacon of light she came to me." Choking on sobs, she continued, "If you won't fight for us, fight for her, Aidan."

Her grief consumed her, and for the first time, Rose let the pain of everything take over. Great wracking sobs broke free, and she curled up against his body. Was this her final goodbye to the Fae who held her heart? How could she go on without him?

She wept until there were no more tears. Until every ounce of sorrow left her spirit.

When she was drained of all her pent-up emotions, Rose hiccupped, but refused to leave Aidan's side. Weariness seeped into her bones and spirit, leaving her even more exhausted and empty. There was nothing more she could do or say.

Rose concentrated on the soothing rise and fall of Aidan's breathing and remained by his side for the entire day. Sleep did not beckon her as she waited for him to take his last breath. Their plan had failed. She gently placed her arm over his chest.

Once the last ray of light slipped out of the chamber, Rose whispered the words she thought never to say, "I release you from your pain, my love. Go find the light of *Tir na nÓg*. Be well and watch over me and your daughter. I only ask that you come for me when my time has ended here."

Her heart pounded fiercely, hating what she was doing. Nevertheless, she could not let Aidan continue in this lingering state of torment. Rose had no idea the pain he might be suffering. She was being selfish.

Lacing her fingers with his, Rose placed their joined hands in the middle of his chest and lowered her head. "I shall love *you* until the last star shines in the universe."

"*Mo ghrá.*"

The familiar burr of his voice sent a tremor of shockwave throughout Rose. Was she dreaming? Had he already crossed the void to the afterlife?

The blood pounded in her ears, and slowly Rose lifted her head to gaze into the dazzling lavender eyes she had always adored. "*Aidan*?" Her question barely audible.

"Who else did you expect," he uttered softly.

"Aidan!" she blurted out. Releasing her hand, she cupped his face and kissed him tenderly. "Oh, *Aidan*, you came back to me."

"I was never far away, beloved. Merely…healing."

She hugged him fiercely. Tears she thought spent returned with a vengeance. After several moments, she wiped her eyes. "Can you move? Do you hurt anywhere? Would you like some water?" she asked between bouts of hiccupping.

"I have no pain, though weak. Water, please." He lifted his hand and reached for a strand of her hair. "How I have missed you, *mo ghrá*."

And when Aidan smiled at her, Rose melted at the sight.

Her lip trembled. "And I you, my dear *warrior* husband."

He chuckled softly, and she collapsed against his chest, letting the light of happiness fill her soul.

Chapter Twenty-Four

*"I once stood on the shores of Tir na nÓg, but the song of love lured me back to the land of the living."*
*~Chronicles of Aidan Kerrigan*

Surveying his gorgeous wife in the gardens, Aidan leaned against the stone pillar. He breathed in the late summer air and relished in the energy of the land beneath the soles of his bare feet.

He had spied Rose earlier in the day from his window attempting to coax a rabbit from the vegetable garden. Hours later, she continued to work and chatter to the animal. Little did she know the rabbit had a burrow and was content to live and eat from the full bounty of vegetables. If she thought to banish him from the area, she would be the loser in this sparring match.

Even a simple task of watching her brought him joy. He'd heard her words daily from the haze of life and death. It was those very words that kept him reaching out toward her and not retreating to the other side. Though the pain was excruciating, he fought to return. In truth, it was her final words when she spoke of their child that brought him fully to consciousness. However, since that day over two weeks ago, Rose had not mentioned the child she now carried in her womb, and he pondered why she kept the knowledge to herself.

"The battle has been fought before and Sir Rabbit

has declared victory," he announced, enjoying the view of her bent over as she snipped some chives.

Rose gave a startled cry and dropped her basket. Turning around abruptly, she glared at him. "What are you doing outside? And how did you manage the stairs?" Pointing to his bare feet, she added tersely, "And without shoes? No shirt?"

"My strength has returned tremendously, thanks to the healing care of you and Aelish. And since the air is warm there is no need to wear clothing and shoes." Though, he would never admit to gritting in pain as he stumbled down the last few stairs.

She eyed him skeptically and sauntered toward him. "So there was no pain?"

"Slight," he lied.

"Tired of your bed?"

He arched a brow seductively. "You were not there naked beside me."

She teased her tongue out along her upper lip and stepped closer. "You know the rules."

"I have no *rules* when it comes to you." Without giving her time to protest, Aidan reached out and grasped her around the waist. Crushing her to his chest, he nuzzled the soft spot below her ear, inhaling her floral scent mixed with the earth.

Rose gripped his shoulders with a moan. He plundered her mouth, devouring the sweetness he craved.

After several moments, he broke free. "Let me make love to you."

She gave him a skeptical look. "Are you strong enough to carry me upstairs?"

"That was not the bargain," he argued, cupping her

heavy breast through the flimsy material of her blouse. He lowered his head against her forehead. "If I was able to make my way down the stairs, you can allow me to give you pleasure."

"As much as I have missed you, I believe we should wait." Rose pulled out of his embrace and wandered over to a bench beneath the shade of an elm tree. She patted the place beside her.

Strolling to her side, Aidan refused to sit. He might be in a weakened condition, but he refused to let this pampering continue. Clasping his hands behind his back, he let his gaze travel out beyond the garden. The trees swayed gently in the breeze.

She tugged on his pants. "I have something I'd like to tell you and don't want to hurt my neck by looking up at you."

Aidan smirked, doing his best to keep the humor from showing, but failing miserably. "Then stand beside me. I have been in a prone position far too long."

"It's good to see your stubbornness has not diminished with your time in a coma," she chided.

He lowered his head to look upon her beautiful features. "Nothing about me has changed, except for my magic. My strength is returning. You were wise in taking me away from Ireland."

Rose stood on top of the bench and wrapped her arms around his neck. "I know you'll miss Ireland, but what about the magic?"

He sighed heavily, noting the wariness in her tone. "No. Though it will be an adjustment."

Trailing a finger across his torc, she then placed her palm on his chest, "I'm glad a few of your tattoos have remained."

"The ones on my arms denote my lineage. They can never be removed."

She exhaled softly and glanced away.

Taking a hold of her braid, he slowly unraveled the mass.

"What are you doing?"

"Waiting for you to make your announcement, so I can carry you up to our bed chamber."

Rose tried to push away, but he held her firmly in his grasp as he continued to unravel her hair.

"I don't know what you're referring to." Her face took on a rosy glow as she stared at him.

"*Liar.*"

Her defiant stance faltered. "You seem to have all the answers, so why don't you tell me."

Fear seized him. Was something wrong with the babe? Aidan could no longer remain silent. He cupped a hand over the soft swell of her abdomen. "Is…there something wrong with our child?"

Her face transformed into one of horrified shock. "No! Absolutely not! But how did *you* know about the baby? No one knows, not even my sister."

Aidan cupped her face gently. "I heard your confession while you were trying to get me to wake. Why have you not said anything?"

She sighed. "We never discussed children. I wasn't sure of how you would take to my sudden pregnancy. Frustrated, exhausted, and attempting to make one last plea to get you to wake, I blurted out the confession."

Dropping down to his knees, Aidan placed his ear against the growing womb. "I am happy beyond words." Even without his magic, he could make out the strong heartbeat of his daughter. His Fae senses remained intact.

He stood, brushing kisses across her face. "You have given me the greatest gift besides your love. I shall cherish this forever."

"I was torn for many weeks. Scared, unsure."

He gripped her chin firmly. "After what we have both been through, never be afraid of anything, beloved. I pledged my body to protect and shield you. My love to carry you to the stars."

"Aidan, you endured far more pain. You were stripped and made mortal. I can't even imagine."

He snorted in disgust and moved away. Fisting his hands on his hips, he settled his gaze upward. "Regardless of the life span of a Fae, we do eventually die. What my body went through was a shortening of my life threads. The quantity of years does not matter. It's how you spend them and with whom." He turned and faced Rose. "With you by my side, these shall become the best years of my life. I have no regrets loving you."

She stepped off the bench and went to his side. Reaching for his hand, she placed a kiss inside his palm. "Make love to me, my husband."

Rose let out a startled gasp when Aidan lifted her into his arms. "Never underestimate my strength again. And *never* set down rules on when I can cherish your body, *mo ghrá*. You will always lose."

****

Light drizzle blanketed the land as Aidan watched a pair of geese sweep down to the river below. He'd spent most of the day cherishing and loving his wife's body, and reassuring her he was capable of fulfilling his husbandly duties. Peace and contentment filled the void which had been present in his life. There were no misgivings on loving Rose.

*This is now my destiny.*

Folding his arms over his chest, he smirked at the intrusion behind him. "Good evening, Liam."

"By the hounds, I thought your magic was stripped within your torture chamber," protested the warrior and coming to stand next to him.

Aidan shrugged dismissively. "The magic is gone, but not my Fae senses or what flows through my veins."

"I cannot fathom why they had to go to extreme measures to torment you," stated Liam tersely.

"To set an example, so no other will attempt to thwart the law."

"Many remain loyal to you."

He glanced casually at Liam. "They must be persuaded to transfer their loyalties to Flynn. I chose him as the next leader. You can guide the others to accept their new leader. Speak first with Conn and Rory."

Liam rubbed a hand over his chin. "The council will not accept him, and the warriors refuse to acknowledge another leader chosen by the nine members. It has become a heated debate on both sides."

Frowning, Aidan turned away from the window. "Has the Brotherhood ceased to function?"

Wandering over to a chair, Liam sat. "No. On the contrary, we continue to complete missions given to us by Flynn. We have an emissary to handle the liaisons between the Brotherhood and the council."

A tremor of unease settled inside Aidan. He had no desire to see the Brotherhood fail on his account. "Who is the new emissary?"

"Elder Loran."

Curiosity replaced worry. "Why would he step into a heated position?"

"To honor your last requests. Even if the council disagrees with Flynn, Loran has acknowledged his desire to have the Brotherhood continue with the honorable codes you set in place. He's determined to keep Flynn there until another is chosen."

"Officially, many years shall pass before the chosen one steps into his role as the leader," confessed Aidan.

"What do you know?" demanded Liam, leaning forward in his chair.

Aidan realized he had shared too much. Nevertheless, he wanted to reassure Liam. Pulling out a chair from his desk, he sat down. "Prophecies yet to be fulfilled."

A shadow of annoyance crossed Liam's face. "The Queen has shared her visions with you?"

"No. The High Seer did long ago. And do not ask me anymore. It was privileged information in my early years. There are moments in life when sacrifices are required, so that future events are established for a greater purpose."

Liam nodded slowly and sat back in his chair.

Silence hovered in the room like an unwanted companion between the two warriors. Aidan had no more words to share with the Fae. Their actions and deeds were separate. No longer would he concern himself with the laws of the Fae kingdom. They did not pertain to him. His future belonged here in the mortal realm. This was now his world—one where he could forge a new path with Rose and their child.

"What are your plans here in Scotland, specifically at Balleycove?" asked Liam.

Barely registering the warrior's question, Aidan blinked, bringing his focus to their current conversation. "I plan on continuing my work with the university. There is a position on the board, which I'm contemplating on filling. I already have an office there, but will gladly be able to work from my home, too."

"An interesting prospect. Care to have an assistant with you?"

He studied the warrior from across his desk. "What are you proposing?"

"There is much I can learn from you. If Rose is now under my guardianship—"

"Only if I die," corrected Aidan and quickly added, "The Brotherhood will not allow you anywhere near me."

"On the contrary, the warriors are all in agreement. This is the reason for my visit. Call it a *partnership*. I can use the excuse I am Rose's guardian." Liam gestured outward. "I can keep the digs to within the parameters of information, and in doing so this will prevent another incident."

"Like the one with Rose and the Standing Stones," concluded Aidan, folding his arms over his chest.

"Exactly. Besides, do you not wish to keep your pulse against the vein of the Fae realm?"

"I'll never return to Ireland. Therefore, I cannot fathom keeping up with the intrigue of the kingdom."

Liam held up his hand. "There is no need. I can always share what is happening there with you, and send messages to certain family members. Bring you any herbs, medicines from the kingdom."

Aidan smiled wistfully. "How does my *sister* fare these days?"

"She sends her love." Liam produced a pouch from thin air. Tossing it onto the desk, he said, "Some herbal remedy to help with the headaches. And before you ask, she did not share why you are suffering from these maladies."

Arching a brow at the warrior, Aidan fingered the delicate package. "It's the residual effects from the cleansing of my body. My sister understands much."

A glint of humor shone in Liam's eyes. "Sorry, but I refuse to pass along the kiss she gave me as well."

"And what of King Ansgar?" asked Aidan, leaning back in his chair.

"In seclusion," responded Liam quietly.

*I have failed you, my king. For that, I am sorry. Forgive me, but love triumphs over even your great reign.*

Pushing away from the desk, Aidan stood. "I would welcome your aid. We might be able to garner you a position on the staff at the university as well. You'd have to provide credentials and other materials."

Shrugging, Liam suggested, "Or I can be your assistant?"

"Why don't you consider being an intern, learning from a scholarly professor," added Aidan, moving toward him.

"Always the leader, right?"

Extending his arm toward his friend, Aidan replied, "Will this pose a problem?"

Liam gripped his forearm. "Until you pass from this earthly realm, I shall honor you as my leader."

Aidan gave his friend a curt nod. "Then may it be a long and prosperous arrangement, Fenian Warrior."

Chapter Twenty-Five

*"I have no desire to unwind the past to the day of that extraordinary eclipse. Only a determination to press forward in the knowledge that true love can conquer anything."*

*~Diary of Rose Kerrigan*

Brushing a hand over the silken snowy material of her gown, Rose smiled at her reflection in the long mirror. "A splendid day to get married," she uttered softly.

Her hair shimmered in the early morning sunlight streaming in through the window of Aidan's chamber. Lily had taken over an hour to braid a variety of flowers with ribbons into her hair. Never could Rose have imagined she could look so beautiful. And it was all for the Fae she loved.

She fingered the moonstone pendant around her neck. Aidan had presented her with the gift two nights ago, after he had made exquisite love to her. He admitted it was a gem he had kept for thousands of years. As their quaking bodies settled from their lovemaking, he drew it forth from under a pillow and slipped it over her head. Her body tingled at the sensual memory.

Heat flushed her face as she crossed to the window, searching for the elusive Aidan Kerrigan. Since her sister and all the women from the Society descended on Balleycove several days ago, they had banished Aidan to another set of rooms far away from the one she now occupied.

Rose leaned against the window ledge, recalling Aidan's stern expression and verbal lashing. He even threatened to toss them all outside the gates of Balleycove if he was not able to be with his beloved. If not for her soothing touch, Rose believed he might have made good on his words.

"Are you waiting for your knight to come parading by?" asked Lily, entering the room.

Rose laughed, but not before stealing one final glance in all directions for her Fae lover. Moving away from the window, she reached for her bouquet of red roses with baby's breath tucked in between the flowers. "So where is he?"

"Where he's supposed to be. Waiting for you at the far end of the garden overlooking the river with the druid."

"Wonderful. We were fortunate to find Bryan at this time of year. Usually, he's making a pilgrimage to sacred places in Scotland."

"Doesn't he retreat at Samhain to one of the Standing Stones in Northern Scotland?" asked Lily, moving to her side.

"He chose a farther place off the mainland. I hear he's venturing to Orkney this year."

"A rugged, but dramatic landscape. Good for him."

Lily fussed over her hair one last time and checked all the buttons that trailed down the back of her gown. "I can hardly wait to see Aidan's face when he sees you." She started to giggle and clasped a hand over her mouth.

"And why is that so funny?"

Her sister gripped Rose's shoulders. "Because he's going to have a fit trying to pry apart the tiny seed pearl buttons from your gown with his massive hands."

Rose sighed in delight. "Perhaps he'll rip it from my body."

Letting out a gasp, Lily wagged a warning finger in front of her. "After I spent *hours* hand-sewing each one on? You would not dare permit him. When you're ready to leave the celebrations, come find me, and I'll help you out of the dress."

"Absolutely not! I'm not going to have you prepare me for my wedding bed like they did in medieval times," quarreled Rose.

Lily opened her arms wide. "Look around you, Rose. You're living in a grand medieval castle. Except your *brawn* knight is a Fae."

"Yes, it is a stunning castle." She paused and touched her sister's face lightly. "Thank you for everything. Dear sister, where do I begin? Let's start with my dress, which is straight from a medieval time-period, to preparing food, decorating the Great Hall— and far too many others to count. I love you."

Lily's lips trembled. "Do not make me cry. If you have not noticed, I'm wearing make-up."

"Of course, I did. And you're beautiful. Although, I must confess you're a beauty without any, Lily."

A lone tear trickled down her sister's cheek. "See, now I'm ruined."

Rose reached for a tissue from the box on a nearby table. Handing it to her sister, she waited until she composed herself. "I meant every word. I love you, my beautiful sister."

Lily engulfed her in a hug. "I'm so happy for you, though I wished you would have sent for me when Aidan was in a coma."

Rose sighed wearily. "We've gone down this conversational road. I had Aelish with me, and you were dealing with Society issues."

"I still can't believe the woman is a *Fae*," admitted Lily. "You should have witnessed my stunned look when you told me on the phone before we departed for here. It's another secret we'll have to keep from the other women."

"Does it bother you to know who she is?" inquired Rose, studying her sister's features.

Shaking her head slowly, Lily responded, "Not at all. It only makes her more enduring to me, and I'm honored that she has chosen to stay on longer."

"Good."

Standing back, she gave one final inspection and a tweak to her dress. Pointing to Rose's feet, she frowned. "Where are your satin slippers?"

"I want to feel the earth beneath my feet."

Her sister clucked her tongue in disapproval. She dashed over to the bed and retrieved the ivory beaded slippers. "You can remove them when you're under the trellis. The garden has had some recent animal visitors, and they've left their mark upon the land."

Rolling her eyes, Rose permitted her sister to slip the slippers onto her feet. "They're only rabbits."

"Rubbish. I think the deer have entered, along with others, including Thor. I tried to keep the dog from scurrying about in that part of the garden, but he's a trickster. Don't be surprised if you find him at Aidan's side during the ceremony."

Grinning, Rose replied, "Maybe they've come to witness the wedding of a human and Fae."

Lily's eyes grew wide. She drew close as if she were about to impart a great secret with Rose. "I thought his powers were taken?"

"I have learned to never underestimate the man *or* Fae." Rose gestured outward. "Lead the way, sis."

As Lily made her way out of the room, Rose took a deep breath in and released it slowly. Clutching her bouquet to her chest, she followed her sister. Slowly and steadily, her steps took her along the corridor where tapestries of ancient centuries greeted her in passing. She took her time descending the stairs, and when she journeyed beyond the massive oak doors, her heart started to beat rapidly.

With each step leading her closer to her Fae, goose bumps traveled over her skin in anticipation. Upon entering the garden, her heart truly did stop for a fraction of a second. Aidan stood in front of the trellis—the arches overflowing with red, yellow, orange, and pink roses. Recalling her sister's words, Thor sat regally next to the Fae.

Aidan stood in his usual powerful stance, hands clasped behind him. Yet, it was the clothes that spoke volumes to Rose. His sleeveless ivory tunic matched the color of her dress to perfection. Edged around the collar and bottom of the tunic was a silver pattern reminiscent of those markings on his arms, which denoted his royal lineage. His pants were of the same material, though in black. The contrast was magnificent—like the Fae who stood before her.

How honored she was he had chosen this attire for

their wedding day.

Aidan arched a brow, and smiled fully as she approached. Rose's breathing hitched, and she melted to her very core. The man oozed a raw sensuality. She thought she couldn't love him more, but she was wrong. This day brought a new meaning to their world. He had given up everything all for her. *All for love.*

And the child she carried was her gift to him.

Holding out his hand, Aidan waited. Doing his best to remain rooted to the ground proved to be difficult the moment his beloved stepped into his view. She was a radiant vision with the sun casting a golden halo around her. Him a hardened warrior, brought to his knees by his love for her. He'd endure the pain of his torturous prison endless times to be with the woman who captured his heart and soul. Never would he be parted from her again.

Her fingers were warm and scented with the roses she carried as he brought them to his lips. "I shall treasure this moment forever, *mo ghrá*," he uttered in a hoarse voice, raw with emotion.

"And I, too," she whispered in return, handing Lily her bouquet.

Her smile was a rainbow of promises yet to be fulfilled.

Placing her hand in the crook of his arm, Aidan led her underneath the trellis.

The druid, Bryan dipped his head in greeting. Closing his eyes, he lifted his arms upward. "We are gathered here in this sacred part of the land. Nature abides everywhere. She is present, along with those who will witness the handfasting of Aidan Kerrigan and Rose MacLaren. Their love has brought them to this sacred union. As each has confessed to me, they have already stated their vows to one another, but will do so once again for all those gathered." The druid withdrew a silver and gold cord from his robe.

Aidan took Rose's hand into his and held it outward. They watched as the druid draped the cord around their wrists.

Taking a step back, Bryan nodded to both. "You may pledge your vows."

Bringing their joined hands to his chest, Aidan stared into the depths of his beloved's eyes. "As I have declared once before, I had no compass when it came to love. It was a foreign emotion and one I had no wish to explore. It took a chance encounter under a rare occurrence for my heart to find love. Always, will my body protect, love, and serve you, Rose. You have brought me home. When the time comes for me to take my last breath, I shall await you at the entrance to eternal youth."

He withdrew a ring from his pocket. As he slipped it on Rose's finger, Aidan lowered his voice. "The circle of our love is forged in the waters of my homeland and the red stone from the caves where the great beasts once resided."

"Aidan, it's gorgeous. I love it!" She smiled seductively and dipped her fingers into the bodice of her gown.

The blood pounded in his veins as she removed a silver ring with etchings similar to the markings on his body. Humbled by her gesture to honor him in this fashion, he fought the tide of emotions in front of so many witnesses.

She took his hand and slid the ring over his finger.

"With this ring, I seal my love to you always. Let it be a symbol of the old and new—of the past and present. I honor both within you."

He kissed the ring and drew her close to him.

She trembled under his touch, but her voice remained strong and firm. "From the moment you lifted me into your arms, my soul truly felt at home. My heart beat for the first time with our first kiss. And when our bodies joined, we wove a thread of love so powerful that not even death can rip it apart. My home is here with you on this earth, until the time comes to either wait *or* meet you on the shores of the Summerland. I love you, Aidan—forever."

He leaned his forehead against hers. "There are no words to express my undying love. Only in my deeds, actions—" He winked and continued "—and to cherish your body."

Noting the blush staining her cheeks and neck, Aidan brushed a kiss near her ear. "Even now, I long to carry you away."

"Your chambers or beneath the shade of the elm trees by the river?" she asked in a throaty whisper.

Before Aidan had a chance to capture her succulent lips, Bryan coughed, alerting them that the ceremony had not concluded.

Giving the druid a smile, he stepped back and held their joined hands outward.

The druid approached. "Aidan and Rose, as your hands are bound together, so are your lives and souls, which are melded in a union of trust and love. Like the radiant stars above you, allow them to be a source of light. With the land beneath your feet as a solid foundation to keep you steady on your path of growth, may your love flourish, even in the darkest times. Let your binding vows you speak today strengthen your union in this marriage of two souls, and may the Goddess bless you on your journey."

After removing the cord, he gestured outward to the gathering. "May I present Aidan and Rose Kerrigan."

A resounding cheer and applause swept through the garden, surrounding the joyous couple.

Aidan slipped his arms around his wife's waist, bringing her against his body. He scanned her lovely features, committing to memory each detail of this glorious day.

"What are you waiting for, my *knight*? Permission to steal a chaste kiss?"

Letting out a growl, Aidan covered her mouth hungrily, showing his beloved that there would never be chaste kisses from him.

Not now. Not ever.

Epilogue

Twirling the wine in his silver goblet, Aidan waited patiently for the first star to enter the evening sky. It had become a ritual ever since his return above. Never would he forget his heritage or love for his people. The door to his previous life closed eons ago and a fresh one blossomed before him. A new home forged with his beloved by his side. Anger was banished by the love for his wife.

On a deep sigh, Aidan lifted the cup up to the glittering star. "You are the sentinel that leads the other guardians who have gone to the great realm in the cosmos. Continue to shine over us, Great Dragons." After draining the wine from his goblet, he wandered back inside the library.

He reached for the letter from the university and smiled. After a month of negotiations, his elevated position had been granted. As part of a select group of professors, he would oversee a unique archaeological department researching new digs. Reaching for a pen, Aidan scribbled his acceptance on the contract.

"An interesting and fascinating arrangement," he uttered in the hushed silence of the room and dropped the pen.

He picked up the flower on his desk, eager to present it to Rose.

Reminiscing about past digs and their relation to

historical events, Aidan proceeded along the corridor heading to the kitchens. When he entered, he frowned. Expecting his beloved to be preparing the evening meal, he found the rooms dark and quiet.

Quickly exiting, he searched for Rose in the separate sitting room. When he found no trace of her scent, he paused at bottom of the stairs. Had she taken ill? Last he had seen her was in the stables with the horses hours ago.

Taking the steps two at a time, he made his way to their chambers. As he approached, he drew his hand behind his back with the flower.

When he pushed open the doors, he halted. A fire crackled in the giant hearth. But it was the vision on the velvet coverings in front of the blaze that drew the breath from his lungs. Her shawl barely covered the sheer lavender gown she wore underneath. The moonstone around her neck glittered in the soft light. Instantly, the blood heated in his veins.

By the hounds, he'd never grow tired of seeing Rose.

She tilted her head to the side. "Are you done with your work in the library?"

"Yes."

"Signed the contract?"

He nodded slowly.

"Good. Then I believe we need to celebrate. I thought we could eat our meal before the fire in our room. We've been having chilly evenings, and I was longing to have a fire in here."

"*Meal?*" he croaked out, oblivious to anything but the enchanting beauty sitting there.

She patted the spot next to her in invitation. "Yes. I

have mushroom and onion pasties, a variety of cheeses, olives, apples, nuts, and…"

"And?"

Her eyes crinkled with mischief. "I strolled down to the cellar. Your collection is extensive." She held up a bottle. "Is it whisky? A type of sherry? The amber glass is exquisite."

Arching a brow, he replied, "You do realize you've chosen a rare vintage?"

"Strange, the label doesn't have any words. Only this symbol."

"Then you understand it is from the Fae realm?"

Smiling, she nodded. "I came to that conclusion."

He crossed the room and sat down next to her. Taking the bottle from her delicate hand, he lifted it to the firelight. "Made from the waters near my home, I have saved this elixir for a time I deemed appropriate. In truth, I've forgotten all about this passion liquor."

"Ahh…so it is not whisky?"

Aidan smiled, setting the bottle down. "No. Quite the opposite, it's a powerful aphrodisiac. Have I not shared the story of when King Arthur requested a certain amber liquid to bestow upon his wife on their wedding day?"

"You have yet to reveal that fascinating story, husband."

"A great tale for another time," he suggested.

Rose laughed. "Then let's save the story and *amber liquid* for another time, say after the birth of our daughter. All I wanted was a sip, since I wasn't going to indulge." She glanced behind him. "What are you hiding?"

Aidan brought forth the flower.

Her mouth gaped open in astonishment. "How? There are no colors like this in the world." She brushed her fingers over the flower. "Each petal is different."

He placed the delicate silver and lavender rose in her hand. "I have been practicing daily. My magic of the land has returned, though not as powerful as before. Learning to become one with the earth has taught me many lessons, some I had forgotten." Exhaling softly, he cupped her chin.

While she held the gift against her chest, Rose's eyes misted with unshed tears. "It's lovely, Aidan. What a powerful scent, too."

"My love for you." He pushed the shawl off her shoulders, letting the material slide to the ground. "For now, I have no need for additional drink to increase my heady desire for your body." Tapping the bottle, he added, "If I drank one glass, we would not be leaving this room for several days."

A crimson blush stained her cheeks. "Goodness, all the possibilities."

Aidan nibbled along her bottom lip. "*All* the positions—ecstasy that can have you soaring to the stars."

"Have I not already experienced that sensation, my Fae?" she asked provocatively, rubbing her face over the stubble on his cheek. "Love this new look and feel."

Arching a brow, his hand slipped down to cup her breast. "Then I'll endeavor to keep this rakish look to appease you, *wife*."

"I love you, husband," she uttered tenderly.

Capturing her face in his hands, Aidan showered kisses around her lips. "As I love you, beloved—to the stars. You swept into my life like a magical spring breeze and illuminated my soul, opening up a void which I refused to view."

When her sigh entered him, Aidan sealed his vow with a kiss worthy of his love.

## Note from Author

The great Aidan Kerrigan was a tale I feared to write. When he first appeared in the story, *Dragon Knight's Medallion*, I panicked. I did not know he was a Fenian Warrior until he walked through the crowd of people at the airport to greet his daughter, Aileen. His presence loomed mighty and grew with the previous stories in the *Legends of the Fenian Warriors*. Regardless, I knew then that his and Rose's love story had to be told. With each Fenian Warrior's story, I shared a layer about this Fae. Little did I know when I penned his first line of dialogue that he was the leader of the Fenian Warriors, came from royalty, and his sister was Queen of the Fae realm.

He chose not to reveal any of this to me. And this is why I became terrified. What more could he share? Well, dear readers, Aidan made it simple. He told me to write a love story. ***"For you see, love is greater than all the power attained in the world—be it human or Fae."***

Therefore, I took you back in time to when he was the leader of the Brotherhood. To when this great warrior had no blemish to stain his life and love flipped his world upside down.

Eventually, Aidan and Rose will depart Scotland and make their home with their young daughter at the Society of the Thistle in Boston, Massachusetts. If you've read *Dragon Knight's Medallion*, then you know the reasoning behind this move.

I truly hope you've enjoyed the final book (for now) in the *Legends of the Fenian Warriors*.

Coming this holiday season, I'm taking you back to

289

the Dragon Knights of Urquhart and their friends, the MacFhearguis clan, specifically Patrick MacFhearguis. It's time to weave a spell of love over this rugged Highlander in *To Weave a Highland Tapestry*.

# Coming in December 2019

# *TO WEAVE*
# *A HIGHLAND TAPESTRY*

*Turn the page for a sneak preview…*

Mary Morgan

## Prologue

When the ancient MacFhearguis clan settled near the Great Glen in Scotland, the Chieftain wished to bless the land and his castle, known as Leòmhann—*the lion*. Druids came from far away, bestowing their approval over stone, land, and people. Afterwards, they took part in a grand feast. Drink and food overflowed in the Great Hall. The bards recounted the tales of their Chieftain and his people, while the children listened in rapt attention. Minstrels played songs of past triumphs, and the dancing and feasting lasted for countless days.

*However*, another tale lay buried within the stone walls of Leòmhann and only those brave enough could recant the true account.

And so it was whispered there were those in the clan—weavers from an ancient order from the west—not happy with the Chieftain's refusal to offer a gift to the Fae who had graced his land before him. Or his lack of interest to take a wife from one of the tribes who followed their belief. Though he honored the old ways, the Chieftain deemed their requests a foolish act. He argued that the druid's blessing fulfilled their needs and hardened his heart against them.

On a cold autumn morn, he banished these irritating women to the forest, fearing they would weave ill thoughts among the other people.

Saddened by this act from their Chieftain, the

women grew concerned that the Fae may not give their own blessing and their people would be left without a compassionate and wise leader. Regardless of his order to silence them, they sought another path to right this injustice.

Gathering around a bonfire on a moonlit Samhain eve, each woman brought with them one long golden thread from their looms. On a whispered prayer, they knotted them all together. Traveling deep into the forest far away from Leòmhann, they came upon a young yew tree. As they swayed softly, the women wrapped the knotted threads around the tree. After they were done, they joined hands and sang out as one.

"Seasons will ebb and flow and battles shall be fought. The loom of the land shall not see rebirth. From left to right, the strands of time will knot and break. Only when a weaver threads the true color on a winter full moon night, shall the land, stone, and clan be cleansed."

Smiling, they embraced each other—deeming their prayer had been received by the Fae. As the leaves rustled beneath their feet, none of them ever fathomed that the true master weaver to claim the heart of a MacFhearguis would not appear for over eight hundred years.

And as the centuries passed, the legend of the Yew tree became more of a curse, and the land around Leòmhann suffered.

**Other books by Mary Morgan**

**Order of the Dragon Knights ~**
Dragon Knight's Sword, Book 1
Dragon Knight's Medallion, Book 2
Dragon Knight's Axe, Book 3
Dragon Knight's Shield, Book 4
Dragon Knight's Ring, Book 5
~*~
**Legends of the Fenian Warriors ~**
Quest of a Warrior, Book 1
Oath of a Warrior, Book 2
Trial of a Warrior, Book 3
~*~
**Holiday Romances ~**
A Magical Highland Solstice
A Highland Moon Enchantment

.

## A word about the author...

Award-winning Celtic paranormal and fantasy romance author Mary Morgan resides in Northern California with her own knight in shining armor. However, during her travels to Scotland, England, and Ireland, she left a part of her soul in one of these countries and vows to return.

Mary's passion for books started at an early age along with an overactive imagination. Inspired by her love for history and ancient Celtic mythology, her tales are filled with powerful warriors, brave women, magic, and romance. It wasn't until the closure of Borders Books where Mary worked that she found her true calling in writing romance. Now the worlds she created in her mind are coming to life within her stories.

If you enjoy history, tortured heroes, and a wee bit of magic, then time-travel within the pages of her books.

Visit Mary's website, where you'll find links to all her books, blog, and pictures of her travels.

http://www.marymorganauthor.com

www.ingramcontent.com/pod-product-compliance
Lightning Source LLC
Chambersburg PA
CBHW070053030726
47506CB00002B/445